DELIGHTING THE DUKE

Dukes Done Wrong
Book 4

Alexa Aston

ARE YOU SIGNED UP FOR DRAGONBLADE'S BLOG?

You'll get the latest news and information on exclusive giveaways, exclusive excerpts, coming releases, sales, free books, cover reveals and more.

Check out our complete list of authors, too!

No spam, no junk. That's a promise!

Sign Up Here

www.dragonbladepublishing.com

Dearest Reader;

Thank you for your support of a small press. At Dragonblade Publishing, we strive to bring you the highest quality Historical Romance from some of the best authors in the business. Without your support, there is no 'us', so we sincerely hope you adore these stories and find some new favorite authors along the way.

Happy Reading!

CEO, Dragonblade Publishing

Additional Dragonblade books by Author Alexa Aston

Dukes Done Wrong Series
Discouraging the Duke
Deflecting the Duke
Disrupting the Duke
Delighting the Duke
Destiny with a Duke

Dukes of Distinction Series
Duke of Renown
Duke of Charm
Duke of Disrepute
Duke of Arrogance
Duke of Honor

The St. Clairs Series
Devoted to the Duke
Midnight with the Marquess
Embracing the Earl
Defending the Duke
Suddenly a St. Clair
Starlight Night

Soldiers & Soulmates Series
To Heal an Earl
To Tame a Rogue
To Trust a Duke
To Save a Love
To Win a Widow

The Lyon's Den Connected World
The Lyon's Lady Love

King's Cousins Series
The Pawn
The Heir
The Bastard

Medieval Runaway Wives
Song of the Heart
A Promise of Tomorrow
Destined for Love

Knights of Honor Series
Word of Honor
Marked by Honor
Code of Honor
Journey to Honor
Heart of Honor
Bold in Honor
Love and Honor
Gift of Honor
Path to Honor
Return to Honor

CHAPTER ONE

Deerfield Park—September 1796

"DO YOU HAVE to go away next week, Hart?"

Aaron Hartfield ruffled his little brother's hair. "Yes, Percy. Big boys leave home in order to go to school. You can come with me next year. I will look after you and protect you and make sure you feel at home."

Percy's eyes grew round. "Will you?"

"Of course, I will. That's what big brothers are for."

"Did Reg take care of you when you went to school?"

He bit his tongue. His mother had asked him never to say an ill word about Reg. Especially to Percy or their younger sister, Ada. Hart found it harder to do as time went by.

At fifteen, Reg was the oldest of the Hartfield children and destined to be the Duke of Mansfield someday, a fact he never let the others forget. Reg had never taken on the role of protector for any of his younger siblings. If anything, he antagonized them. Or ignored them. There was nothing in-between.

When Hart left Deerfield Park and accompanied Reg to school, he had held out the slim hope that Reg would think to take care of him. How wrong he'd been. Reg had nothing to do with his younger brother. When the boys a year ahead of Hart had bullied him unmercifully, Reg never lifted a finger to stop their cruelty. It was a lesson Hart never forgot.

"You have your tutor. Be sure to study hard this year with him," he encouraged Percy. "You want to be prepared academically. The curriculum is demanding. It's best to show them you are up to any challenge."

Percy sighed. "It's a whole year before I'll get to go with you. That's a long time."

Even at ten, he knew the hours and days passed differently during various times. Since Hart enjoyed school, those months always seemed to fly by. He could imagine, though, how slowly they must go for Percy. Ada was only three and still in the nursery. He knew his little brother must be lonely.

"Would you like to ask Cook to pack a hamper for us?" he asked. "We could have a picnic by the lake."

Percy looked uneasy at the suggestion. "Do we have to swim?"

"Not if you don't want to," he said, knowing Percy, at six, was still afraid of the water and only rarely got in, never further than his knees.

Hart loved the water. Swimming in the lake was only second to riding for him. Water terrified Percy, though. Even as a baby, he would scream at the top of his lungs when dipped into his bathwater. He had never grown out of his fear. Hopefully one day, Hart would be able to teach Percy to swim. He didn't want other boys making fun of his younger brother.

"Let's go downstairs," he suggested. "After we pick up these toy soldiers."

The two cleared the floor, packing away the soldiers. Hart had outgrown playing with them but continued to do so to please his little brother. They went to see Cook, who stopped rolling out a pie crust, and personally supervised what went into the basket.

"Have fun, little lords," she told them as they set out from the kitchens.

The lake was about three-quarters of a mile north of the house. Hart helped Percy spread out the blanket they had collected before they left, placing it under the shade of an oak tree. The tree was on a tall bank that overlooked a portion of the lake and gave them a pleasant view. He opened the hamper and lifted out cold legs of roasted chicken, apples, and two pear tarts. Cook had included two jars filled with lemonade and he opened one, handing it to Percy, who drank greedily.

They sat under the tree, eating and talking about school and what it would be like when Percy accompanied him next year. Hart told Percy about his favorite instructors and what was expected of first-year boys. His brother asked a hundred questions, which Hart patiently answered. Percy didn't get much attention. Their father and mother rarely spent time in the country with their children, preferring to be in London for the Season. When home, the duke closeted himself in his study most days, only admitting Reg, his favorite since he was the heir. The duchess spent her time reading or writing to friends, occasionally calling for Ada and lavishing brief bursts of attention on her youngest child. The two were gone for a two-week stay at her sister's house and wouldn't even be back to tell Reg and Hart goodbye before they left for school early next week.

Percy yawned noisily and Hart suggested he curl up and take a nap.

"What will you do?" Percy asked, rubbing his eyes.

"I think I will go for a swim while you rest."

"I don't have to go?" Percy asked anxiously.

"No. You stay here."

His brother did as he was told, slipping off his shoes and curling up on his side. He was already fast asleep by the time Hart had stripped off his clothes. With a running start, he hurdled off the edge and landed in the water. It was chilly but he relished the feel of it and he began kicking, using long strokes to carry himself across the lake.

It took several minutes to reach the opposite bank and he waded out, breathing heavily. Plopping onto the ground, he stretched out his legs and placed his hands behind his back to brace himself as he lifted his face toward the sun. The warm rays sank into him and he grew drowsy, closing his eyes as he basked in the sunlight.

Then he heard a voice carrying across the water. His eyes flew open and he brought a hand up to shade them, wondering if Percy had awakened and called out to him. Hart peered across the distance and saw two figures on the bank, one short and one much taller.

Reg.

He leaped to his feet and shouted, "Leave him alone!" His gut was telling him that Reg, his older brother, was up to mischief.

With so great a distance, he didn't think Reg had heard him and he yelled even louder.

"Stop!"

This time, Reg looked up. Hart could see he had his hands on Percy and now lifted him. Hart could hear his younger brother's screams.

"No! Don't! No, Reg!"

Then Reg swung Percy back and flung him into the water.

Percy didn't know how to swim.

He scrambled into the water, panicked, and began swimming hard and fast back across the lake. He could hear Percy screaming and Reg's laughter. Though he drew closer, Percy's protests seem to weaken.

Then they ceased.

Hart raced through the water and reached the opposite shore. Reg stood looking down from the bank.

"Where is he?" Hart demanded, panic rising as his eyes skimmed the surface.

"I tossed him in. He needs to stop being such a baby. Hartfields aren't cowards."

Hart whipped his head around, "Percy! Percy!" he cried.

The water was still.

He dived back in, searching, surfacing, and plunging in again, his hands searching the water.

Then he brushed against Percy and latched on to him, towing

him toward the shore. Dragging Percy out of the water, he saw his little brother wasn't breathing and his head was at an awkward angle.

"No!" he screamed. "No. No. No."

He pushed on Percy's chest. Lifted him and turned him to his side. Brought the heel of his hand down hard on Percy's back.

Nothing happened.

"Breathe, dammit. Breathe, Percy," he demanded, shaking his brother by the shoulders.

Percy's head lolled.

Hart eased his brother back to the ground. He sat in a stupor.

Percy was dead . . .

He gathered his brother into his arms and began rocking him. He talked to Percy, babbling nonsense. The body grew cold in his arms.

"My God!"

With bleary eyes, he looked up. His father stood there, Reg by his side.

The duke pried Hart's fingers away and lifted Percy into his arms. "My boy."

"Hart let him drown," Reg said.

The numbness that had filled him fled in an instant, replaced by a rage so great that Hart leaped to his feet and slammed into Reg. He pounded his brother with his fists, seeing nothing but red.

"Stop!" a voice cried as strong arms jerked him away.

It was the duke who had pulled him off. He had obviously set Percy down.

Anger still bubbling within him, he said, "Reg did this, Father. He threw Percy in, knowing he couldn't swim."

Reg pushed to his feet, his nose swollen, blood running from it, staining his cravat and shirt.

"I did not. I came upon them. I saw Hart force Percy into the water. He shouted to me that he was teaching Percy how to swim."

"You are a *liar!*" Hart roared, flinging himself at Reg again.

Once more, his father pulled him off and shoved him away. He glared at Hart and said, "Put your clothes on, you bloody blighter." Mansfield leaned down and scooped up Percy, gazing upon him tenderly.

Standing his ground, he said, "Reg is lying. He is the one who tossed Percy into the water and did nothing to save him. He killed Percy."

The duke shook his head, storm clouds in his eyes. "You are a bitter disappointment to me, Aaron. First, to force your brother to swim when you knew he was terrified of the water. Second, to have the audacity to blame Reginald for your actions. You are a disgrace to the Hartfield name."

"He must be punished, Father," Reg said, rubbing his jaw. "Sent away. Why, he might harm Ada next and that would kill Mother. She dotes on her so."

Hart shook his head. "Neither of you cared one whit for Percy. I am the one who loved him. I've always looked out for him."

"How can you say that? You killed him," Reg taunted. "You should be locked away."

The duke shook his head, bringing Percy close to his chest. "No. It won't do to have my son to be known as a murderer. We shall say this was an accident. That Percy wanted to learn how to swim to please us. That he suffered a cramp and went under and drowned on his own."

He turned and glared at Hart. "As for you? I am a perfect duke with a perfect son. I have no room in my life for the imperfect. I have heard of a place for boys such as you. Ones who have done unspeakable things and cannot be trusted around their families. It is called Turner Academy."

A chill ran through him. He had heard whispered rumors of such a place. How it housed vile, wicked boys who had done terrible things and been sent there in order to protect their families.

"I will see you sent there," the duke said dismissively. He turned, carrying Percy, and walked away.

Hart watched them, a hard lump in his throat. Bitter tears stung his eyes and poured down his cheeks.

"Cry," Reg said softly. "It won't bring him back."

He looked at his older brother, who had always needled him. His energy sapped, he could only fall to his knees.

"You always thought you could protect him. You didn't, did you?" Reg taunted. "You have to live with the knowledge that you could have saved him—and you didn't."

Hart's head fell to the ground. He cursed Reg and his father and even God for letting Percy drown.

Finally, he stumbled to his feet and threw his clothes on haphazardly. He glanced to the blanket, where the remnants of their picnic lay. Picking up the jar that Percy had held, guzzling lemonade, the liquid running down his chin, he unleashed an unearthly scream and tossed the jar into the lake.

He should have been the one who died today. He hadn't kept Percy safe as an older brother should have.

Hart didn't think he would ever forgive himself.

And he vowed to one day make Reg suffer for what he had done.

CHAPTER TWO

Turner Academy—June 1801

HART PLACED HIS pencil on the desk and blew out a long breath. He glanced about the room and saw he was the only pupil left. Rising, he brought the pages of his examination to Mr. Morris, his mathematics tutor.

"How do you think you did, Mr. Hart?"

He pushed a hand through his thick, chestnut hair. "Actually, I believe it's the best I have ever done, Mr. Morris. Thanks to Donovan."

Morris' eyes twinkled. "Mr. Donovan is a very good friend to you."

Hart grinned. "He spent enough time pounding theorems and equations into my head." He paused. "Do you think you might have the results before we leave for Markham Park?"

The tutor nodded. "I have evaluated the exams as they have come in. You will know the mark you achieved before you set foot inside the carriage, Mr. Hart."

"Thank you," he said, hoping he had done as well as his gut told him.

He left the classroom and found Donovan pacing in the corridor.

"Well?" he demanded.

Hart sighed. "I feel really good about it," he told his friend.

"You should. I spent enough time going over everything with you. You knew it forward and backward going in." He threw an arm around Hart's shoulder. "Let's go back to the room. We'll be leaving soon."

"I just don't understand how numbers make such sense to you," he said as they made their way through the large manor house which served as the school they had attended the past five years.

"You should. It's how you are with languages," Donovan told him. "You soak them up with ease. I can't conjugate a verb to save my soul, while you rattle off past participles and future present tense without even having to think about it."

They entered their dormitory room. Miles sat on his bed patiently waiting, his trunk already packed. He was the most organized of the five Turner Terrors. Wyatt haphazardly threw items inside his trunk, while Finch meticulously folded each piece of clothing and rested it gingerly inside.

He loved these boys as brothers. They had all been sent to Turner Academy five years ago, abandoned by their families and placed into the hands of the Turner brothers, co-founders of the school. Hart had dreaded coming here, having heard a bit about the type of student who attended Turner Academy. Boys who had done terrible things and were shipped off to Kent so they wouldn't embarrass their families at better known public schools.

Miles had been accused of shooting and killing his beloved younger brother when it was his older brother, a marquess and future duke, who had pulled the trigger. Wyatt's older brother, also heir apparent to a duke, burned down the family stables, causing over two dozen horses to be lost in the fire. Wyatt, too, had been blamed for the incident. Donovan's father, the Duke of Haverhill, believed his son caused his wife's death instead of the poacher who had encroached upon the duke's lands and left a trap in which the duchess stepped into.

Then there was Finch. None of the Turner Terrors knew why he had been banished from Sommerville, his family home, and dumped at the academy. Finch was the only one who had never shared his tale of woe in the years they had been together. Still, he was the most loyal of all the Terrors and protected them with a fierceness that made all the other pupils give the Terrors a wide berth. No one bullied them. If they had, Finch would have beaten the offender to a bloody pulp.

Wyatt slammed his trunk shut as Finch closed his carefully. Hart and Donovan had finished packing earlier while the other three were in different exams.

"How was the mathematics exam?" Miles asked. "I know you were worried."

"Hart did well," Donovan answered. "We need to head downstairs. I'll go look for Mr. Smythe."

"We can carry our own trunks," Finch said. "We are old enough and strong enough. Mr. Smythe has more to do than wait upon us."

The boys all had a great deal of respect for Mr. Smythe. He was a former soldier who was a jack-of-all-trades at the academy. Besides performing a variety of tasks, Smythe managed to spend time with each individual boy. He listened to them and dispensed sage advice when they solicited it. He was everyone's favorite, though Mrs. Josiah came in a close second. Her cooking was the best any of the boy's had ever experienced.

Finch hoisted his trunk up, resting it on his shoulder. The others followed suit and the five brought their trunks downstairs to the foyer, where a familiar liveried footman waited.

"I'll see to those," he said.

The footman served the Earl of Marksby, where the boys now headed. While most of the other students returned to their homes during holidays, the Turner Terrors never did. They spent every day at the school with each other. None of them ever received a letter from home nor had any visitor stop by the school to inquire about their health or progress. They were dead to their families. Because of that harsh reality, they had chosen to forge a new one of their own making. Hart trusted his four friends and considered them the brothers of his heart.

"No," Finch insisted. "We can take them outside and help you load them into the wagon."

"Very well, Mr. Finch," the footman replied.

This would be the fifth summer the boys had gone to Markham Park, where they would spend two weeks with the earl and countess. This was the first summer, though, that they would be the only academy students present. The rest were all going home. Some wouldn't return when autumn came, being sent instead to other schools or on to university.

Home no longer existed for Hart and his companions. Turner Academy had become their world.

It surprised him as they took their trunks outside to only see a single coach and cart. Usually, the earl sent more than one of each since the Turner brothers and their wives, who served as housekeeper and cook at the academy, accompanied them to Markham Park. Lord Marksby had been the one over twenty-five years ago to give the Turners the money in which to start up their school and the earl enjoyed visiting with the men and their wives each summer.

They finished placing their trunks in the wagon and when he turned, Hart saw that all four Turners, along with Mr. Morris and Mr. Whitby, who taught languages, were lined up. Confusion filled him.

"A word, Mr. Hart," called Mr. Morris.

He trotted over. "Yes?" he asked eagerly, his hands behind his back, fingers crossed.

Donovan joined him. "How did he do, Mr. Morris?"

"I shouldn't be sharing another boy's scores with you, Mr. Donovan," the mathematics tutor gently chided. "However, I will inform Mr. Hart that he passed with flying colors."

Donovan threw his arms around Hart. "See? I told you that you could do it."

A rush of pride rippled through him. He turned and said, "Thank you, Mr. Morris."

"I fear I had little to do with it. Mr. Donovan seems to be the better tutor. In fact, you scored only second to Mr. Donovan. You placed higher than all the other boys except for him."

"What?" Joy filled him. "That is the same as taking first prize for me." He thrust out a hand and Mr. Morris took it. Hart pumped enthusiastically. "Thank you!"

He turned and his fellow Terrors cheered, slapping him on the back and telling him how proud they were of him.

After they settled down, Mr. Nehemiah said, "It is time for you to leave, boys."

"Aren't you coming?" Miles asked.

"Not this time," Mr. Nehemiah said. "Since it is only the five of you left at school during this summer holiday, Lord Marksby has extended his invitation for you to remain the entire time."

"What?" Wyatt cried.

Of all of them, Wyatt loved going to Markham Park the most.

"Yes, you will be there all summer," Mr. Josiah seconded.

"And his lordship is paying for us to go on holiday to the Lake District," Mrs. Nehemiah said. "So, you boys are to be on your best behavior. Is that understood?"

"Yes, Ma'am," they all echoed.

Mrs. Josiah raised a hamper and handed it to Hart. "Here are a few treats for the journey."

He bit back a smile. It was only an hour to Markham Park. Instead, he said, "Thank you, Mrs. Josiah."

"You are growing boys and need your nourishment," she told him.

"It's time for you to leave," Mr. Nehemiah said. "We will see you come September."

The five said their goodbyes and climbed into Lord Marksby's elegant carriage.

As the vehicle took off, Hart opened the basket and distributed its contents. Though they had eaten a filling breakfast only a few hours earlier, they easily finished what Mrs. Josiah had sent.

Soon, the carriage turned and made its way up the drive to Markham Park. Hart alighted first, spying Lord and Lady Marksby waiting to greet them. The others spilled out and the five went to meet the earl and countess.

"We are delighted to have you here for the summer," Lord Marksby said.

"It wouldn't be summer without a visit from the Turner Terrors," Lady Marksby added, her laughter tinkling.

"You know that nickname?" Wyatt asked.

"Of course, we do," the earl said. "Though it doesn't seem fitting at all. You boys are the best behaved of the lot. We look upon you as our sons."

His words touched Hart. The Marksbys were childless. The Turner Terrors were, in effect, orphans.

"Thank you, my lord," he said on behalf of the others. "We enjoy our time at Markham Park and the attention you lavish upon us."

"Come inside," the countess urged. "Cook has prepared all your favorites."

They followed the couple inside and despite having snacked on the way there, the boys gobbled up everything in sight. When the meal ended, Lord Marksby cleared his throat and they gave the earl their attention.

"We will stay at Markham Park for two weeks and then go to London."

"London!" Donovan cried. "Why, none of us have ever been to the city."

"Lady Marksby and I thought as much. It is time to put a little town polish on you. We will take advantage of riding in Hyde Park, as well as go to several museums."

"Museums?" Miles piped up, his face lighting with interest.

Hart chuckled. Miles loved history more than anyone in all of England. Going to museums and seeing artifacts would make him very happy.

"We'll also walk through Mayfair," the earl continued. "You

must be exposed to classical architecture. We will take in the Tower of London, as well."

"And don't forget," the countess added, prodding her husband.

"Oh, yes. We must stop for ices at Gunter's."

"What are ices?" Finch asked warily, his forever suspicious nature coming out.

Lady Marksby chuckled. "It will be your favorite thing, Finch. I promise."

"Then after a few weeks in town, it will be back to Markham Park," the earl finished. "And then you will return to Turner Academy for the new term."

Hart couldn't help but grin from ear to ear. This summer promised to be the best of his life.

CHAPTER THREE

London—November 1812

HART WENT STRAIGHT from the London docks to the address on the letter he had received at the beginning of the month. It had come from the same solicitor who had paid the bills for his education at Turner Academy and university. The one who had purchased the army commission for him once he had graduated. He had never heard from Mr. Griffin in the years that followed.

Until now.

The letter had been penned in July but hadn't reached Hart for almost four months. Wellington's army had been on the move, especially after the victory at Salamanca in July. The British Army had then entered Madrid in early August and pushed as far as Burgos before retreating again to Salamanca and then finally Ciudad Rodrigo. No wonder it had taken so long for the news to reach him.

News of death.

Griffin's letter wasn't clear as to the order of things but Hart knew two facts. His father, the duke, and his brother, the marquess, were deceased.

Major Aaron Hartfield was now the Duke of Mansfield. Owner of Deerfield Park in Surrey and who knew how many other estates throughout England.

Ambivalence filled him. As did doubt. Hart had only known war for so long that he was almost afraid to return to Polite Society. Not that he had ever truly been a member of it. Reginald had seen to that. To Hart's banishment from Deerfield Park and the blame for Percy's death. It riled him that he would never be able to seek the revenge he had wanted for his beloved brother. Hart had wanted to confront Reginald. Make him suffer.

All his life, he had seen everything in black and white, no shades of gray. Something was either right or it was wrong. There was no in-between. Attending Turner Academy had only strengthened his stance. The tutors at Turner Academy had seen that he was a principled boy, one for whom honor, duty, and integrity were his calling cards. Hart would never compromise his moral code. He would sacrifice himself for the greater good of a righteous cause.

That had been his belief when he had gone to war against Bonaparte. The army had bred into him an even stronger sense of duty. At the same time, however, he had seen the immense suffering of soldiers on both sides of the bayonet. Years at war had wearied him. He was so very tired of all the fighting and still didn't see an end in sight. It was almost a blessing in disguise to receive Griffin's note informing him of his changed circumstances and pleading for Hart to come home immediately to England and assume the mantle of responsibilities that came with being a duke. Not just any duke. One of the wealthiest and most powerful dukes in all of England.

Now, guilt filled him. Guilt for leaving his men behind to fight a war that might never cease. Guilt for the euphoria that filled him, knowing he would no longer have to dodge bullets and compose letters to the parents and wives of his fallen soldiers. Guilt for delighting in the deaths of the two men he despised. If left to his own intentions, Hart would probably go and dance upon their graves.

He cleared his mind. Hate did no good. He had hated Reginald and his father for years before he saw that hatred only poisoned him and he did his best to abandon it. His changed circumstances had led to the greatest friendships of his life—the Turner Terrors. He had spent every day for over ten years in his fellow Terrors' company. Four of them had left Finch behind in England as they went off to war. Finch had no one to purchase his military commission and instead had accepted the offer of the living from the Earl of Marksby, a mentor to the Terrors throughout their formative years.

The remaining Terrors had marched off to war and found themselves stationed together in various outfits, still able to cajole and commiserate with one another on almost a daily basis. The only exception was Wyatt, who sometimes took on the role of spy or scout for Wellington. Wyatt would disappear for a stretch of time and then return to the fold, keeping secret where he had been and what he had been sent to accomplish.

Ironically, one by one, the other three Terrors had received similar notifications as Hart had. Miles, their acknowledged leader, was the first to return to England when his drunken brother, the Duke of Winslow, was thrown from his horse and killed on the spot. Wyatt was the next to depart from the Peninsula. Never the best at writing letters, Hart only knew that Clive, Wyatt's older brother and the Duke of Amesbury, had turned up dead, making Wyatt the new duke.

Finally, Donovan had returned to England. The two of them had been celebrating their elevation in rank when Donovan's life changed. His father and brother had drowned. Donovan was now the Duke of Haverhill, a name he despised and would now always be known as. His friend had been despondent, losing a brother he had idolized and been kept from seeing or contacting for many years. Hart had sent Donovan on his way, telling him to be a good duke and good man, the kind his brother Sam would have been proud of.

Three friends. Three soldiers. Second sons who had become dukes.

And now Hart joined their company.

Curiosity filled him as he wondered how Mansfield and his heir apparent had died. Had they perished together, as Donovan's relatives had in a carriage accident? Or separately? Had Reginald died first and then their father—or the other way around?

Soon, he would have answers to his questions. No one would dare keep the truth from a duke.

He arrived at the solicitor's office and caught his reflection in the window before he reached for the door's handle. Perhaps he should have shaved before departing the ship which had brought him back from Spain but it was too late now. His thick hair was wind-tossed from standing on the deck, watching their approach to England and then inland to London up the Thames. His uniform, the only clothing he owned, looked worse for the wear, rumpled and stained.

It didn't matter. He was a duke now. Dukes could go about looking however they pleased and ignore society's rules. Though it would be nice to finally have a decent bath. He couldn't remember the last time that had occurred. Hart smiled to himself, wondering what Griffin would make of the new duke.

He entered the offices and went to the first desk he saw. The clerk glanced up and blinked twice.

"May I help you?" he asked, a slight frown on his features.

"I am formerly Major Hartfield—now the Duke of Mansfield. I wish to see your employer immediately."

Suddenly, the man shot to his feet, his features changing radically. "Of course, Your Grace. If you will have a seat—"

"I won't need it since I expect to see Mr. Griffin at once," he curtly replied.

"Yes, Your Grace," the clerk replied nervously. "Please. Wait here. I will be back shortly."

The clerk raced from the room as if he had seen the Devil himself. Hart chuckled. Wyatt would have joined in the laughter. Miles would have disapproved of Hart's arrogant behavior. Donovan would have been bored.

And what of Finch? How would Reverend Finchley have

handled the situation?

Hart was close friends with each of the Terrors, probably the closest to Donovan. Of them, though, Finch was the one he felt he knew the least about. All the Terrors had shared their stories of why they had been sent to Turner Academy. All except Finch, that is. To this day, it remained a mystery among them why the blond, angelic Finch had been sent to a place with a reputation for accepting wayward boys.

The clerk returned, this time with his employer in tow. Hart didn't recognize Griffin but didn't think he would. After all, other than his one trip with Lord Marksby and the Terrors to London almost ten years ago, Hart had never set foot inside the great city.

"Ah, Your Grace, it is so very good to see you have returned safely from the Continent," the white-haired man said. "Would you care to come to my office? Might you wish for some tea?"

"Nothing for me, thank you. Lead the way."

The older man said, "This way, Your Grace."

Already, he had been called *Your Grace* four times. He supposed it was something he would have to get used to. That, at least, was tolerable. The moment he was referred to as Mansfield, however, would be a difficult one. He supposed every man had his own cross to bear. In this case, his would be thinking of the man who had fathered him—and hadn't believed him—when he'd spoken the truth about Percy's death.

Fresh anger sizzled through him at the thought of Reginald getting away scot-free without having to pay any kind of price for Percy's death. That Reginald had lived for so many years without ever having paid the proverbial piper stuck in Hart's craw.

Ushered into Griffin's office, Hart took the proffered seat and said, "Before anything, tell me about their deaths."

The solicitor closed the door and took a seat behind his desk. He pulled in a long breath and exhaled it slowly before answering.

"I am afraid you are walking into a bit of a scandal, Your Grace. Nothing of your doing, of course, but tongues do have a tendency to wag within the *ton*. Hopefully, by next Season when Polite Society reconvenes in London, the events of last July will be mostly forgotten."

He didn't reply. Hart had learned to merely sit in silence when he wanted information from someone. His glare usually caused them to continue speaking, revealing whatever he wished to know.

"You see, the marquess found himself in a bit of a pickle."

Hart crossed his arms over his chest. "I don't want you to prettify the facts, Griffin. I merely want those facts. I can make my own judgment of them. The truth, please. Unvarnished."

The solicitor's head bobbed up and down. "I see. Well, then I suppose I will be more frank. The marquess had a terrible reputation among the *ton*. He was known as the worst of scoundrels."

"Examples, please."

"He had gotten more than one woman with child and ignored them afterward. He had numerous affairs with women without regard to discretion. It was the last of these affairs that led to his demise."

Griffin paused, claiming his handkerchief and dabbing his forehead nervously.

"Your brother engaged in an affair with Viscountess Garner. You may not realize, having been at war and not in Polite Society, that *affaires de coeur* are tolerated as long as both parties are discreet and the lady in question has provided the expected heir. In this case, the viscountess had done her duty, with both an heir and a spare. She was known for engaging in the occasional affair. Nothing serious."

"How was this time different?" he asked, curious how an affair could lead to Reginald's demise.

"The marquess unfortunately spoke about the affair publicly upon numerous occasions. This news got back to Lord Garner. The viscount issued a challenge, which was accepted. The choice of weapons was pistols. Seconds arranged for the place and time the duel would occur. A doctor was engaged to be on the scene in case either participant was wounded."

Griffin stopped and mopped his brow again. His eyes darted about nervously.

"Just tell me, Man. I will not blame you as the messenger but I do need to know what occurred."

"Yes, Your Grace." Griffin licked his lips. "Lord Garner was known for being a terrible shot. Your brother had a reputation for knowing his way around guns. For some reason which no one understands, the two men agreed not to turn and fire at will. Instead, alternate shots would be taken, which allowed your brother, the challenged, to fire first."

Hart understood immediately. Garner, being a poor shot but desperately wanting to defend his reputation and that of his wife's, had allowed Reginald to go first. If Reginald wounded his challenger, satisfaction would be reached and both men could have left the field with their honor intact. No second shot would need to be fired.

"Continue," he urged.

Griffin cleared his throat. "The marquess arrived shortly before five that morning in a state of drunkenness, according to witnesses."

"He didn't feel Lord Garner had a chance."

"I suppose not," Griffin agreed. "The viscount appeared shortly thereafter and the two men took their assigned spots on the field. Your brother could barely stand at this point and fired his pistol. Some say he waved the gun in Garner's direction and was so drunk he missed. Others stated he deloped."

"He deliberately missed," Hart said, shaking his head in disapproval. "Because he thought his opponent was not worth shooting."

"Yes, Your Grace. That practice is specifically banned and yet occurs upon occasion. In this instance, Viscount Garner felt horribly slighted and shouted this aloud. Then he took aim and fired his own weapon.

"It struck your brother directly in the heart."

Satisfaction filled Hart. He might not have been the one to put the bullet into Reginald but he was glad this Lord Garner had.

Griffin continued. "Those present were shocked that the viscount managed to even hit his opponent, due to his lack of skill, much less strike true and deadly. The doctor raced to the fallen man and after a moment, declared him dead. Lord Garner fled England for parts unknown. Lady Garner retired to their country estate with her two sons. It is rumored she will return to London for the upcoming Season."

"And my father?"

"His Grace received the news of his son's death and retired to his rooms. Shortly afterward, his valet discovered him to be dead. The *ton* says that Mansfield died of a broken heart."

At least Hart now knew the story. He didn't care about the gossip that surrounded his family. He was his own man and would make that clear to Polite Society.

"What else do I need to know?" he inquired.

"Regarding their deaths? Both are buried in the family plot in Rumsford, Your Grace."

He had no intention of visiting either of their graves. "What of my mother and Ada?"

Griffin frowned, stirring uneasily in his chair. "I suppose you wouldn't know."

"No, I wouldn't know anything, Griffin. I was sent away from my home for a crime I didn't commit. All contact was cut off." He paused. "Tell me."

"Her Grace passed on about five years ago. She is buried next to her husband."

"And Ada?"

Hart had tried not to think of his little sister, innocent in all that had occurred. Still, he had each year on her birthday, imagining when she was old enough to ride. To have a governess. To make her come-out. To wed.

"Lady Ada died years ago, Your Grace."

The solicitor's words were like a physical blow. "What?"

"I cannot remember exactly when. She was quite young, though. Five or six, I'd say. I believe it was her heart."

He remembered how delicate and frail Ada had always appeared to be. How late she had walked. How her nursery governess carried her everywhere even after Ada learned to do so.

"She is buried next to your mother."

Hart bowed his head. He supposed he would have to go and see his sister's grave at some point. His mother's, too. Neither had been home at the time of Percy's drowning. Hart used to wish his mother would arrive at Turner Academy. Not to take him away but just to see him. To tell him she loved him and that she was sorry for him being accused of something she knew he would never have done. As the years passed, though, he knew that visit would never come. The duchess had favored Percy and then Ada and had never given Hart much thought. He finally realized it was for the best. He had brothers in the Terrors. He needed no more family than they.

He swallowed and raised his head, seeing Griffin was studying him. "Go through everything now, Griffin. My holdings. My finances. My investments. I need to know what I possess beyond my title and what obligations I will need to fulfill."

As the solicitor droned on for the next three hours, Hart grew dizzy with just how much he possessed. Estates. Race horses. Investments in both England and overseas.

"We can meet again to continue our conversation, Your Grace. I fear I have wearied you with all my lengthy explanations."

"Very well. Nine o'clock tomorrow?"

"If it is convenient with you, it is convenient with me, Your Grace."

"Point me in the direction of a reliable inn, Griffin. I am in sore need of a bath and a hot meal. And a tailor, I suppose. I am wearing the only clothes I possess and they won't be suitable for society."

The solicitor appeared startled at his request. "You have no need of an inn, Your Grace. You have a beautiful London townhouse in which to stay when you come to town."

"I see."

It hadn't occurred to Hart that he had a place in London since he had never visited it before. Of course, his parents left for months at a time to partake in the Season when he was a boy and he supposed it was where they had always stayed.

Griffin offered to accompany him to the townhouse and smooth the way for him with the servants but Hart declined. He asked for the address and then walked there because he didn't think he had enough to pay for the hackney cab's fare.

He knocked on the door and a butler opened it. When he explained who he was, he gained admittance. The next few hours were a blur. He was put into a bath in the duke's rooms, which had been cleared of all personal possessions. A tailor arrived and measured him, promising to have an appropriate outfit at the house early tomorrow morning before he left to visit with Griffin again. He dined in his rooms on shepherd's pie and a rich claret and then fell into bed, naked, relishing the feel of the feathered pillow and clean bedclothes.

Though he was bone weary, Hart lay looking at the ceiling for a long time, wondering just how much his world would now change.

CHAPTER FOUR

Rumsford, Wiltshire—January 1813

OLIVIA FINISHED MAKING her bed and smoothed the coverlet. She was ready to leave her small bedchamber for the warmth of the kitchen. Winter had been colder than usual this year but nothing like the winters at Riverburn, her childhood home in Lancashire in the north of England. Thankfully, those years were behind her. She had found a home with her uncle and had lost all contact with her father.

Not that he even remembered who she was.

Olivia had been the only child from the marriage of Lord and Lady Rivers. As a female, she was deemed unimportant from birth. Her father only was interested in getting an heir. Olivia had thought if she could be clever and impress him, he might pay her a bit of attention. She had excelled at her studies with her governess and on the handful of occasions when she did see her father, she braved his wrath for even speaking to him and tried to share what she had learned.

It hadn't mattered. He didn't want to listen to her or have anything to do with her, especially after Higbee came to Riverburn when Olivia was nine. Her cousin had lost his father, who was in the military, and Lord Rivers, despairing of getting an heir off his wife, had brought the boy to live with them, believing his nephew was destined to be his heir apparent. At twelve,

Higbee was already tall, handsome, and quite intelligent. The boy became her father's world. If Olivia had been ignored before, she was now treated as an outcast.

Because of it, she had begun to take comfort in food. She ate everything in sight and even slipped down to the kitchens at night to find whatever was available. She had a terrible sweet tooth and indulged it whenever she could. Her mother, who had been the most sought after beauty of her come-out group, bemoaned Olivia's weight gain, as well as her ordinary looks. The criticism only made her eat more.

Olivia's own come-out had been a disaster. At eighteen, she was awkward and clumsy and vastly overweight. Though she had a large dowry, she lacked for dance partners and couldn't seem to make friends with any of the other girls. By Season's end, she had had no offers and doubted any would be coming along in the future.

When her mother contracted the pneumonia that autumn and quickly passed, it had brought Olivia some relief not to be attacked at every turn. Her father had agreed to allow her to go to her uncle and aunt in Wiltshire to help her get over her supposed grief.

Olivia never returned home.

She had spent every spring and summer with her relatives for as long as she could remember. Uncle Theo and Aunt Beryl were more parents to her than her own ever were. They happily took her in each Season while her parents attended all the social events of the *ton*. Every August when they came to collect her, she cried and begged to stay longer and was always refused.

Coming to Wiltshire had changed her life. With no one criticizing her and being showered with love, Olivia stopped overeating. She had slimmed down tremendously and actually blossomed, growing into her looks. While she would never be a great beauty as her mother had been, she could now look in the mirror without feeling shame. Fortunately, she didn't have to think of her looks very often. In Rumsford, she was valued for who she was. No one in the village minded that she was more intelligent than most people. She got over her shyness, helping Aunt Beryl with parish affairs. Soon, Olivia had gained confidence and an abundance of friends.

She loved her life now. The only shadow had been Aunt Beryl's passing last summer. She had been talking to Olivia one moment and was gone the next. Though she and Uncle Theo grieved, they knew Beryl was in a better place. Never had a kinder, sweeter woman walked the face of the earth.

Rubbing her hands together to try and warm them, Olivia left her bedchamber and went to the kitchen, where her uncle already sat at the table. She frowned, noticing again how thin he had become. He had seemed to lose his appetite after his wife passed and no matter what Olivia and Cook made to tempt him, he didn't seem interested.

"Good morning, Uncle Theo," she said, stopping to brush a kiss upon his cheek before taking a seat to his right.

"How did you sleep, my dear?" he asked, pouring her a cup of tea.

"Quite well though I placed an extra quilt over me last night."

"It has been cold since before Christmas," he noted.

Cook placed a plate before Olivia and she thanked her, digging into the hearty breakfast. She appreciated food now and didn't use it as a crutch. She wouldn't eat again until teatime.

"I'm off to the village," Cook announced as she slipped a basket over her arm. "Need to get more eggs and milk. We're also short on flour and sugar."

"Would you like me to go with you?" Olivia asked.

"No, my lady. You've got the Altar Guild meeting this morning. That's more important."

They finished up breakfast and Olivia rose to clear the table and wash the dishes.

"Wait," Uncle Theo said, placing an arm on her forearm. "We need to talk."

She sat, wondering what it might be. Usually, she helped him in putting together his weekly sermon and perhaps he wanted to seek her advice on it since they hadn't yet begun this week's. In fact, for several months now, she had managed the bulk of each sermon. She enjoyed being able to use her mind and make meaningful connections between the Scriptures and how to incorporate them into everyday life.

"We have visitors coming," he shared.

"Oh, does Cook know? When will they arrive? If it is around noon, perhaps we should serve them luncheon. Or an early tea," she mused.

"I doubt they will stay long." His brow creased and he fell silent.

Worry filled her. "What is it, Uncle Theo? What is troubling you? Who are these visitors?"

"Your father and cousin."

Olivia felt as if she had been slapped. "What? Why?"

She hadn't even thought of her father and cousin for months until this morning. She never heard from either of them. It was as if they no longer existed. When she had first come to stay in Wiltshire, she had dutifully written her father once a month for the first year. When her father's secretary had finally written to her telling her that the earl was too busy to maintain a corre-spondence—even though he had never answered a single one of her letters—Olivia had quit pretending to be the obedient, submissive daughter and ceased writing to him. Her father had never checked upon her even once. Never invited her to return to Riverburn at any time, whether for the Christmas holidays or on a more permanent basis.

Now, he was coming here. To Rumsford.

And with that spiteful Higbee.

Not only had her cousin been the golden child and male her father had longed for, he was cruel to Olivia. She had hoped Higbee would become a big brother to her. That they would ride together. Talk. Share secrets.

Instead, Higbee belittled her at every turn, making fun of her the more weight she gained. He would hide bugs in her bed and inside her shoes. Shred her hair ribbons. Put salt in her teacup. All of that she could tolerate. But he had gone beyond mere teasing. He had locked her in the basement for a day, threatening to break her arm if she told on him. As a warning, he had wrenched her wrist before he did so. He would push her when no one was looking. Kick her and she would fall. Everyone at Riverburn thought Olivia was clumsy because of her bruises—when all along, they had been the result of Higbee's doing.

A boy who was a bully would be much worse as a man. The thought of Higbee accompanying her father to Wiltshire now had her in a panic. The earl she could have calmly met. Her cousin, however, was a much different story.

Olivia sprang to her feet, absently collecting the dishes and taking them to the dishpan. She would wash them. Doing the dishes always soothed her.

"Olivia, please. Come and sit," Uncle Theo begged. "There's more to discuss before they arrive."

She whirled. "More?" Her belly roiled at the thought. Her uncle knew something. Something that he hadn't shared with her.

A loud knock sounded from the other room.

"They're here," Uncle Theo sighed.

She marched to the parlor and took a seat. She refused to be the one who welcomed them. Olivia placed her hands in her lap, one atop the other, trying to steady her racing heart as her uncle shuffled to the door. She almost fled the room before he opened the door but would not act as a coward. For whatever reason they had come, she would meet them head on.

Her father pushed his way into the vicarage, Higbee on his heels. In the years she had been gone, the earl's hair had turned from being threaded with bits of gray to completely gray. His face was more lined than before. Other than that, he looked the same.

Higbee had filled out, though. He had fully reached manhood, standing over six feet. He wore a beautifully tailored coat of dark blue and fawn breeches that showed off his muscular legs. His face had matured and she knew many women would consider him to be quite handsome.

"Good morning," Uncle Theo said to the pair before closing the door.

"Where is she?" the earl said, still not bothering to greet his own flesh and blood. His eyes searched the room and fell on her. "Get up, Girl. Go find Lady Olivia at once."

She realized that he thought her a servant. Olivia had never been much interested in clothes and she'd had no income during her stay with her aunt and uncle. She only had a few gowns now that she had slimmed down and those were serviceable, not fashionable. In fact, she had no idea what London fashion now dictated for a woman of Polite Society to wear. She had been in the country five years and never planned to darken a ballroom again.

Rising, she curtseyed and said, "I am Olivia, Father."

He frowned, looking perplexed by her statement. "Nonsense," he proclaimed. "The chit is a butterball."

She had never heard the word before but knew it was highly unflattering.

"I am your daughter," she repeated firmly, glaring at him, trying to keep her temper under control.

Higbee took a step toward her, studying her. "By God, Uncle—she is! Look at her eyes. They're the same bluish-gray." He shook his head. "You certainly have changed, Cousin. Last time I saw you, you outweighed me. Why, you look almost fragile now."

She might look fragile but she had a spine of steel. "Why are you here?" she demanded.

Her father's eyes cut to his brother. "You haven't told her?"

Uncle Theo shook his head. "Perhaps we should all take a seat."

"Told me what?" she asked, stepping to him.

Her uncle took her hand and pulled her to the settee. They

sat and the other two took a seat. The parlor suddenly seemed smaller than usual.

Squeezing her hand, Uncle Theo said, "I am sick, Olivia."

"No," she said, her voice a whisper as dread filled her.

"Yes. The doctor diagnosed it just before Beryl passed last year."

"Is that why you have no appetite?" she asked, her eyes beginning to fill with tears.

"Yes."

"How . . . how long do you have?"

He sighed. "The best guess is two or three months. Possibly less." His gaze met hers. "I am the one who wrote to your father, Olivia. He has come to take you home."

She shot to her feet. "No! I want to stay with you, Uncle. I must care for you."

"That won't be necessary," her father said, his tone bored.

Olivia turned to him. "I don't care what you say. I *will* care for Uncle Theo. He has been more a father to me than you ever were."

Uncle Theo took her hand and pulled her back to the settee. "It has already been arranged. The bishop knows and has spoken to the new duke regarding the living. A new vicar is being sent, along with his family. They will inhabit the vicarage. I will go stay with Mrs. Feldham. She has agreed to look after me until the end."

Olivia liked the widow and knew her to be caring and considerate but she couldn't allow this. "I won't be separated from you," she said stubbornly.

"I am afraid you have no say in the matter," Higbee said. "You are a woman and you will return with us today."

She whirled, her anger surging. "Why do you care, Higbee? You have never liked me. It shouldn't matter to you—or Father—whether I spend my time with Uncle Theo or not. You have made no effort these past five years to inquire after me. Why now?"

Higbee glanced guiltily at her father. A look passed between the two. One she didn't like.

"What do you have planned?" she asked, her tone cold.

"You are going to partake in the upcoming Season, Olivia," the earl said. "You will wed by Season's end."

She snorted. "Do you already have a groom picked out for me?"

Higbee laughed. "No, but it will be easier now. Why, from what I am told, you were the laughingstock of your come-out group, Cousin. At least now you have grown into your looks and I won't have to be responsible for you."

"I see." She glanced at her father and back to Higbee. "You are trying to get your ducks all in a row. You don't want to have me around once Father passes. I would be your responsibility then. The fat, maiden cousin who only grew older, year by year. One who frequented your dinner table and embarrassed you in front of your friends who gossiped about me."

Her cousin flushed and Olivia knew she had guessed correctly.

"We are doing you a favor," her father said. "Theodore wrote to me of his illness and begged me to do my duty by you. This way, you won't have to watch him slowly die, as you did your mother."

Anger surged through her at the loss of control over her life and having to be parted from her beloved uncle.

"Do you think I really cared about her? With all the barbs she threw my way? She harped on what a disappointment I was to her and belittled me at every turn. Told me how I was an obese ugly duckling and that no man would ever want me. I was relieved when she passed. It freed me from her taunts and allowed me to leave Riverburn. Not that you ever noticed. You paid me no attention when I lived there and never bothered to respond to a single letter I wrote you once I left."

Olivia stood again. "Go, the both of you," she said firmly. "I will care for Uncle Theo."

Both her father and cousin rose. "That is not an option, Olivia," her father said sternly. "Comments have been made. You know how the *ton* loves to gossip. There are rumors you are dead. That I banished you. That you are now an actress or even a whore in a brothel. I don't want any taint of gossip to affect Higbee's chances of making an excellent match."

He stared hard at her. "You will come with us. Today. You will attend the Season. You will wed. You will refrain from speaking poorly of me or your dear cousin, who has nothing but love and respect for you."

She knew she had no choice in the matter. Women never did.

"I will go and pack," she said dully.

"Let the maid do that," Higbee said, sniffing.

Olivia looked at him with narrowed eyes. "She is only here once a week. Would you care to wait until Thursday for the packing to be accomplished?"

He looked shocked. "Then who does . . . oh, you do," he said knowingly. "Bloody hell. My cousin is a maid."

She turned and left the room, hurrying to her bedchamber.

"I will not cry," she said, gritting her teeth. "I will not give them the satisfaction of seeing me as weak."

Opening the wardrobe, she took out her small group of gowns, placing them on the bed, along with her other belongings. It was a sparse collection. She thought back to her one Season and all the gowns, chemises, and stockings she had possessed, most of which she had left behind when she'd fled to Wiltshire. The lone trunk she had brought with her five years earlier sat in the corner. She removed the books that sat atop it and unlocked it. Folding her clothing, she placed it within the trunk, including the extra pair of shoes that she wore in warmer weather. The books also went inside. They were her uncle's but he would want her to have them.

Finally, she took the small miniature of her aunt and uncle from its place beside her bed. Aunt Beryl said they'd had it painted shortly before they'd wed. In it, the pair looked so young and alive.

This is how she would choose to remember them. Full of life and love for each other.

And her.

Olivia returned to the silent parlor. No conversation occurred.

"My trunk is ready," she said to no one in particular.

"I will have the footman fetch it," Higbee said, leaving the parsonage.

"Say your goodbyes," her father commanded and followed his nephew out the door.

Tears blurred her eyes as she looked at her beloved uncle. She took his hands.

"This is the last time we will see one another," she said softly. "I doubt they will let me return for your funeral."

"You have no need to do so, my darling girl," Uncle Theo said. "Remember me as I am and move on to a new, fuller life. Do not let them bully you as to whom you should marry. You will know him. Your heart will know his."

He leaned close and pressed a kiss to her brow. "You came to us for so many years, over those many springs and summers. And then Beryl and I were fortunate enough to have you in our lives year-round. Do not be sad, Olivia. I will go to Beryl and we will watch over you. Stand strong. You have grown into a lovely woman, both inside and out. You will take your special charms and make others very happy."

"I don't know what I will do without you," she said, desolation filling her.

"You will go on. 'Tis what we all do after great loss. And you will be stronger for it. You have learned life's true lessons here. How to be kind to others. How to give of yourself and expect nothing in return. How to take joy in simple things. Keep those things fast."

Her throat swelled with emotion. "I will," she choked out.

"Then let us see you on your way." He reached into his pocket and pulled out a small pouch. "Take this."

When he passed it to her, she heard the jingle of coins.

"Oh, I can't. You will need this to pay the widow for your care."

"Actually, your father is providing the funds for that so I am giving you all that I have."

Olivia hugged him. "That is very generous."

"You will need it. My brother may provide you with a wardrobe for the Season but he won't think of the little things you'll wish for, such as books."

"You know me so well, Uncle Theo."

He smiled. "You have been as my own child, Olivia. I am grateful for the time we have spent together."

She slipped the pouch inside her reticule and her cloak about her. Uncle Theo walked her out the door. The footman entered once they left. Then Olivia moved back, glancing inside one last time at the place she had been her happiest.

She turned and they walked toward the carriage. Her father and cousin were already inside. She thought them horribly ill-mannered not to even tell Uncle Theo goodbye, especially knowing he hadn't long to live.

Olivia faced him. "I will write to you."

He smiled. "I will look forward to receiving your letters. But not too many of them, my dear. Spend more of your time living life and not writing to me about it. Promise?"

"I promise," she said solemnly.

The footman returned and fastened her trunk to the carriage. He faced her. "Ready, my lady?"

"One more moment."

She flung her arms about Uncle Theo. "I love you so very, very much."

"I love you, my sweet girl."

Olivia broke away and took the footman's offered hand. He helped her into the carriage and she sat. Immediately, her eyes went to her uncle.

The driver started up the vehicle and Uncle Theo smiled wistfully as he waved farewell to her. She waved back, biting her lip, reminding herself not to cry. She watched out the window until her uncle and the vicarage were a mere speck on the horizon and then continued to train her gaze at the passing scenery.

Olivia would keep her promise to Uncle Theo. She would live the life she wanted, as much as she could within the confines of Polite Society. She wouldn't try to hide her bluestocking tendencies, as she had during her first Season. Others would either accept her—or they wouldn't. She wouldn't change for them. Instead, she would always be true to herself.

It would be the way she honored Uncle Theo and Aunt Beryl's memory.

CHAPTER FIVE

London—March

OLIVA SAT AT the silent breakfast table, watching the two men who had taken her away from the happy life she had known. They had rarely acknowledged her presence. That first morning in London after Higbee had discarded the newspaper he was reading, she had politely asked for it.

He'd refused.

Her cousin had told her it was entirely unnecessary for her to have access to a newspaper, citing that true ladies knew nothing about current affairs and shouldn't care to. When she had corrected him, saying she was very interested in topics such as politics, he had given her a dismissing look and gone back to his breakfast.

She was tired of being left out of everything. Of going practically nowhere, other than the dressmaker's shop, where she had more fittings today.

"Are you ever going to receive any new gowns?" Higbee asked, startling her. "You have worn the same handful of rags ever since we came to London."

"They are perfectly suitable," she snapped. "And I am waiting on my fittings to be completed in order to receive my new gowns."

In truth, she should have already gotten most of her new

wardrobe. She didn't know why Madame La Renn was dragging her feet and decided she would confront the modiste this afternoon.

Higbee cleared his throat, gaining his uncle's attention. "You're going to have to wear appropriate clothing to *ton* events. You don't want to embarrass us or yourself."

"Your cousin is right," her father said.

"Uncle, you must also demand that Olivia keep conversation to suitable topics," Higbee said.

"Just what topics do you deem suitable?" she asked. "I suppose politics, economics, and discussions regarding rights for the lower classes are considered unsuitable."

Her cousin looked taken aback. "Of course, they are." He thought a moment. "The weather. Yes, that is a safe topic."

"I can't talk about the weather for an entire conversation," she pointed out. "If I am to find a husband, I must learn something about him."

"I can help in that," Higbee said. "Already, I have told a few of my friends from university about you." He looked to the earl. "Although, Uncle, you might have to increase the chit's dowry in order to make her more appealing to the right gentleman."

"I am not a chit!" she cried, standing and tossing her napkin upon the table.

"Sit," her father commanded.

Reluctantly, Olivia reclaimed her napkin and returned it to her lap as she took her seat again.

"I don't care to meet any of your friends," she said, sniffing. "If they are your friends, that is reason enough for me to dislike them."

"See, Uncle?" Higbee said. "She is impossible."

Her father glared at her. "You will do as you are told. Your cousin and I will help to find you a proper husband."

"You . . . what . . . does that mean you are choosing him for me?" she asked, outraged at the thought.

Her father shrugged. "We know who is and isn't appropriate

in society. It is your job to sparkle and attract the right man."

"Sparkle?" She laughed.

"Yes, sparkle. As your mother did. You are to look and act your best at all times. I expect nothing less from you. The gentlemen that ask to court you must be approved by me or Higbee. Only then will they be allowed to call on you or take you on various outings."

Despair filled her. She realized her father and cousin would only be interested in the wealthiest men of society for her. Money meant nothing to her because she'd had none her entire life. Her simple life at the parsonage had suited her well.

Riled at the thought of having no say in her future husband, Olivia said, "I suppose you will want me to find not only a wealthy man but a titled one, as well."

"Of course," Higbee agreed. "Marriages are meant to bring opportunities between families."

"Then I suppose an earl won't be good enough. I should aim for a marquess—or a duke," she quipped.

"I doubt you could land a duke with your independent streak," her father said. "Dukes aren't men who wish to be challenged, least of all by their wives." His face grew stern. "I am warning you, Olivia. Do not behave in an untoward manner at social events."

"I know never to be alone with a gentleman, Father. I remember that much from my come-out Season."

"No one would have wanted to be alone with you then," Higbee said gleefully. "You were a tub of lard."

His words hurt her but Olivia kept silent.

"I expect you to do as your cousin has suggested," the earl continued. "Restrict your conversations to a limited group of safe topics. Do not display any of your bluestocking ways."

"But if I don't truly converse with a man, how am I to know his true character?" she complained.

"That is where Higbee and I will step in. We will judge if a man has character enough to court you."

Olivia knew all they would be interested in was how lofty a title he possessed and how much wealth he possessed. Despite her tendency to defy them, she vowed not to consider a baron or viscount as her husband since he wouldn't be allowed to woo her. Getting to know them would only prove fruitless in the long run and might hurt the man, not to mention herself.

She had already dreaded the Season but now she felt all choice was being removed from her. She could only hope to find a man her relatives approved of that also might fit her criteria of what she wished for in a husband. She wanted a moral man. One who was kind and thoughtful. Loyal to his family and friends. A man who might actually admire her mind and not think her some silly plaything.

Rising, she said, "If you will excuse me. I have the week's menus to plan with Cook."

Olivia left the breakfast room and retreated to what had been her mother's sitting room. She had rarely been allowed inside it as a child. It still felt odd to her to be sitting in it but she knew it was a place her father and cousin would avoid. The room had become her retreat these past two months, ever since she had been taken from Wiltshire.

As expected, Cook joined her and they discussed the week's menus. The rich fare had been hard for Olivia to become accustomed to after years of dining upon simple, country food. She had incorporated some of that into a meal or two each week. So far, no one had complained. Once they decided upon what to serve, Olivia wrote out the meals for Cook and gave her the copy.

"Thank you for all you do, Cook," she said with sincerity.

The older woman smiled broadly. "It's nice to be appreciated, my lady."

Next, Olivia took out parchment and wrote to Uncle Theo. She did so twice a week. She didn't have much to tell him about because she hadn't done much during her time in London. Instead, she reminisced during each letter about happy times they had spent together, often including Aunt Beryl in her recollections. She hoped her uncle appreciated receiving her letters. Already the ones he sent to her showed how he had deteriorated. His handwriting, always so neat and meticulous, had altered into a scrawl. The length grew shorter with each one she received. Soon, she knew he would be gone.

And then she would truly be alone.

She summoned a servant and asked that the letter be posted immediately and then settled in with a book for a few hours before her noon appointment at the modiste's. She would rather be reading than having Mary, her new lady's maid, experiment with various hairstyles for the upcoming Season.

Olivia lost herself in the book, a history of Ancient Greece, and was surprised when Mary appeared.

"It's time to leave for our appointment, my lady," the servant told her. "Come, let me pin on your hat. I've also got your shawl, umbrella, and reticule. The skies are threatening but there's been no rain as of yet."

She let the maid fuss over her and then they left the townhouse. The carriage awaited them and the driver drove them to Madame La Renn's shop.

As they disembarked, Olivia saw the look exchanged between Mary and the footman and said, "I am going to be here for some time, Mary. Perhaps you would rather stay in the carriage instead of standing inside the shop for hours." Glancing at the footman, she said, "Why don't you keep Mary company?"

"You might need me, my lady," Mary protested unconvincingly.

"If I do, then I will send for you. You will only be a few feet away."

Olivia entered the dress shop and was glad Madame greeted her personally. She thought since she had no chaperone to guide her, despite being three and twenty, the dressmaker had been taking advantage of her.

"Madame La Renn, this will be my fourth time to come to your place of business. Once was for taking my measurements and selecting fabrics, while the next three have been for fittings. I find it odd that I have yet to receive a single gown."

The Frenchwoman frowned. "But surely you realize—"

"I realize that you are dragging your feet, Madame. My father's money is just as good as the next customer's. By day's end, I expect at least a good dozen day gowns or more to have arrived at our residence."

The modiste nodded. Olivia noted approval in her eyes. "Of course, Lady Olivia. Many are already completed. Others will be fitted today, including all of your evening wear. It is why I asked you to reserve several hours for the process today. I myself will supervise your fittings."

True to her word, Madame kept Olivia until shortly after half-past three, guaranteeing that she would send a wagon with gowns and all of the undergarments, gloves, and stockings that had been purchased, as well as several reticules.

"Have you purchased any hats yet, my lady?" the modiste asked.

"I was waiting to see how my gowns turned out before I did so."

The woman reached for a card and presented it to Olivia. "This is a milliner that I trust. She is two blocks from my shop. I give her my highest recommendation."

"Thank you, Madame. I look forward to meeting her—and receiving my gowns."

She left the dress shop and moved toward the carriage. The stairs still remained in place but Olivia wasn't ready to climb them yet and return home. Instead she knocked on the carriage's door.

The footman opened it, looking a bit rumpled, as did Mary, whose face was flushed.

"I wanted to tell you that I am through at Madame's and have decided to go to the bookshop that is three doors to the north. I will browse for a good while, perhaps an hour or more, and then be ready to return home."

"Yes, my lady," the pair murmured, still looking guilty.

Olivia didn't care. Servants had a hard life. If these two cared for one another and she had allowed them to steal several hours this afternoon in which they could be together, she was happy to do so.

She moved down the pavement and had to cross the entrance to an alley to reach the bookshop. She glanced down it and, a few feet away, saw a group of four boys huddled in a circle, bending over. Then she heard a high-pitched shriek.

"What are you boys doing?" she shouted, stepping toward them.

They sprang apart and she saw they held lit matches in their hands. One of the boys held an ebony kitten by the scruff.

"Are you torturing that poor creature?" she demanded.

"What's it to you?" the tallest one asked. He reached out and shoved her.

Olivia staggered back a few feet, appalled at the boy having put his hands on her.

"I demand an apology, young man, and then you are to let that poor kitten go."

"Who do you think you are?" another boy asked, the one holding the struggling kitten. He dangled it beside his leg as the other two boys faced her, their fists balled.

Though fear tugged at her, she said, "I am Lady Olivia Knight."

The leader guffawed and the other three boys snickered.

"Ladies don't dress like that," the tall one said, playing to his audience.

She glanced down at her simple country gown and worn boots, both of which had seen better days.

"It doesn't matter how I am dressed," she told them. "I am who I said I am. Lady Olivia Knight. Daughter of the Earl of Rivers. You must stop what you are doing at once. Give me the kitten," she demanded.

"Or what?" the leader said, taking a threatening step toward her.

For a moment, she thought the boy, who couldn't be more than nine or ten, might strike her.

Because of that, she struck first.

Olivia swung the reticule attached to her wrist, hitting the boy on the side of his head, stunning him. With the umbrella she carried, she slammed it into his face, directly into his nose. Blood spurted everywhere and he cried out in surprise. The other boys moved toward her as one. Fear filled her.

Then they looked as if they had seen a ghost. The one holding the kitten threw it at her and, somehow, she managed to catch it as they rushed past her.

She didn't know what had happened because her entire focus was on the kitten. It was coal black but she could see where part of its tail had been singed. The two front paws also had been burned. Tears filled her eyes at the cruelty she had witnessed. Cuddling the kitten to her chest, she turned.

That was when she saw the very imposing man standing directly behind her.

CHAPTER SIX

HART LEFT HIS London townhouse for a walk, once again ready to explore a city he knew little about. He had come to town at the urging of his fellow Terrors and their wives, having spent the Christmas holidays with the group at Hillside, Donovan's country estate.

It still unnerved him to see his friend missing part of his arm and hand. Donovan had been in a carriage accident and the limb had been pinned under the weight of the vehicle. To save his life, amputation had been necessary. Wynter, Donovan's wife, still bore a faint scar on her cheek from the accident. To think of all the risks Donovan had taken in war, only to come home and lose his hand and forearm, chilled Hart. Still, his friend hadn't seemed to care, being in remarkably good spirits. Part of it was due to having married his beautiful wife, while the rest was because Wynter had just presented her husband with a son in late November. The couple had named the boy Samuel, to be known as Sam, after Donovan's beloved brother.

Spending the holidays with all the Terrors, save Finch, had been the balm Hart's soul needed. It was good to reconnect with the men who had been his friends since childhood. They had gone through much together. It didn't surprise him that Miles had married. He was the most responsible of the Terrors and would have thought immediately that he needed a duchess and an heir. Meeting Emery and seeing how well she complemented

Miles assured Hart that his friend had made a successful match.

Emery had served as Wildwood's de facto steward and had taught not only Miles but Wyatt and Donovan about estate management. She was friendly and efficient and had passed along several ideas to Hart, which he had asked his own steward, Patterson, to implement. Between meticulous notes Emery had provided for him and his daily meetings with Patterson, Hart believed he had a good handle on the state of affairs at Deerfield Park. Patterson had been its steward for three years and had brought some important changes to the estate. Coupled with advice from Emery, which Patterson was implementing with enthusiasm, Deerfield Park would thrive for many years to come.

What did surprise him was the fact that both Wyatt and Donovan had wed so quickly. The pair had been the libertines of the Terrors. Even though they had become unexpected dukes, the alacrity with which both men wed had startled him. Once he met Meadow and Wynter, however, he could understand why his friends had snatched up the beauties, who were as warm, intelligent, and caring as Emery. The time spent getting to know the three women allowed him to see the advantages of marrying.

Hart had fallen in love with the three new little Terrors. Ben was the oldest at seventeen months and the image of Miles. Little Leah, born last summer, favored both Wyatt and Meadow. The newest addition, Sam, was all Donovan. Hart had found himself going to the nursery to see each of the children, often finding his friends there playing with and holding their babes. Each of the three men did so with ease, even Donovan with his one-armed approach.

It had caused envy to brew within Hart. He had never been the jealous sort, his friends having little to nothing as he did, having been cast out from their family homes and sent to Turner Academy. Even where women were concerned, Hart didn't mind when a barmaid was more attracted to Donovan or Wyatt, who actively pursued the fairer sex and even competed for them with each other.

What Hart found himself longing for was what he saw between the couples. The way they looked at one another. The casual touches. The subtle ways they communicated with one another without conversation. It was obvious each of his friends had made love matches. The men were not only besotted with their wives but their children.

And Hart wanted that. Desperately.

It was why he had agreed, at the women's urging, to come to London for the Season. While he would have preferred to remain at Deerfield Park and go through spring planting and summer harvest, he knew Patterson more than capable of running the estate. Coming to London to peruse the Marriage Mart was his mission in life now.

Hart had tired of war. He felt beat down by it. He wanted to be revitalized and find a woman as appealing as the Female Terrors, as he'd come to think of them. He doubted he would be as fortunate in finding a woman of both beauty and intelligence but if he had to choose, he would favor intelligence. Looks faded, but a woman he could converse with as their relationship matured over the years was something he was interested in.

Wynter had told him he would find love and when he did, he would know it. Hart doubted love was in the cards for him. It had already struck thrice among the Terrors, and so the odds were against that. Still, he had high hopes he could find a decent match among the ladies of the *ton* since dozens of them were to make their come-outs this Season. He wanted to be settled with a wife and children, perhaps a few dogs, happy in the country, and leave the shadow of war that stained his soul far behind.

He had already spent most of today with his solicitor. There never seemed to be an end to business dealings. Sitting behind a desk—even sitting, period—was not something he was fond of. Hart now walked the London streets for a good two hours, enjoying stretching his legs and being caught up in the rhythm of the city before he decided to make his way home since the skies had turned dark and ominous.

Passing an alley next to a bookshop he had stopped in a few days ago, he saw a group of boys and the back of a woman. One boy moved menacingly toward her and before Hart could act, the woman swung her reticule into the boy's head. Her other arm swiftly came up and the boy howled as Hart saw blood sprout from his nose.

Hart glared at the boys, who caught sight of him and rushed past the woman. Her head bent and she cooed softly before turning around and spying him. Her eyes widened and he was drawn in by them. They were a bluish-gray and had depths he suddenly wanted to explore. He took in the rest of her, petite with blond hair and an oval face. She was very pretty though her mouth trembled. She wore an old shawl and a gown of faded blue which had seen better days.

A faint *meow* sounded and they both looked to the furball she held close to her. Hart stepped forward.

"Is it your kitten?" he asked softly.

The woman shook her head, dropping her gaze to focus on the black furball. "No, I came across those boys on my way to the bookshop. They were torturing the poor thing, lighting matches and holding them to it."

An expletive escaped his lips and he apologized.

"No need to apologize, my lord," she told him. "I have a few choice words to call those ruffians myself."

Hart didn't correct her. He had been *Your Graced* enough so that he was sick of hearing it. Instead, he touched the pad of his thumb between the ears of the kitten. Despite its mistreatment, he heard it purring.

"She likes you," the woman murmured, smiling at the kitten.

"You know it's female?" he asked.

"No. Do you know how to tell?"

"I do. If you'll let me see it."

She hesitated a moment and then handed the kitten over. "Be careful of her front paws," she cautioned. "They are burned as is some of the fur on her tail."

He investigated briefly and announced, "You are right, Miss. The kitten is female." He handed it back to her and said, "Those paws need to be looked at, though."

"Oh, I know what to do."

Despite just having met her, he said, "I only live two blocks from here. Would you like to take the kitten to my townhouse and see to it there?"

She bit her lip and a rush of desire rippled through Hart, surprising the hell out of him.

She took a few steps to reach the mouth of the alley. Glancing down the street, she looked back at him. "All right, my lord. Lead the way."

If she had been gentry, he would have offered her his arm. As it was, she cradled the kitten and merely fell into step beside him.

"It's just around this corner, Miss . . ." His voice trailed off.

"Knight," she supplied. "Miss Knight."

"Well, Miss Knight," he said. "My townhouse is up here on the left."

Hart watched as she realized the enormous, stately building was their destination. To her credit, she merely nodded.

"I will assume your staff will have everything I need."

"Undoubtedly."

He opened the door and found a startled footman standing by the door.

"Your Grace!" he cried.

The woman beside him tensed slightly but she kept her poise.

"Show me to the kitchens, please," she said to the footman.

When he frowned and looked at Hart for direction, Hart said, "I'll take you to them."

His arrival in the kitchens caused a stir. Hart told Cook, "This is Miss Knight. See that she has what she needs."

"Yes, Your Grace," the large woman said.

Immediately, Miss Knight sprang into action, dictating orders, rattling off a list of things she wanted as she balanced holding the kitten and setting down her reticule and umbrella. Hart supposed by her manner and dress that she must be a governess, used to being in charge. He remained to the side as she bathed the kitten's paws and singed tail in cool water.

By now, a scullery maid had collected the whipped egg whites Miss Knight had asked for and brought them in a bowl. She dipped the kitten's paws and coated the tail with that. Then she took the clean cloth she received and dipped it into a strong tea, which Cook had just finished brewing. Miss Knight pursed her full lips and blew on the cloth, again causing a stir of desire within Hart. She had appeared to be pretty to him at first. Now, she became more attractive by the minute as she ministered to the tormented kitten.

She looked around. "Is the axle grease here yet?"

"Coming," another scullery maid replied as she opened the door and a young groom hustled inside with a bucket.

Drawing closer, Hart asked, "Why axle grease?"

"It is made of animal fat and beeswax, which has been thinned with turpentine. It will create a sterile seal and keep out infection."

"I see. Here, let me help," he said, taking the squirming kitten and holding it steady while she coated the injured areas.

"Cloth, please," Miss Knight commanded. "And the scissors."

She took the linen square and cut it, fashioning small booties for the kitten, which she slid over its paws.

"The ribbon?"

A maid handed it over and Miss Knight clipped it to the size she wanted, tying lengths of it around the kitten's legs so the linen bandage would stay in place. She did the same to the now-quivering kitten's tail. Hart continued stroking the poor thing, his heart going out to it.

Miss Knight sat and lifted the kitten from him, placing it in her lap. He swore he saw gratitude in the kitten's eyes as it began to purr again.

"The warmed milk?"

Cook herself set the saucer on Miss Knight's thigh and

stepped back. Seeing it wobble, he leaned over to steady it, holding it by the edge, the back of his fingers resting against her thigh. Something passed between them and she frowned, looking at him oddly and then quickly away. She moved the kitten slightly and it began lapping at the milk, slowly at first and then hungrily.

That's how Hart wanted his first kiss with Miss Knight to be. Slow. Full of exploration. Then heating up greedily.

He blinked.

He had no business kissing a governess. One he had met not more than a quarter-hour ago. He didn't deal in foolishness.

Still, he kept his gaze on her, watching her face light up as the kitten continued to eat.

"There, Midnight. Good girl."

"So, you have already named her?"

"Yes. Though why, I haven't a clue. I doubt I will be able to keep her."

She blinked away what he thought might be tears. Of course, being a governess, she wouldn't be able to keep any kind of pet in the household where she served.

Determination filled her face. "I will try to do so, however." She looked back to Cook. "Was a basket found?"

"Yes, Miss." Cook handed over the wicker basket. "Lined with flannel cloths, just as you asked."

Miss Knight smiled. "Thank you, Cook. You and His Grace's staff have been most helpful. Midnight and I are most grateful."

She slipped the kitten into the basket and stroked it a few times. The furball's eyes drooped and then shut. Miss Knight closed the lid to the basket and stood, slipping her reticule upon her wrist again and collecting her umbrella.

"I will be off now, Your Grace. Thank you for your help with the kitten and those unruly boys." She chuckled. "I thought I was the one who had scared them off but I realize now that you lurking at the mouth of the alley did the job for me."

Without further ado, she stood and briskly made her way

from the kitchen. Hart watched the sway of her hips for a moment, enjoying the sight of them swishing from side to side, then he strode after her.

By the time he caught up to her, she had reached the foyer and he asked, "Might I take you home?"

She flushed. "No. I was meeting a friend at the bookshop. I should return there."

The nearby clock chimed five times.

"The bookshop will be closed by the time you reach it."

"Still, my friend might be waiting for me. I must go. Thank you again for your help, Your Grace."

"I will accompany you."

He thought annoyance flashed across her face but if it did, she quickly hid it and nodded.

"Let me carry Midnight for you," he said, easing the basket from where it hung on her arm.

"Thank you."

They walked the few blocks to the bookshop and he returned the basket to her.

Glancing around, he said, "I don't believe I see your friend. Are you certain I cannot offer you a ride home?"

"No, thank you. I believe I will remain here a few more minutes in case she comes, after all. Goodbye, Your Grace."

He felt dismissed and nodded. "It was a pleasure to meet you, Miss Knight. Stay out of alleyways—else you might collect more than a kitten the next time."

She laughed, rich and throaty, causing a frisson of delight to run through him.

Hart turned and reluctantly left her. As he rounded the corner, he decided to go back and at least ask where she was employed. He would use the kitten as an excuse, saying he might want to come see if it had recovered from its injuries.

When he reversed course and came around the corner again, he saw Miss Knight already gone from where she had stood. She hurried down the pavement as if the Devil himself were after her.

Hart began following her.

She was met by a footman and what looked to be a maid. Quickly, he ducked into the doorway of a shoemaker's shop and, from his hiding place, leaned out a touch in order to see what was happening.

The maid's hands were flying in the air, as if she were scolding Miss Knight. Then the footman helped her into a carriage, with the maid following. Hart stepped back, waiting for the vehicle to pass in the street. As it did, he saw no distinguishing marks on it though the team of horses pulling the carriage was a fine group of horseflesh.

As the carriage rolled past him, he stepped out to watch it, wondering why a governess—or whatever she was—had use of such a fine vehicle.

Hart also wondered why she had lied to him.

There had been no friend. Miss Knight had been eager to return to this area because a carriage already waited to take her home. Curiosity filled him. Not much had caught his attention since he had been home, certainly not a beautiful upper servant.

Hart wondered how he could go about locating Miss Knight—and finding out exactly who she was.

CHAPTER SEVEN

*W*HY HAD SHE *decided to hide her identity?*

Olivia lay in bed, gently stroking the kitten that slept upon her pillow. Soon, Mary would be coming in to help her dress for the day. The maid hadn't seen Midnight yet. No one in the household had. But Olivia was going to have to do something with her soon.

She had left the kitten in its basket and gone downstairs to dinner last night, sitting on her father's left, as usual. Immediately, he had sneezed once she sat down. Several times. The earl had wrinkled his nose.

"Have you been in the stables touching any of the barn cats?" he asked, his tone accusatory.

"No, Father. You know I do not ride. I have no need to go to the stables."

Lord Rivers sneezed again. "Drat! Somehow, the smell of a cat has gotten inside. I can't abide the beasts. Their fur makes me sneeze uncontrollably."

Guilt filled her—and then a small feeling of satisfaction as he continued to sneeze repeatedly.

He pushed to his feet. "I will eat at my club."

"I'll join you, Uncle," Higbee said, giving her a smug look as he followed his uncle from the dining room.

Olivia had asked that her meal be sent up on a tray since she was now alone, along with a glass of warmed milk to help her sleep. She had torn up tiny bits of the roasted chicken and fed them to Midnight, who ate them daintily. The kitten also drank a good portion of the milk. The poor thing must have been starving. She didn't know how old Midnight might be but the kitten would still need caring for until her paws healed. Even then, Olivia couldn't see turning the creature out onto the streets. She had determined to speak to the head groom in their stables tomorrow after breakfast and see if Midnight could join the other cats her father referred to.

She found a small puddle of urine which the kitten had left and cleaned it up with a handkerchief before placing the kitten inside her basket again. She washed her hands and face thoroughly since Midnight had slept next to her all night and then allowed Mary to dress her once the maid appeared.

Going to the breakfast room, she found only Higbee present.

"Where is Father?" she asked, a little worried that he wasn't here.

"His valet says he is a bit under the weather and breakfasting in his room. I hear his eyes are almost swollen shut. He blames cat dander and avoids the creatures at all cost."

Higbee went back to his newspaper. Fortunately, their London butler had taken a liking to Olivia and saw that she received the newspapers each day, placing them in her sitting room after Higbee discarded them. It was wonderful to read the London newspapers on a daily basis, which carried much more information than the country one which came out once a month and only carried news of local affairs. She always left the newspapers in her sitting room and the butler retrieved them, replacing them with the next day's editions.

Once she finished eating, Olivia returned to her room to collect the basket and took it to the stables, asking a young boy to summon the head groom. When he arrived, she told him of the injured kitten she had found and how she'd ministered to it, only to learn that the earl was sensitive around cats, making her unable to keep the kitten inside the house.

"We can always use another mouser," he declared. "How did you tend to its injuries?"

"It's a she. Her name is Midnight."

Olivia explained what she had done and the groom nodded sagely. "Seems like you did what was needed, my lady. I'll have my missus keep Midnight in our rooms until she is healed and is a bit older. You're welcome to come and visit her there or in the stables."

"Thank you. I was worried Midnight wouldn't have a home."

Returning to the house, she went to her room and rang for Mary, telling the maid they were going to the milliner's. She had taken the carriage yesterday in the hopes of being able to bring gowns back from Madame La Renn's. Though she hadn't, the modiste had been good to her word and a wagon appeared shortly before six last night, filled with every gown Olivia had ordered. Mary had enjoyed putting them all away, exclaiming over the beautiful cuts and materials used.

Not wanting to ask for the carriage again since the milliner's shop wasn't but a ten-minute walk, she put on her new spencer, a deep blue and perfectly tailored to fit her. It was warmer than her ancient shawl. The new gown she wore made her feel quite pretty, as did the matching reticule. Now, all she needed was a much better hat than the one Mary placed upon her head and pinned into place.

"You're looking right smart, my lady," Mary praised. "I'm going to burn your old gowns."

"No, don't do that. Perhaps someone in the household might have need of them."

Mary's lips twitched. "My lady, they are threadbare and faded in color. No one will want them, not even the lowest servant." She paused. "Your shawl is old but nice. I wouldn't mind having it."

"Then it is yours."

"Thank you," the girl said, going to the shawl and wrapping it about her, a satisfied smile on her face.

They proceeded to the milliner's shop, referring to the address on the card Olivia had received from Madame La Renn.

"I may be some time," she warned her maid. Reaching into her reticule, she produced a coin. "Why don't you look for a cart with hot crossed buns and treat yourself? Come back in an hour."

Mary beamed. "Thank you, my lady. You are very generous." She accepted the coin and waited to leave until after Olivia entered the shop.

Glancing around, she saw three women together. The tallest of them handed a hat to one with silver-blond hair and said, "Try this one on, Wynter."

The woman did. "What do you think?"

The third said, "I think Donovan would love you in it. The blue brings out the blue in yours eyes."

The blond smiled at her friend. A pang of envy struck Olivia. She wondered what it would be like to have friends to go shopping with or to museums or to Gunter's for ices. She had longed to do all those things during her come-out Season and hadn't made any friends that she might accompany around town.

"May I help you?" a voice said.

She turned and guessed this was the proprietress of the shop. "Mrs. Hamlin?" she asked.

"Yes," the woman with dark hair and light eyes replied. "Might you be Lady Olivia?"

"I am," she said, unsure how the woman knew Olivia's name. "Madame La Renn sent me to you."

"I know. You must have made a good impression upon her, my lady. Madame only sends her very best customers to me."

The milliner's words surprised her.

"Why don't you browse the shop while I fetch the list?" Mrs. Hamlin said.

"The list?"

"Yes. Madame sent a list of every gown she has produced for you in order to give me a better idea of your needs. I will bring it now."

The milliner left, disappearing through a curtain. Olivia shook her head and then realized the other three occupants in the store were staring at her. Her cheeks heated.

"You must have made a wonderful impression in order for Mrs. Hamlin to take you on," the tallest said. "She is quite particular in whom she accepts as a client. Why, three years ago, she wouldn't have seen me at all. I was living in the country, helping to run a large estate, with no idea that I would marry into the *ton*."

"You helped run an estate?" Olivia asked, awestruck.

"My father was the estate manager for the Duke of Winslow," the woman explained. "He grew ill and I took on more of the work as time progressed."

"Until she took on the duke," the blond said, smiling. Olivia saw a faint scar on her cheek, which did nothing to mar her beauty.

"Yes, I did," the tall woman said. "And we are both quite happy together."

"Oh!" Olivia exclaimed, not knowing what to say.

"Forgive me for not introducing myself. I am the Duchess of Winslow. These are my good friends, the Duchess of Haverhill and the Duchess of Amesbury."

She stood there, thunderstruck, to be in the company of three duchesses.

The Duchess of Winslow gently asked, "And who might you be, my lady?"

"Uh . . . I am . . ." She had to think a moment. "Lady Olivia Knight, Your Grace. Your Graces. It is indeed such a pleasure to meet you."

Both of the other duchesses stepped forward. The one with glossy brown hair said, "We are equally pleased to meet you, Lady Olivia. Might you be attending the Season this year?"

"Yes. It is why I am in need of hats. I have been living in the country for the past five years, after my come-out Season, and I am only returning to town now."

"Oh, did you wed?" the Duchess of Haverhill asked.

"No." Olivia felt herself flush. "My mother passed and I went to live with my aunt and uncle in Surrey. Uncle Theo is a vicar. Or he was. He is too ill now to tend to his parish."

"I am sorry to hear that," the Duchess of Winslow said.

"It is the reason I have returned to London," Olivia confided. "My father wishes for me to have another Season. He is insistent that I wed."

The three women looked at one another. She had no idea why they exchanged such a look—or what it meant.

The Duchess of Amesbury smiled. "Since you have been gone from town for so long, you might not know many people. We are happy to extend our friendship to you."

Olivia was touched. She didn't recognize either duchess from her own come-out Season and thought they must have just preceded her since they looked close to her age or slightly older. The Duchess of Winslow had said she wasn't a member of Polite Society before her marriage. To think she might go into this Season not only knowing a few women but possibly claiming friendship with them meant a great deal to her.

She returned the smile. "I would be delighted to become acquainted with you, Your Graces."

"Then you must come for tea," the Duchess of Haverhill said. "So that we might get to know one another. Are you free this afternoon?"

Startled, she said, "Yes, I am. I would be happy to take tea with you."

"Then it is settled." The duchess provided Olivia with her address, asking that she come at four o'clock. "Enjoy your hat shopping," she said. "We will talk all about it when we see you later."

The duchesses left the shop and Mrs. Hamlin stepped forward. "You are fortunate, my lady. Those three are very influential and most kindhearted. If they take you under their wing, I am certain you will find a husband of your liking by

Season's end."

"You heard our conversation?"

"That your father wishes you to wed? Yes, I did. And we must find the perfect hats for you to wear to attract the right kind of suitors."

An hour later, Mary came into the shop as Olivia was finishing up her discussion with Mrs. Hamlin. They had gone over the list Madame La Renn had provided and looked at various hats displayed in the shop. She had chosen several she liked and then worked with the milliner as she sketched a half-dozen more that would be particular to Olivia.

"I will see that your choices from my shop are delivered this afternoon," Mrs. Hamlin said. "As to designing the others, I will get them to you by the end of next week, in time for the Season's opening."

"I am very grateful, Mrs. Hamlin. I know little about fashion and appreciate your guidance today."

"Any time, Lady Olivia. I hope we will have a long and fruitful relationship."

She walked back with Mary, who pumped her for information about the various hats she had chosen and chattered about once again trying new hairstyles to see which would complement each of her mistress' new gowns.

This time, Olivia agreed and they returned to her bedchamber, where she allowed the maid to fiddle with various hair arrangements for over two hours.

Finally, she said, "I am going to tea today, Mary. Please select a gown for me."

The maid did so and altered Olivia's hair slightly to suit the gown. She thanked the servant and went downstairs, asking the butler where her father was and then going to his study. Rapping on the door, he bid her to enter.

The earl and Higbee sat together. Both arched their brows as she came in. Her father's eyes looked only slightly swollen.

"I was hoping to use the carriage this afternoon, Father," she began. "I have been asked to tea by a friend."

"You have friends?" Higbee asked, looking perplexed. "Who?"

Trying to sound nonchalant, she said, "The Duchess of Haverhill."

Her cousin's jaw dropped. "You know a duchess?"

"Yes. In fact, I am friends with three of them," she exaggerated, only hoping that claim would come true over the following weeks. "Both the Duchess of Amesbury and the Duchess of Winslow will also be in attendance today. Thankfully, my new gowns have arrived so I will be suitably dressed."

She turned back to her father. "May I have use of the carriage, Father?"

"Of course," he quickly replied. "In fact, I may need to escort you."

The last thing Olivia wanted was to bring her uninvited father along.

"I don't think you would be interested, Father. None of the dukes will be there. We are going to be discussing the hats we all purchased at Mrs. Hamlin's shop this morning."

She launched into excruciating detail about hats. Seeing her father's eyes glaze over, she knew she had won.

"You are right, Olivia. I think it best if you go to tea by yourself. However, I would like to meet these friends of yours. And their husbands."

Of course, he would. Lord Rivers was always chasing after and trying to befriend titled, powerful men. Dukes would be the ultimate prize. She didn't know what her father would make of these three women, however. Already, they seemed far different from anyone she had met during her come-out Season. Not that she previously met any duchesses or had been extended an offer of friendship from any ladies in the *ton* during her single Season. Olivia hoped she truly might make friends with these three. If not, at least she would be acquainted with them and be able to spot a friendly face when the Season began.

At a quarter to four, she came downstairs and went out the

front door to the waiting carriage. She was wearing a new gown and carried a matching reticule. She knew her hair to be stylish, thanks to Mary's ministrations. Her confidence soared as the carriage took her several blocks away.

They arrived at the Haverhill townhouse and Olivia squared her shoulders and knocked upon the door.

The butler greeted her by name. "Ah, Lady Olivia. Her Grace is expecting you. The Duchess of Amesbury is already present."

"And here I am," the Duchess of Winslow called out behind Olivia.

She linked her arm through Olivia's, telling the butler there was no need to announce them.

"Shall we?" the duchess asked, leading her up the stairs.

Olivia decided the three must see each other frequently to be so at home and not needing to be announced. She had never heard of such a thing but, once more, it distinguished these women from others.

They entered the drawing room and she was touched when both duchesses present greeted her with a kiss to her cheek.

"Please, have a seat," the Duchess of Haverhill said. "I hope you are hungry. My cook has been trying out some new tarts."

"I have never met a tart I didn't like," Olivia said and the three chuckled.

Already, she felt relaxed in their presence and forgot to be nervous in such illustrious company. She found herself enthusiastically discussing current events for the first time since she'd left Uncle Theo's and silently warned herself not to talk so much. She knew she had a tendency to dominate a conversation when she was interested in a topic but as they spoke, her new acquaintances actually seemed interested in her opinions. They discussed everything from politics to children's teething. All three women had little ones and Olivia delighted in hearing stories about them.

"I haven't been around children much but I would love to see your babies, Your Graces."

The Duchess of Winslow shook her head. "This won't do.

There are simply too many duchesses here. How are we to know whom you are speaking to?" She smiled. "I am Emery. Please call me by my name. It will lessen the confusion and I would feel much better relaxing the usual formalities."

"Oh, I was hoping we would do so," the Duchess of Amesbury said. "I am Meadow."

"And I am Wynter," the Duchess of Haverhill added.

With wonder, she said, "Then you must call me Olivia. I do love all your Christian names. And they seem to fit each of you so well."

The door opened and two very handsome men appeared. One looked to be about six feet. He had chocolate brown hair and hazel eyes which were so focused on Meadow that it seemed as if he saw no one else. He came and greeted her with a kiss to her cheek. The other gentleman, a few inches over six feet, had dark hair and piercing blue eyes. He was also missing the lower part of his left arm, which she could see by the way his coat was pinned. She wondered if he might have lost it while at war. He came and kissed Wynter's brow and then looked at Olivia with a friendly gaze.

"Darling, this is Lady Olivia Knight. Olivia, my husband, the Duke of Haverhill."

She rose and curtseyed and he took her hand. "It is a pleasure to meet you, Lady Olivia." He glanced to his companion. "Wyatt, come here."

The duke was kissing his wife's hand. "Yes?"

"Come meet Lady Olivia. This is Amesbury."

She curtseyed again and this second duke also took her hand. "Meadow says you are friends. It is nice to meet you, my lady."

"Lady Olivia will be attending the Season," Emery said. "She has been living in the country for several years. We aim to find her a husband."

Her cheeks flooded with heat. "Oh!" she declared, worried that these women thought her some kind of project.

"Lady Olivia knows quite a bit about politics," Wynter told

her husband. "We were discussing the recent policies the prime minister has implemented and she clarified several points for me regarding Lord Liverpool's stance on paying off the country's war debt."

"She also likes children and can't wait to meet ours," Meadow added.

The dukes exchanged a look and then Haverhill said, "Of course, our Sam may only be four months old but he is already brilliant. You will see so when you meet him. If this weren't his usual naptime, I am certain he would be in the midst of you ladies, stealing all the attention."

"Our daughter, Leah, is eight months now and can crawl faster than I walk," bragged Amesbury, looking every inch the proud papa.

Emery chuckled. "Well, I must throw in that my Ben, who is seventeen months now, is walking and likes to chase our dogs. He only says a few words, though."

Amesbury laughed. "He *is* Miles' boy. I will wager Miles was also one who said little when he was young until he had something important to say. Come to think of it, he is still the same way."

"Where is my husband?" Emery asked. "I thought you were together."

"We left Miles and Hart at White's," Haverhill said. "They were looking at some crop report."

Emery's eyes lit up. "Oh, I do hope Miles will bring it home with him."

The two men laughed and Amesbury said to Olivia, "No one enjoys a good discussion regarding crops more than our Emery."

The dukes joined them for the remainder of tea and by the time Olivia left, she felt comfortable in their presence, as well. As she rode home in her father's carriage, she couldn't help but glow with happiness. She had made plans to meet the three women at a bookshop tomorrow and then they were going for ices at Gunter's afterward. She had never made plans with women her own age and was almost giddy.

She arrived home and as she entered the townhouse, her father greeted her.

"This came for you," he said, holding up a letter. "I received word as well. Theodore is gone."

Suddenly, all the elation Olivia had felt rushed from her as tears formed in her eyes. The man who had been both father and friend to her had passed. With Uncle Theo and Aunt Beryl gone, she felt adrift and very much alone.

"Thank you," she said softly, accepting the letter he handed to her.

"Higbee and I will be traveling down for the funeral the day after tomorrow."

No mention was made of her accompanying them. Olivia knew oftentimes women weren't allowed at funerals. It didn't matter. She would mourn in her own way.

Taking the letter to her bedchamber, she read Mrs. Feldham's words of Uncle Theo's final days and death and how his last thoughts had been of Olivia, wishing she would find happiness.

She curled up on the bed, holding the miniature of Theo and Beryl, and cried a river of tears.

CHAPTER EIGHT

OLIVIA PRESSED THE cold cloth to her eyes, hoping the swelling would subside. She had remained in her room last night for dinner, refusing the tray Cook sent up, preferring to be alone. She had cried many tears, both sad and happy. The sad ones were for how she felt in losing Uncle Theo. The happy ones had been as she recollected the good times she had spent in her uncle's and aunt's company over many years. They had loved her from the start, never judging her, simply showering her with love and affection.

She supposed she should go downstairs to breakfast, though, instead of moping in her bedchamber. Recalling her promise to Uncle Theo, Olivia was more determined than ever to live her life. She would throw off the restrictions her father had placed upon her when she had first arrived with him in London. She was an adult and would be treated as one.

Ringing for Mary, she washed her face and promised herself there would be no more tears. In the future, she would celebrate Uncle Theo and Aunt Beryl and not focus on their deaths.

Mary dressed Olivia for the day. The day gown's neckline was lower than she preferred. In fact, many of the gowns Madame La Renn had created exposed far too much skin as far as Olivia was concerned. Perhaps it lingered from her time when she was overweight and wanted to hide as much of herself as she could. She searched and found a fichu that complemented the dress and added it before going to the breakfast room.

Instead of ignoring her as usual, Olivia saw both her father and cousin look up as she entered the room. When her father said good morning, she nearly fainted. Taking her seat, a footman brought her tea and another footman provided a plate of toast points and eggs, her usual breakfast. She thanked them and concentrated on her food, knowing she was about to be pumped for information.

"How was your afternoon tea?" the earl asked pleasantly.

"It was quite good," she said noncommittedly, adding a lump of sugar to her tea and stirring.

"So, there truly were three duchesses present?" Higbee asked.

"Yes." She slathered jam on a piece of toast.

"And?" her cousin urged.

Olivia looked up, a bland expression on her face. "Yes?"

"Don't toy with me, Cousin," Higbee chided.

She took a forkful of eggs and chewed thoughtfully before saying, "I am not toying with you, Higbee."

"You are deliberately being obtuse."

"About?"

He cleared his throat. "What did you and Her Graces speak of at tea yesterday?"

She didn't fight her smile but gave in to it. "Ah, we had an excellent time. We spoke of hats and fashion. Oh, and politics. Especially the new policies the prime minister is wishing to push through Parliament."

"What?" Higbee almost shouted. "You didn't!"

Her father frowned sternly. "You have been told to speak of appropriate topics, Olivia. I seriously doubt—"

"I wasn't the one to bring up politics, Father," she said innocently. "The Duchess of Amesbury did. She is quite informed regarding current events but so is the Duchess of Winslow and the Duchess of Haverhill. And the Duchess of Winslow is very knowledgeable about estate management. Why, I didn't have to say much at all. Those three ladies knew as much or more than I did."

Her father harumphed, his way of showing dissatisfaction without calling her out.

"I fail to see how a duchess would care to discuss politics," Higbee said.

"Then you are truly short-sighted, Cousin," Olivia said. "It seems to be a regular topic of conversation among these three. As was fashion. And their children. The dukes seemed quite proud of their children."

"The dukes were there?" her father sputtered. "I thought you said they wouldn't be at tea."

"I didn't think they would. Two of them, Haverhill and Amesbury, came in just before tea was over. They had been at White's with friends. Both men were very amiable and spoke of their babies with great fondness."

Higbee snorted. "Men don't care anything about babies."

"Well, Haverhill and Amesbury certainly seemed to. Haverhill even knew it was his son's naptime."

"Are you going to have tea with them anytime soon?" the earl asked. "You are always welcome to invite them here."

"I am seeing them this afternoon at two o'clock. We have plans to go to a bookshop."

Olivia decided to leave out the part about sharing ices at Gunter's. She was afraid if she mentioned it, both her father and Higbee would show up unexpectedly and ruin the outing for her.

"This is delightful," her father proclaimed. "My daughter befriended by three duchesses. Oh, it will be quite easy to find you the proper husband once your friendship with them is made known."

"I don't want to trade on my friendship with them or anyone else," she snapped. "And I want to start going places. You forbid me from going to any lectures or museums when I first arrived in town and I have sat in this house for over two months with nothing to do. My new friends like to get out and if they ask me to go somewhere with them—such as our outing to the bookshop today—then I am going. I am of age, Father. I don't need you to order me about."

She saw he controlled himself, knowing he hated her speaking up and wishing to disavow her and her independent streak. Now that she was friends with influential people, however, he kept quiet. At least she hoped she would remain friends with the three women. She had longed for friends for so long. While she had made friends back in Rumsford, there hadn't been anyone her own age she had become close to. That's why she cherished her time at tea yesterday with Wynter, Emery, and Meadow. They were alike—and yet different enough—to create stimulating conversation. She hoped once the Season began that their friendship would continue.

Then again, they were duchesses. Their lofty positions in Polite Society meant that not many others would be admitted to their exclusive circle. Olivia would have to be happy with whatever they offered and prepare herself for the time once the Season began to be discarded.

Breakfast was finished in silence and, when it ended, she excused herself, retreating to the sitting room, where she had placed several books from her father's library. He would never know any of the volumes were missing from the shelves. She thought the only reason he ever went into his library was to drink brandy with his friends. Olivia buried herself in a history of the Roman Empire and then switched to the newspapers when the butler brought them to her. She culled the pages with interest, seeing all kinds of things she could discuss with her new friends during today's outing.

At the appointed time, she made her way downstairs. Her father was waiting in the foyer.

"You didn't ask for the carriage but I asked for it to be readied for you," he said, surprising her.

"Thank you, Father, but I won't be needing it."

"You will not walk to your appointment, Olivia," he said firmly.

"Oh, I don't plan to. Her Grace, the Duchess of Winslow, is calling for me."

Shock filled his face as their butler answered the door. He turned and said, "Lady Olivia, Her Grace's carriage is here."

"I will walk you out," the earl said.

Knowing she couldn't stop him, she merely nodded.

As they approached the ducal carriage, Emery waved and lowered the window.

"Is this your father, Oliva?"

"Yes, Your Grace," the earl said smoothly. "I am Lord Rivers."

"It is lovely to meet you, my lord," Emery said graciously.

"This is the Duchess of Winslow, Father."

Wynter leaned over. "And I am the Duchess of Haverhill, my lord. It is a pleasure to meet you."

Meadow appeared in the other window. "Good afternoon, Lord Rivers. I am the Duchess of Amesbury. I must thank you for sharing your delightful daughter with us. Lady Olivia is such an interesting conversationalist. I was telling my husband how much I enjoy her company. You have done an excellent job raising her. She is both kind and intelligent."

"Why . . . thank you, Your Grace," her father managed to say, looking taken aback.

"I will see you later, Father," Olivia told him, accepting the footman's help in handing her up.

As the carriage drove away, she said, "It is so very good to see all of you."

"We are happy you could join us today," Emery told her. "I have seen your father at *ton* events but have never been introduced to him."

"Oh, he was very eager to meet the three of you," she informed them. "I must tell you that I am not close to him in the least. Being born a female caused him to turn his attention elsewhere. Sometimes, I believe he struggles to recall my name. He is close to my cousin, Higbee, his heir apparent."

"I am sorry to hear that," Wynter said. "I despise men who do not value women."

"Don't be sorry for me. I spent every Season with my aunt and uncle while my parents came to town. Then I lived with Uncle Theo and Aunt Beryl these past five years." Olivia paused. "I only came to London because of my uncle's severe illness. I received a letter yesterday after I returned home that he had finally passed."

Meadow took her hand and squeezed it. "We are sorry to hear that, Olivia. Would you rather not come today?"

"No, I do want to get out. Uncle Theo and Aunt Beryl were my true family. When I left Surrey in January, Uncle Theo made me promise to enjoy my future. To take every opportunity I had to learn and grow. He warned me not to be sad at his passing because he would be with Aunt Beryl again. I was not to mourn for him but rather celebrate his life."

"Your uncle sounds like a very wise man," Emery observed. "I know it is hard to be without him, though, especially since you were so close."

"He and Aunt Beryl will live on in my heart. Uncle Theo believed I should get on with my life. He hoped I would find a husband and start a family of my own." She shook her head. "I must warn you that my father—and Cousin Higbee—are typical of members of Polite Society in that they are enamored by titles and riches. They are encouraging my friendship with you three. Not because they are happy that I have met interesting women with whom I have something in common but they are hoping the mere knowledge of my friendship with powerful duchesses might bring eligible suitors to my doorstep."

Olivia sighed. "I understand if you wish us to part company over this matter."

"Let your father ruin our budding friendship?" Wynter snorted. "We will be friends because we like you, Olivia. All of us do. You are a breath of fresh air and so very clever."

Meadow smiled. "And if men are attracted to you merely

because you are friends with us, you will soon figure that out. I have a feeling you will find a husband this Season. One you will truly care for. One you will love."

"Oh! I am not looking for love," she said. "I merely wish for companionship with a man who can respect my mind and allow me to follow pursuits dear to my heart. I would hope he would be honorable and kind."

"But you wouldn't be afraid to love?" Emery asked. "I will admit it is terrifying to open your heart and soul to a man. I was truly frightened doing so. I found, though, when I gave my heart to Miles that everything else was suddenly right in my world."

"You are fortunate to have found a love match, Emery," Olivia said. She glanced to the other two. "I believe you also found love matches. They are rare, however. I hope I can find a good man. One I can respect. That will be enough. And I hope I can find him sooner rather than later. If not, my father has said he and Higbee will step in and make a match for me."

The carriage slowed and she realized they had reached the bookshop.

Meadow smiled warmly. "Do not worry, Olivia. You are bright and beautiful. I have a feeling the right man will suddenly appear."

"Uncle Theo said I would know the right man. That my heart would know his."

"Oh, that's lovely," Wynter proclaimed. "But books are calling our names."

"And then ices," Meadow said, a glint of mischief in her eyes.

The four descended from the carriage and entered the bookshop, Emery slipping her hand through Olivia's arm. The gesture warmed her. Just having met and beginning to know these three gave her hope that this Season would be drastically different from her first.

Chapter Nine

HART ACCOMPANIED HIS fellow Terrors to Tattersall's, at Hyde Park, just outside the city. Though only open to the buying public on Mondays at this time of year, an exception had been made. When a duke was involved—much less four of them—he was fast learning exceptions became the ducal rule.

He was looking for a new mount for the city. He liked two he'd left behind at Deerfield Park and had used his carriage to travel to London. After he had inspected the horseflesh in the town stables of his friends, they had all insisted he venture with them to Tattersall's, where they and the rest of the *ton's* gentlemen purchased their horses.

Mr. Tattersall was knowledgeable and friendly. He had an ease about him that most men didn't when dealing with gentlemen of such high rank. That alone made Hart want to put coin into Tattersall's pocket, not to mention the prime horseflesh on display.

The four were led about the stables, taking horses from their stalls into the covered alleys and then a select few into the courtyard. Two grooms led the horses Hart was interested in, with each taking turns riding the horse about the yard as the Terrors watched with interest. When Hart narrowed it to two choices, he mounted each horse himself and rode it in order to get a feel for the horse's gait and temperament.

He swung from the back of the second and tossed the reins to the groom, rejoining his friends and Tattersall.

"Any idea which you might prefer, Your Grace?" the owner asked, seeming confident that a sale would be made.

"I haven't a clue," Hart admitted. "I like them both for different reasons."

He looked from one horse to the other, wondering how he could make up his mind and if he should sleep on the decision.

"You don't have to choose," Miles pointed out. "You are a duke now, Hart. You can afford both."

A slow smile spread across his face. "I hadn't thought of that," he proclaimed. Looking to Tattersall, he said, "It will be both."

Wyatt slapped Hart on the back. "A good choice."

"See? There are advantages to being a duke," pointed out Donovan.

Tattersall told Hart he would have both horses bathed and groomed before they were sent over. He agreed to the purchase of saddles the owner recommended and told Tattersall to send the bill to him.

"I don't have a secretary as of yet but I will see you paid immediately."

"Thank you, Your Grace. That is always appreciated." Tattersall touched the brim of his hat and excused himself.

Hart frowned. "That seemed odd."

"What? The part about paying your bill?" Miles asked. "Tattersall is lucky. He is paid with more frequency than most other merchants of any type of good, be it clothes, boots, or horses. He will not allow any additional purchases from his stables unless prior bills have been settled."

He was still confused, knowing he was missing something. "Explain this."

"Many of the *ton* wait months to pay their bills," Wyatt shared. "And just as often, a good deal of them don't pay at all. Merchants can wait years to be paid for goods and services."

"That's abominable!" Hart proclaimed.

"It may be but it is the way of Polite Society," Donovan said quietly. "Many times, heirs gain their titles only to learn they are mired in debt that goes back a decade or more."

"What an appalling thing to do to people," he said. "I will never allow that."

"I learned when I became Amesbury that Clive dragged his feet on paying the servants their wages, both in London and throughout the various country estates. It was the first thing I saw to once I was made aware of the situation. Good help is hard to find. I certainly don't want to run anyone off due to holding back their wages. Servants work the hardest of all and deserve timely compensation."

"You made good choices today, Hart," Miles praised. "I myself would have purchased both mounts."

He shook his head. "It is a bit hard getting used to having the luxury to purchase two mounts. The five of us were poor as church mice while we were at Turner Academy and then university. Sometimes, it boggles my mind to think I hold so many lives in the palm of my hand and that I alone am responsible for the welfare of so many."

"It will grow on you," Miles assured him.

"I agree," Wyatt said. "Miles takes to responsibility like a duck to water and always has. But even Donovan and I have learned a great deal in our short time as dukes. That sense of gravitas permeates you sooner rather than later."

"Marrying Wynter helped me with that," Donovan shared. "Settling into marriage with a woman I see as my partner gave me someone to talk to about it all."

"I was the same with Meadow," Wyatt said.

"Emery taught me—and the others—about estate management," Miles said. "She has been a steadying influence on me."

Hart chuckled. "You all are walking advertisements for the state of matrimony."

"We are," Wyatt said, nodding with enthusiasm. "Becoming a duke when I least expected to do so was bloody hard. Falling in love and letting go was even harder. But I am a better man and duke because of Meadow."

Hart sighed. "I know you have all made love matches. They can't be easy."

His soul whispered to him that it would be impossible for him to do so. He had shut a door that sealed off any emotion he felt long ago. It was if the war had stripped him of the possibility of feeling. Though he yearned for what his friends had, he didn't believe it was a possibility for him.

"It isn't easy. It's the hardest thing in the world," Donovan declared. "You have to strip yourself bare and be willing to be seen by a woman. Really seen by her. Not the veneer you coat yourself with and present to the world. The you with all walls torn down."

"It is emotional suicide," Miles continued. "To open up. To be willing to allow yourself to be so fragile. So vulnerable."

"You all make it sound horrible," he said.

"It is horrible. Terrible at first," Wyatt said. "But when your heart and body cry out to be joined with someone you know you cannot live without? You must succumb and allow love inside. It is the hardest thing I have ever done but I will never regret letting down my guard and allowing Meadow to see me, warts and all."

"Warts?" Donovan scoffed. "Try letting your loved one see you without a limb. Now, *that* is bloody difficult."

They argued playfully as they returned to Wyatt's carriage, which had conveyed the four of them to Tattersall's.

"If you are going to White's now, you may drop me at home instead," Hart told them.

"Tired of being social already?" Donovan asked. "It is usually Miles who doesn't want to be at the club."

Miles snorted. "We would all rather be home with our wives and children. Don't pretend that I am the only one."

"Well, I have no wife or children nor do I believe I will any-time soon. What I do have is a mountain of paperwork to peruse."

"Not before a treat," Wyatt said. "My coachman has instructions to take us to Gunter's."

"Gunter's?" Hart asked. "The place with those ices?"

"The very one," Wyatt confirmed. "Remember the first time Lord and Lady Markham took us there? Finch wasn't sure at all about it."

"And he became the one most smitten with going there," Donovan recalled. "Has anyone heard from Finch lately?"

They spoke about their friend for a while and Hart knew he owed Finch a lengthy letter, which he would compose once he returned home.

The carriage pulled up in Berkeley Square, which seemed vaguely familiar to him even after all these years away.

"I say we go inside for a hearty tea instead of mere ices," Miles suggested. "Looking at horses has triggered my hunger."

"I agree," Donovan said. "Gunter's Tea Shop it is!" He added, "Wynter tells me it is the only place in town where a male may escort a female without benefit of a chaperone."

Hart certainly wouldn't be escorting any ladies to tea here anytime soon. He already dreaded the Season because he thought his friends, being deliriously happy with their wives, would push him to find a bride, as well. While he knew he needed to find a duchess in order to provide an heir for the title, he wondered if he should give himself some time before doing so. The war had ravaged his soul, more than he would care to admit to anyone, least of all his fellow Terrors. He supposed he should be in a better frame of mind before he sought a wife. It wouldn't be fair to any woman to ask her to live with the foul moods which sometimes descended upon him without notice. Hiding them from his friends was one thing. Trying to keep them from a wife was quite another.

They disembarked from the carriage and made their way across the street, entering the tea room. Suddenly, Donovan was waving and grinning.

"There. Across the room. We must join them."

His three friends moved away and Hart fell into step, glancing up and seeing Wynter. As they drew closer, he saw Emery and Meadow accompanied her. Another woman was in their company but her back was to them as they approached.

"Greetings, ladies," Wyatt said. "What a grand coincidence. We have been looking at horses and Hart has purchased two. I am sure he is ready to tell you all about them."

The fourth woman had glanced up at Wyatt as he spoke. Something about her profile seemed familiar.

Then she turned.

It was Miss Knight.

OLIVIA FELT THE color drain from her face as she spied the handsome duke she had met a few days ago.

Of course, he would be in the company of three dukes. Dukes probably spoke to no one else but dukes.

She hadn't known his name because he never introduced himself. By his dress, she had seen he was a gentleman and had called him *my lord*. Only when they had arrived at his townhouse and the startled footman had addressed him as *Your Grace* did she learn he was a duke. By then, it seemed too late to inquire which dukedom he controlled. Her attention had been focused on the ailing kitten. That was what had been important to her, not the forbidden sin of accompanying a gentleman back to his home. A small part of her knew it was wrong but she had pushed aside her better judgment in order to help Midnight.

Olivia had thought they would never meet again. Even if they attend a few of the same *ton* events together in the weeks to come, she had no one who might introduce them. Besides, she had been dressed not much better than a servant. The duke would never have believed her to be a lady.

Until now. Circumstances had thrown them together in a most unusual way.

His gaze locked on her and she felt the blood rush to her cheeks. Olivia glanced away and saw Haverhill brushing a kiss upon his wife's cheek.

"What a pleasant surprise, Darling," he said and then looked to the others, greeting them, before his eyes landed upon her.

"Ah, Lady Olivia. It is good to see you again. You met Amesbury the other day. Let me introduce you to my other friends."

She rose, locking her knees to keep from toppling over as she saw others in the tea shop look on with interest.

"May I present the Duke of Winslow?" Haverhill said.

Sweeping into a curtsey to the duke with golden brown hair and sky blue eyes, she raised her gaze as Winslow took her hand.

"I am happy to meet you, Lady Olivia," he said, a look of earnest about him. "My wife has done nothing but sing your praises since making your acquaintance."

"Her Grace is being too kind," she said.

Haverhill cleared his throat. "And this is the Duke of Mansfield. Hart, this is Lady Olivia Knight."

She recognized the name. Hart. When she had been at tea yesterday, Haverhill had said he had left Miles and Hart at their club. Hart must be some kind of nickname for her white knight.

Olivia curtseyed again but as the duke took her hand, he said to the others, "We have actually met."

"You have?" asked Emery. "How delightful. Come join us and tell us about this meeting."

Her blush now extended from her cheeks to her roots as the men took chairs from the empty table next to them and brought them over. Since each duke seemed to want to sit beside his wife, the women shuffled around until Olivia found herself bunched between Amesbury and Mansfield. Mansfield's knee rested against hers as they crowded together, causing her leg and then her body to grow hot. How could a man's knee be scalding?

"Tell us, Hart," Meadow urged. "How you and Olivia encountered one another."

The duke turned his head and she saw the ghost of a smile

playing about his sensual lips.

"Would you rather share our tale?" he asked her.

"There is really no *our* to it," she said. "I found an injured kitten as His Grace was passing by." Olivia's gaze fell to the table, not wanting to elaborate and hoping the duke would have the good sense to drop the matter.

"Lady Olivia is being far too modest," Mansfield said. "The kitten in question was being tortured by a group of ruffians. She charged in and demanded they cease at once."

"How brave of you, Olivia," Wynter said admiringly.

"It wasn't brave at all," she protested. "Actually, more foolish."

"Because the leader stepped forward and looked as if he would do her harm," the duke continued. "I was passing nearby and ready to step in but Lady Olivia dispatched him with her reticule and umbrella. He left that alley with a throbbing head and bloody nose."

"Bravo, Olivia," Emery praised.

"The others followed suit," the duke concluded, "leaving the kitten—now named Midnight—with the lady. By the way, how is Midnight? Did you keep her?"

She grew even warmer under his attention. "She is well. My father has a problem with animal dander and so Midnight is being cared for by our head groom and his wife. Once she is healed from her injuries and a bit older, he told me she would be a mouser in the stables."

He smiled—and it took her breath away.

"I will have to come see her sometime."

"Did you escort Lady Olivia and Midnight home, Hart?" asked Winslow.

Olivia tried to catch his eyes before he spoke but she was unsuccessful.

"Actually, we first went to my townhouse," Mansfield revealed. "You should have seen Lady Olivia spring into action, ordering servants about, calling for what she needed to minister to the tiny furball. Why, she was so confident at giving orders that I thought her to be a governess."

He smiled at her again and her heart sank. Without realizing it, he had ruined everything for her.

She shot to her feet. "I am very sorry, Your Graces. I know I should never have accompanied the duke to his personal residence. It simply isn't done. An unmarried lady had no business entering his townhouse unchaperoned." She swallowed painfully. "I am ashamed of my behavior and I understand that you will no longer wish to pursue any type of friendship with me. Please, feel free to ignore me when you see me at social events."

Olivia snatched up her reticule and fled the tearoom.

CHAPTER TEN

HART WATCHED, STARTLED, as Lady Olivia raced from the table.

"What the devil?" he asked aloud. "Why would she do that?"

Emery's eyes scolded him though she kept her tone light. "You have embarrassed Olivia in front of her friends, Hart. She's right. She should never have accompanied you back to your place. If that fact became known, she would be ruined."

"Bloody hell. I didn't even know she was a lady. She was dressed meanly. It was why those boys even thought to attack her. And she called herself *Miss* Knight," he added in his defense. "How was I to know—"

"You know now," Miles said sternly. "The least you owe her is an apology." He paused. "But I think you owe her even more."

He did. "Excuse me."

Hart left his friends, hurrying from the tea shop. He saw Olivia, her shoulders hunched, standing a few feet from him. Just as he started toward her, she stepped from the pavement as if to cross Berkeley Square—but she did so blindly, not having checked the traffic. He heard the shout of a coachman as he approached, trying to warn her off.

Olivia looked up.

And froze.

His heart racing, Hart quickly made up the short distance between them, yanking her to safety just as the carriage roared past them. He took a few steps back until they were safely on the pavement again. She trembled in his arms.

Bending to her ear, he said, "You are safe."

For a moment, he held on to her, reluctant to release her. Her curves called out to him, as did the light floral scent surrounding her. If he had his druthers, he would have kissed her. But somehow, he'd already embarrassed her in her front of her new friends. He certainly wasn't about to repeat doing the same on a public street.

Easing his arms from her, he took her hand and tucked it into the crook of his arm so that she would have him to hold on to for support.

"I understand you are upset. Would you like me to escort you home?"

Instead of gratitude, anger flickered in her eyes. "Oh, that would be exactly what I don't need, Your Grace."

Olivia broke away from him and started down the pavement.

Hart rushed to catch up.

She stopped, glaring at him when he did. "No, Your Grace, I am not going to get into your carriage and ride it in—alone—with you. News will already get out how I went to your home. My father will hear of my disgrace. It will be a miracle if any gentleman is foolish enough to offer for me."

Once more, she started down the street. Again, he hurried after her.

"Stop following me!" she said loudly and then looked around, seeing she had drawn the attention of passersby. "I mean it," she uttered quietly.

The pattern occurred again, with Olivia marching off and Hart following, this time at a discreet distance.

She stopped. He ran into her.

"This will never do," she said. "You have already humiliated me."

"How did I do that?" he asked. "I am genuinely puzzled. Let me walk with you and have you explain it to me. You are upset and it is because of me. I wish to make amends."

She didn't reply but started walking. He fell into step beside her.

Grudgingly, she said, "You know the rules of Polite Society."

"Actually, I don't," he told her.

She frowned, her head cocked. "How could you not?"

"I have been on the Continent. I was a soldier—an officer— until a short while ago. I am a second son who has inherited a dukedom he neither wanted nor expected. I have never moved among the *ton*. I am not familiar with their rules though I assume they are legion."

"Oh." She appeared mollified. "Well, an unmarried lady is never to be alone with a gentleman else she is ruined. It is why ladies are not to go off into darkened corners so that men can kiss them."

"This has happened to you?"

"Of course not!" she scolded. "I know the rules. I never should have accompanied you home the other day."

"Is that why you told me you were Miss Knight and not Lady Olivia?"

"Yes, in part," answered begrudgingly. "But poor Midnight was suffering so. I did not want her to lose a part of her paw or ache from the burns longer than she had to."

"You put the health of a kitten above your own reputation."

"Yes, rather foolish on my part, wouldn't you say?"

He paused and she actually stopped alongside him. "I think it is rather noble." Hart took her hand and slid it back into his crook and began walking again. "But who is going to know about the incident? My friends would never say a word to injure you or your reputation. Your secret will be safe."

"They are very kind women," she said. "They might feel sorry for me. It would be wonderful if they did not mention the incident. But I can no longer be friends with them. A woman of loose morals—"

"That does not describe you," Hart interrupted. "And though

I have only been back a short time in England and only recently met my fellow Terrors' wives, they are the best of any females that walk the earth. They won't judge you for putting Midnight's health above silly societal rules."

"Terrors?" she asked, puzzled.

"That is a story for another time."

She shook her head. "There will be no other time, Your Grace. Once you see me home, that will be the end of our short acquaintance."

"What? I don't even get to visit Midnight?"

"You are mocking me."

"I am not," he protested.

"No duke is interested in an injured street kitten."

"Well, this duke is," he said firmly. "I wasn't even supposed to be a duke. I have heard, though, that dukes act as they wish. I am telling you that this duke is highly interested in injured kittens."

She laughed.

He joined in. God, it felt good to laugh. He couldn't remember the last time he had done so.

"You are wrong about those women. They will continue to be your friend. They like you. Those three are loyal to their bones. They will not allow you to walk away." He grinned. "After all, they are duchesses. They will demand your friendship and you will be forced to comply."

She giggled.

He liked the sound of that.

"You mentioned society events. I assume that means you are partaking in the Season."

Hart sensed the change come over her. Though it was only her hand on his arm, he sensed the tension filling her body.

"Yes. I have not done so for many years. Instead, I have been living in the country with my uncle in Rumsford. I would rather be in Surrey than London but I have no say in the matter."

"Rumsford?" he questioned.

"Yes. Rumsford. Are you familiar with it?"

"It is the closest village to my country seat."

"Deerfield Park," she whispered. "Oh, Mansfield. *You* are the Duke of Mansfield."

"Yes, I believe I was introduced to you by my title."

"The Duke of Mansfield was never at Deerfield Park. Neither was the marquess. It was easy to forget about them because they never spent time in Surrey."

That didn't surprise Hart, especially knowing how Reginald had hopped from bed to bed, which would have been more difficult to do in the country versus living in London.

"Who is your uncle? Perhaps I have met him. I started making the rounds of the area after the Christmas holidays, meeting my tenants and others nearby."

"Uncle Theo is dead," she said glumly. "He was the vicar."

"He is dead?" Hart asked. "It must have been very recent because I saw him only last week."

Lady Olivia came to a stop. "You did? Oh, please, tell me about it."

"It is as I mentioned. I felt it important to meet the locals and was calling upon those in Rumsford. I met the new vicar, whom the bishop assigned to the parish since the previous duke had died and I had yet to return from war. He mentioned Reverend Knight, who was being cared for by a widow."

"Mrs. Feldham."

"Yes, the very one. I called upon her and spent two afternoons with your uncle." He smiled. "Oh, he was quite the fellow. Though it was apparent he was ill, he still did his best to be a lively and entertaining conversationalist."

She smiled wistfully. "That is Uncle Theo. He always could make everyone laugh."

Having heard her laugh, Hart wanted to be the one who did so now. Which was the most insane idea he had ever come up with. He barely knew this woman.

"I wanted to care for him until he passed but my father insisted I return to London. He wants me to wed by Season's end so neither he nor my cousin, his heir apparent, will have to be responsible for me. I had lived with Uncle Theo and Aunt Beryl ever since my mother passed from the pneumonia."

"So, you are making your come-out then. You will certainly have something over the other young misses. They will be frightened schoolgirls, while you have polish."

Lady Olivia laughed again. This time, she did not sound amused.

"No, Your Grace, I made my come-out before I left for Rumsford. It was a catastrophe. I received not one offer. Made not a single friend. I hated every minute of it."

He didn't see how that could be the case. Olivia Knight was a beautiful, poised woman. True, five years ago she might have been slightly immature, but most debutantes were fresh out of the schoolroom. Even if she had little to no dowry, he could not see why she hadn't received multiple offers of marriage.

"That is hard to believe, my lady."

"It is the truth. I weighed a good seven stones more than I do now and my mother constantly told me how very ordinary my face was. No gentleman would partner with me and no lady wished to befriend me." She hesitated and then added, "It was why meeting the three duchesses and having them actually be interested in being my friend meant so much to me. My father ignored me my entire life because I was a female. My mother berated me because of my size and plain looks. Neither cared that I was intelligent or starved for their love. I wound up eating myself into oblivion."

His heart went out to her. It sounded as if she had experienced a hard life, at least until she had left to be with her aunt and uncle. At least Hart had found his Turner Terrors. Lady Olivia had had no one.

"I can assure you that Emery, Meadow, and Wynter are not shallow, typical women of the *ton*. They have offered you friendship—and they will stick by you. Neither I nor their husbands will breathe a word of your visit to my townhouse. I realize now that I humiliated you by sharing that part of the story. It was wrong of me."

She gazed at him in understanding. "In your defense, you did not know. The rules of war are far different from those of English society." She paused. "Although I am not certain which might be more vicious."

Hart laughed and she joined in. The blended sound seemed like music to his ears.

Suddenly, he didn't want her partnering with other men, be it dances or in cards. A sense of possessiveness filled him.

Had he found his duchess?

They rounded a corner and she said, "This is my father's house. Thank you for escorting me home, Your Grace. It was kind of you, especially after I ran out in a such a state. I apologize for being so ill-mannered."

"You are forgiven, my lady. But truly, there is nothing for me to forgive. I speak for myself and my companions."

"You are very compassionate, Your Grace."

Lady Olivia stepped toward the door.

I should say something.

But he didn't. He wanted to but Hart found himself tongue-tied.

She knocked upon the door and it was immediately answered by the butler.

"Good afternoon, my lady." The butler glanced at him. "And good afternoon, my lord."

"It is His Grace," she told the servant. "And he is leaving. Thank you again, Your Grace."

With that, the door closed. Hart walked slowly back to Gunter's and entered the tearoom. He stopped in the doorway and watched his friends for a moment. Meadow was feeding Wyatt some sweet. Donovan leaned close and whispered something in Wynter's ear. Miles openly held Emery's hand, something that even Hart knew to be scandalous behavior if done in public.

The three couples looked so happy. They began conversing again. From the looks of it, their conversation was lively. He hated to interrupt and started to leave.

Then he heard his name called and he turned back, walking forward and joining them, taking a seat. The group had demolished what had been a very hearty tea.

"You were gone an awfully long time," Meadow said. "Did you see Olivia home?"

"I did," he replied.

"And?" Wynter prodded.

"And what?" he asked.

"You might as well tell them everything," Wyatt suggested. "If you don't, they will drag it from you, pleasantly or unpleasantly. I have found it is much easier to give in."

"And *you* were the spy," Donovan teased. "Good thing these three weren't working with the French and torturing you for information."

When he hesitated, Emery said, "You were brought here by design, Hart. The Terrors knew we would be here for tea and that Olivia would be present. Yes, we had decided to play matchmaker between the two of you without mentioning it to either one of you."

"Little did we know that you had already met," Meadow said. "That was an interesting tidbit."

"I would have loved to see Olivia take down that horrible boy," Wynter added. "To think they were torturing a helpless kitten. Perhaps Olivia can give us all lessons on how to use an umbrella as a weapon."

"Back to what is important," Emery said. "Did you apologize to her? Did she accept it?"

"She apologized to me," Hart explained. "I tried to tell her she had nothing to be sorry about. She fears she made a huge mistake in bringing Midnight to my townhouse and that the three of you will either gossip about her or give her the cut direct. I told her that would never occur. That you are not like most of your counterparts in the *ton*."

"The poor thing," Wynter said. "I believe she is very lonely. She is quite interesting, though. I do admire her. I hope she will understand that there will be no gossip about her."

"She worried that it would affect her chances at making a match this Season. It seems her father and cousin insist upon her wedding," Hart told them.

"Even though I have yet to meet the cousin, I don't like the pair," Meadow declared. "I think we should take Olivia under our wings and help her to make a brilliant match." She glanced in his direction. "Unless you are interested in her, Hart."

"She is very nice," he said, his voice neutral. "However, I am not certain I am quite ready to wed yet."

The table fell silent and then Emery said, "Then we will make sure she meets the right people. All of you dukes need to think of your other friends and acquaintances so that we might introduce them to Olivia. I would see her happy. She has had little of that in her life, especially now that her dear uncle has passed."

They began debating names of gentlemen to introduce her to. Hart grew more despondent as they did so, proving to himself that he was in no frame of mind to take on a wife.

Even one as intriguing as Lady Olivia Knight.

CHAPTER ELEVEN

OLIVIA WENT TO the sitting room, which was fast becoming her retreat. Her bedchamber only had a single window with heavy damask curtains and remained dark even during the day. Her mother's sitting room had floor to ceiling windows along one wall and she enjoyed the light, airy feel of the room. Even though it was nearing five o'clock, she chose to come here to think.

She believed the Duke of Mansfield had good intentions when he said neither he nor the three duchesses would hold her responsible for her rash behavior of a few days earlier. He couldn't speak for the three women, though. They had their reputations to maintain. Even if they remained silent and never revealed her misstep, they would know that she was someone who could not be trusted to use good judgment. Kindhearted as they were, they would realize she would not be someone they wished to further an acquaintance with. Olivia did believe they would acknowledge her at the first event of the Season if their paths crossed because they were so polite.

Thoughts of the upcoming Season had her rattled. She knew no one else beyond the three duchesses and Higbee, of course. Her cousin had said he would tell some of his friends about her but Olivia had to wonder what he would say—or what he had said regarding her over the years. She chuckled. She doubted Higbee had mentioned her at all. He had been in his last year of university when she made her come-out so he hadn't witnessed what a fiasco it had been. If any of his friends had been present that year, they would not recognize her now because her physical appearance was so radically altered. She wondered if her father had done what her cousin had suggested and sweetened her dowry in order to entice more suitors. That would appeal to the fortune hunters. Olivia hadn't a clue how to fend them off.

Perhaps her father was right and she should allow him to decide who should be her future husband. Dispense with all courtship and merely make a match for political gain. It was what would likely happen in the long run so she might as well get used to the idea now.

A knock sounded at the door and she called out, "Come."

Their butler entered, looking flustered. That alone had her worried because he was always a picture of serenity.

"My lady, you have . . . visitors."

"Visitors? But I am expecting no one."

In truth, she expected no guests because she knew no one in London and had seen no one during her time here beyond the three duchesses. Hope sprang within her.

"Might it be three duchesses?"

"Yes, my lady." He presented her with a stack of cards. "And dukes, as well."

"Oh!"

Olivia flipped through the calling cards and saw her friends had brought their husbands along.

And the Duke of Mansfield.

"I took them to the drawing room and took the liberty of calling for tea, my lady."

"Excellent. I will go see them now."

She rose and smoothed her skirts, her heart racing. They hadn't abandoned her after all. With a song in her heart, she hurried to the drawing room. Entering it, she saw the group gathered about the fire and went to them. The ladies greeted her with kisses to her cheek and warm embraces, while the dukes nodded politely.

"Please, have a seat," she urged.

Once all were comfortable, she added, tears brimming in her eyes, "I cannot tell you what it means to have you come to call."

"Of course, we came," Meadow said. "We were afraid you would think we did not wish to support you. That is far from the truth."

"We are friends, Olivia, and friends stand by one another," Emery said.

"Even when a friend acts unwisely?" she asked hesitantly.

"You saved a poor kitten from being brutalized," Wynter declared. "Its life was at stake. You acted rationally and calmly. From everything Hart said, your quick action made the difference."

"I should like to see your Midnight," Meadow said.

"I would send for her but Father sneezed numerous times and his eyes were swollen merely from sitting next to me at breakfast after I had been around Midnight. He still has no idea I brought her home." She grinned. "I would rather keep it that way."

"Well, I adore cats," Emery said. "I think it might be good for Ben to be around one. He chases after our dogs until they are ragged and he is worn out and fussy. I think if he had a cat who could sit in his lap, it might be calming for him. Might we take your Midnight once she has healed?"

"That would be wonderful," she said, tears brimming in her eyes.

The tea arrived and she poured out for everyone. A lively discussion followed. They talked of bills being presented in the House of Lords and recommendations Emery had made to the Duke of Mansfield, since he was new to estate management. Olivia was very aware of the duke since he had taken a place next to her on a settee. Usually, it seated two ladies with no problem. Mansfield, though, was much larger than a lady, a bit over six feet. Though not as broad as some of his friends, his lean, athletic build was still evident under his beautifully tailored clothes. His thigh pressed against hers, causing her to constantly be aware of him.

Winslow finished up talking about an economic measure Parliament was considering and Haverhill said, "Spoken like a true Terror."

"That term," she said, glancing to her right. "His Grace mentioned it before but I was unfamiliar with its usage. Is this some political party I am unaware of?"

The men all laughed and Amesbury said, "*We* are the Terrors. We met at Turner Academy and Miles christened us with the nickname. The five of us graduated from the academy and went to university together."

"Five?" she asked, frowning.

"Yes, there are five Terrors," Winslow said. "Finch—William Finchley—is a vicar in Kent. He took the living the Earl of Marksby offered after we finished university. The rest of us went to war."

"My uncle was a vicar," she said. "I lived with him and my aunt for the past several years. He recently passed, however. His funeral is tomorrow."

"I met Reverend Knight recently," Mansfield added. "I am sorry I never heard him preach a Sunday sermon. He had a quick wit and keen intelligence."

"Then it runs in the family," Meadow said. "You could be describing Olivia."

"I loved Uncle Theo dearly," she said. "I wish I could attend his funeral but only Father and my cousin are going."

She told a few stories about life with Uncle Theo and the men regaled her with a few tales of their time at Turner Academy. The entire group was in stitches when the door opened and her father and Higbee entered.

Olivia shot to her feet, feeling guilty as if she had been caught doing something she shouldn't have been doing by entertaining the group. Quickly, she thought on how to introduce everyone. With a higher rank, that individual should be introduced first, but with so many dukes? She was at a loss where to begin.

Winslow must have surmised her dilemma as the rest of them rose and her relatives approached.

"We are a large group, my lord, so let us make the introductions with speed. I am the Duke of Winslow and this is my duchess."

The rest followed suited, ending with Mansfield introducing himself. Her father and Higbee looked overwhelmed so she stepped in.

"And this is my father, the Earl of Rivers, and my cousin, Mr. Knight."

"It is indeed a pleasure to meet such an illustrious group gathered under my humble roof," her father said obsequiously.

"Please, join us," Olivia added. "Would you like tea? I can ring for more cups."

"That isn't necessary," the earl said brusquely. "Why would I wish to focus on what's in a teacup when I have such fascinating guests?"

His dismissive attitude of her caused Olivia to withdraw within herself. The others carried on the conversation without her for a few minutes.

"I will look forward to renewing our acquaintance at the first ball of the season," the earl said. "I find your company most refreshing."

Meadow smiled. "We feel the same way about your daughter, Lord Rivers. I have never been one to make friends easily or lightly but I already value Lady Olivia's friendship."

"Perhaps you can help her attract a husband, Your Grace," her father said. "She wasn't able to during her come-out. It's high time she found one and put her bluestocking ways to rest."

"Especially since she is already on the shelf," Higbee added. "She will have quite a bit of competition from the younger debutantes as it is."

Emery gave the two a cool look. "There are men among Polite Society who value a woman who isn't afraid to use her mind. My husband is one of them. I know there are others of the same ilk who will respect Lady Olivia and her opinions. She will be a breath of fresh air among the many immature girls making their come-outs."

An uncomfortable silence filled the air. Olivia knew her father wanted to challenge Emery—even put her in her place—but he was afraid to cross a duchess, especially in front of her duke. Winslow had slipped his hand around his wife's to show his support.

"I have an idea, my lord," Wynter said. "Since your daughter has been missing from society for several years, I believe it would help smooth the way if she had a woman of some importance as her advocate. I would like to be that woman. Although Olivia has already made her come-out and is not in need of a sponsor, I would rather have her by my side as Haverhill and I attend events."

Wynter turned to her. "I think it best if you come and stay with us, Olivia. It would prevent us from having to call for you before each event and we could always go through the receiving lines together. I know there are gentlemen my husband and I wish to introduce you to. Staying with us for the Season would help manage the situation." She turned to the earl and smiled sweetly. "Wouldn't you agree, Lord Rivers?"

Before he could reply, Meadow said, "Oh, that isn't fair. I want Olivia to stay with us." She reached over and took Olivia's hand. "Perhaps you could stay with the Haverhills for a month and then come to us."

"Don't leave us out of the mix," Emery declared. "You can finish up the Season with us. We would be honored to have you as our guest."

She could tell her father was torn by what the women had proposed. "But shouldn't it be up to a father to make certain his daughter has made an appropriate match?" he asked.

The three duchesses laughed heartily.

"My dear Lord Rivers," Emery said. "If you haven't learned

the lesson by now, I am happy to teach it to you. Women are the true power in the *ton*, especially where marriage is concerned. We can steer the right gentlemen toward Olivia, allowing her to make the decision as to whom best suits her. She will have her pick of any man she chooses—with our support."

Emery's words hung in the air, waiting to be challenged. When they weren't, she smiled graciously and said, "I am glad that is settled. I have so many people to introduce you to, Olivia, gentlemen and ladies alike. Why, I believe you may just be the most popular person of this Season. People will clamor for your presence at their events in order for them to be a success."

"Have your maid pack your things tonight," Wynter advised. "They can be moved first thing in the morning. We have much to discuss before the Season begins so you might as well come to stay with us until it starts."

"I say—" her father began.

"That is an excellent idea, my love," Haverhill interrupted. "I, too, enjoy Lady Olivia's company." He looked to the earl. "It is nice that she is of age and can make decision on her own, isn't it, my lord?"

The duke's meaning was obvious even if unspoken. Her father would have to go along with the plan even if he objected to it.

And Olivia felt liberated for the first time since coming to London.

Mansfield rose and they all followed suit. "We should depart. I would hate for us to overstay our welcome." He took her ungloved hand and brought it to his lips, kissing her knuckles. "Thank you for entertaining us, my lady, despite the fact that we had no invitation from you. You are a most gracious hostess."

Warmth spread throughout her at his touch. "You and your friends are always welcome, Your Grace."

"Will I see you at your uncle's funeral?" Mansfield asked.

Olivia didn't understand why he would ask this since she had already stated she would not be in attendance.

Her father asked, "You knew my brother?"

"Yes. Deerfield Park, my country seat, is near Rumsford. I recently met Reverend Knight and am sorry to hear of his passing. I plan to attend tomorrow's services."

"Olivia is staying here. My nephew and I will be attending. Perhaps—"

"Oh?" Mansfield asked, one eyebrow cocked. "I know Lady Olivia was quite close to her uncle. I merely assumed she would be going to tell him goodbye. Closure is so important, I believe, when there has been a death in the family."

"It isn't necessary for her to do so," her father said firmly.

The duke turned to her, his gaze intense. "If you wish to go, I will take you myself."

Though it would be absolutely the wrong thing to agree to, being alone with a bachelor in a coach for the two-hour drive to Surrey, she saw he gave her the opportunity her father had refused her.

"I very much would like to attend Uncle Theo's funeral," she said softly.

"Then we should all go together," Higbee suggested brightly. "It would be a waste for two carriages to go down from London when one would suffice. Don't you agree, Your Grace?"

Mansfield turned to her cousin. "I would be happy to take the four of us in my coach, Mr. Knight. Shall we say ten o'clock? I believe the funeral is at one."

Her father nodded in agreement. "We would be happy to accompany you, Your Grace. All of us," and he included Olivia in his glance.

"Then we should say our goodbyes," Amesbury said.

Olivia was hugged and kissed again as the group departed. She saw her father and cousin leave, accompany the others downstairs. Turning, she found the Duke of Mansfield had remained behind. He offered his arm to her and she took it as they left the drawing room.

"Your father is a bully," he stated.

"Tell me something I don't already know," she said lightly.

"You must stand up to him."

"I have tried ever since my recent return to his household. It will be easier not being under his roof for the next several months. If I am lucky, I may never have to return to it at all."

"You think because you will marry."

"It is a possibility. It is why women place themselves on the Marriage Mart. I truly don't expect Wynter or the others to find me a husband. She was being kind in helping to remove me from an impossible situation. I hope, though, given the opportunity to mingle in Polite Society without my father bearing down upon me that I might meet someone who will respect me."

"What of love?" he asked.

"What of it?" she countered. "I know my new friends all made love matches. I don't really want or expect love, though. I think a good marriage can be based upon friendship and mutual interests."

Though she said the words—and had believed them her entire life—her pulse and heart now raced being near this man. But to think a duke, one as handsome and wealthy as Mansfield, might be interested in pursuing her was ridiculous. And it was even more preposterous to think such a man might grow to love her. She must push aside any such notion. Love was not in play for her.

And neither was this man.

She saw him outside and he was the last to enter the second of the two carriages parked in front of their townhouse.

As the carriages rolled away, Higbee took her arm. "How did someone like you become bosom friends with the highest echelons of society?"

Olivia jerked away and gave him an enigmatic smile. "Wouldn't you like to know?"

She hurried inside and to her bedchamber, where she rang for Mary.

When her lady's maid entered, she said, "You are to pack everything I own, Mary. We will be staying in the Duke of Haverhill's household beginning tomorrow."

CHAPTER TWELVE

Hart climbed into his carriage, having already instructed his coachman to call at Lord Rivers' townhouse before they proceeded to Deerfield Park. He wasn't certain if he was supposed to send word or not of his arrival in order to warn his staff he would be stopping today for a brief time. Since he had made the decision to travel to Surrey so late, he didn't think he should send a messenger. He hadn't wanted to risk one of his grooms' safety by asking him to travel in the dark. If he sent someone this morning, it would only give his staff a short while to prepare. Perhaps it would be better to surprise them and see how things were run in his absence. He didn't expect they would be at Deerfield Park long. Merely to freshen up after their journey south before they went to Reverend Knight's funeral.

He looked forward to spending more time with the intriguing Lady Olivia but hated that he had to suffer being in the company of her father and cousin. The cousin had made no impression upon Hart, while the father irked him to no end. Couldn't the man see what a gem he had in his daughter?

Apparently not.

He thought again to Ada and how his father had ignored her, being the youngest Hartfield child and a female. Actually, Mansfield had ignored Hart and Percy, as well. All his time and attention had been spent on his heir apparent. Reginald had turned out to be far less than he should have been, a disappointment and black mark on the family name.

When he was a father, Hart planned to be as his friends were, happy with either a boy or girl and eager to spend time in the nursery. He smiled, thinking how infatuated the other three Terrors were with their children, bragging on teeth being cut and steps being taken. A part him longed for a large family, one which would be loving and thoughtful toward one another. He would teach both the girls and boys to ride and hunt. His thoughts turned to swimming and how he had once enjoyed it. Hart had never gotten into the water after the day Percy drowned, though. Perhaps it was time he put that incident in the past, especially if he did have children. He would make certain each of them were strong swimmers because he didn't think he could suffer through the death of another loved one by drowning.

The vehicle stopped and he thought about where he wanted Lady Olivia to sit. He had enjoyed being cozy with her on yesterday's small settee, their limbs brushing against one another. His ducal coach, though, possessed long, wide seats so he wouldn't have the advantage of pressing against her. He decided he would rather she sit opposite him, the better to converse. It would also allow him to gaze at her even when they weren't speaking.

The door opened and his footman handed her up.

"Good morning, my lady," Hart said, indicating the seat she was to take.

"Good morning, Your Grace," she replied cheerfully as she settled herself.

Her eyes appeared more gray today in the dark violet gown she wore. It surprised him she was not wearing black and then he panicked for a moment.

What if her uncle's death meant she was now in mourning and would not be attending the Season?

Yet she had given no indication of that. He would make certain to learn today what her plans would be, not wanting to admit to himself that they would determine what his own would be.

The earl entered the carriage and immediately took the seat next to Hart.

"Good morning, Your Grace. What a fine day to be traveling in such illustrious company."

"Good morning, Lord Rivers. Mr. Knight."

The cousin sat opposite his uncle, an eager look upon his face.

"We are delighted to journey with you, Your Grace," Knight said. "Simply delighted."

The two men were as giddy as debutantes making their come-outs simply because they were riding with a duke in his carriage. He despaired of the fawning that would occur over the next two hours.

"Did you see the prime minister's speech in the newspapers this morning?" he asked Lady Olivia, knowing she enjoyed discussing politics and determined to make sure she was included in any conversation that occurred within the confines of the carriage.

"Not yet, Your Grace. What did he say?"

Hart described in detail Lord Liverpool's words as she nodded in agreement and then frowned.

"I don't agree with him on one point regarding the increase in taxes," she began, only to be cut off by her father.

"His Grace is not interested in your opinions, Olivia," the earl chided. "You would do best to keep quiet today."

Anger sizzled through Hart. "As a matter of fact, my lord, I am quite interested in Lady Olivia's opinions. She expresses herself with such clarity and wit. Yesterday's tea was delightful because of her contributions to the conversation."

Rivers frowned. "You are kind to indulge her, Your Grace, but she won't catch a husband that way, spouting off nonsense about the prime minister's policies. She is a female and needs to learn her place."

He saw her mouth tremble slightly. All the confidence she had shown previously seemed to shrink with her father's harsh words.

"I believe Lady Olivia to be charming and informed," Hart said firmly. "Other gentlemen of the *ton* will see this no matter what the topic. Your daughter won't need to catch a husband, my lord. She will be able to choose from men who are attracted to her goodness and intelligence."

Hart cleared his throat and turned his full attention back to her. "Please continue, my lady."

She hesitated a moment, glancing from Hart to her father and then back, before proceeding. As she spoke, she grew in confidence and they wound up having a lively discussion. By its end, her cousin's eyes were closed and he snored softly. Hart looked to the earl, who looked incredibly bored. Encouraged by that, he continued his discussion with Lady Olivia until he sensed that the earl, too, had dropped off. He confirmed it by turning to look at Rivers, whose head leaned against the side of the coach and whose mouth hung slack.

Grinning, he turned back to his companion. "I see we have bored them both into sleep."

"Neither of them likes any kind of political discussion. Father barely tolerates going to the House of Lords for a vote and he is never informed by what is stated in a bill. He votes however his friends do without a thought to the consequences."

"It is too bad that women are not allowed to speak before the House of Lords," he told her. "You have a good grasp on the issues and could easily explain them in simple language to men such as your father. At least we may converse on whatever we wish while they are asleep."

"They should remain that way until we reach Rumsford. They both slept the entire way from Rumsford to London when we traveled together back in January." She paused and then added, "I do want to thank you again, Your Grace, for allowing me to come today. I know oftentimes women do not attend funerals but I am happy I will be able to honor Uncle Theo with my presence at today's service and burial."

"It is an honor to escort you, my lady. Since you are familiar with the area and its people, tell me about it and them."

They spent a good hour discussing the village and surrounding area, including who lived in the neighborhood. She suggested that once he returned after the Season that he should hold a country ball and invite all his neighbors and those from the village.

"A splendid idea. When does the Season actually end? In fact, would you tell me what it is about? I haven't asked my friends and I have no prior knowledge of it."

Her brow furrowed and he thought he had been insensitive, asking her to speak about a time which she herself had revealed was an unhappy one for her.

"It is all right, my lady. You do not have to regale me with what the Season is like. I will learn soon enough."

"No, I don't mind. Hopefully, this time will prove to be more cheerful than my last."

"So, you will participate? Despite your uncle's passing?"

She nodded. "Uncle Theo insisted I do so. He wanted nothing more than for me to be happy. He said to celebrate his life and get on with my own."

"A wise man, your uncle."

She sighed. "Sometimes, it is hard for me to understand how Uncle Theo and Father were related, much less brothers. They were as different as night and day. All right, Your Grace, let us talk about what the Season is like."

Lady Olivia launched into a description of the various types of social events. She was quite witty and painted a clear picture in his mind of the social affairs they would attend.

"Dare I say the whole thing sounds most unappealing?" he asked. "I am not one for small talk. Seeing the same people over and over on a daily basis seems very dull and tedious to me."

"Oh, it won't be," she assured him. "You will be the center of attention every time you enter a room."

He frowned. "Why is that? I only know a handful of people.

My fellow Terrors and then I will probably run into a few people I knew from school."

She laughed and he warmed at the sound of it.

"You will be invited to literally every event because you are a duke—and a bachelor. Single dukes do not come on the market very often. Hostesses will wait with bated breath, hoping you will respond to their invitations and then actually deign to show up. Eager mamas will thrust their darling daughters into your path. You will be expected to dance every dance. The whole of Polite Society will follow your every move at each ball or rout. They will look upon you with interest to see whom you have invited to the theatre or which lady you decide to sit beside at a musicale."

"That is utterly ridiculous," he proclaimed. "Merely because I am a duke now? I can tell you that I am the same man I was and my opinions have not changed from when I was merely Major Hartfield until now."

Interest shone in her eyes. "Ah, so that is where your name comes from. I have heard the others refer to you as Hart."

"I despise my given name. Aaron. I never thought it suited me. I have been Hart practically from the time I could walk."

She cocked her head, studying him. "You do look like a Hart."

"I wish you would call me Hart," he said impulsively, seeing the blush that tinged her cheeks at his suggestion.

"That would be highly inappropriate, Your Grace," she said primly, pursing her beautiful lips.

Lips that he was desperate to kiss.

Hart thought that he had no reason to go through a lengthy Season when the woman he wanted to be his duchess was seated across from him. Lady Olivia was beautiful, intelligent, caring, and interesting. He had no reason to look further because he knew he would never find anyone who would compare favorably to her.

Yet he was reluctant to make his feelings known. This woman had endured a lonely life and suffered through a disastrous

Season, one in which others had gossiped about her and ignored her. She was the ugly duckling who had emerged as a beautiful swan. She lacked confidence, thanks to her father, who seemed to do nothing but criticize or browbeat her at the drop of a hat.

Lady Olivia needed to experience a full Season. The *ton* should see how she had blossomed. She needed gentlemen to fill her dance card. Partner with her at cards. Send huge bouquets of flowers and call upon her, giving her compliments. She deserved the attention, which would hopefully help her learn to believe in herself and see her worth.

Only then would Hart make his feelings for her known. He would tolerate other men paying attention to her because it would bolster her. Lady Olivia needed to move freely through society and let them recognize the jewel she was. Then he would claim her as his duchess. She already fit in well with the Terrors' wives. It would allow him to have a marriage based upon friendship and common interests, as she had indicated she hoped she would find.

As for love? He didn't know if he could love. He had never known it from either parent. Never experienced it in the brief encounters he'd had with other women. All he knew was he felt a strong attraction to Lady Olivia and a fierce possessiveness toward her which made his chest tighten painfully. He yearned to hold her in his arms and kiss those luscious lips.

He would. In time. For now, he would be here for her. En-couraging her. Convincing her she was a woman to be valued.

"What about in private? You could call me Hart then."

She looked startled at his words. "Your Grace, when would we ever be alone? I have told you that is against every rule of Polite Society. If I am going to find a husband, I must adhere more closely than most ladies to these rules. Already, my name being announced at affairs will cause others to titter. There will be a few who remember the homely, overweight girl and still judge me based upon their previous recollections."

"That is monstrously unfair," he protested, hating the idea

that people would speak about her in such a hateful manner.

She gave him a knowing look. "It might be—but it will occur all the same. Many won't remember me because I made such a little impression during my come-out. Those who do are the gossips, the worst in Polite Society. They thrive on ugliness. I, too, am the same person I was, just as you are the army major and now a duke."

"I wasn't supposed to be. None of the Terrors were. We are all second sons who by twists of fate find ourselves holding ducal titles."

"Your friends all seem to have adapted to their titles, most likely because they were comfortable in their own skin before that title came along. You will be the same."

"I fear that I, too, will face gossip," he revealed. "My brother, who was the heir apparent, was a dreadful person. The worst I have ever known. He conducted illicit affairs with numerous married women of the *ton*."

"That happens all the time, Your Grace," she said quietly. "Your brother's actions should not affect you, however, especially since he is gone."

"Those types of couplings are common, I am told, but discretion is of the utmost importance. Reginald wasn't discreet about any of his liaisons. One of the cuckolded husbands challenged him to a duel. The viscount shot Reginald through the heart."

She gasped.

"And when my father received the news of his oldest son's death, he was dead within hours. So you see, my lady, I will also be fighting the hounds of gossip. I want to clear the Hartfield name. My father, as you have noted, was rarely at Deerfield Park. I want to be a better man and take care of the estate and my tenants more than he ever did. I also want to let Polite Society know that this Duke of Mansfield is a man of honor."

"You are right. Some gossip may occur at the start of the Season. They will be curious about you, wondering if you are like your brother. Or even your father. It won't take long for the *ton* to see that you are a man whose word is his bond. Though I haven't mingled in society recently, I know your friends have. They all are perfect gentlemen and a credit to their titles. Being in their company and being known as their friend will also help you escape any taint clinging to you."

Lady Olivia smiled at him and his heart began beating in double time. "You will have your pick of young ladies. If you marry one who comes from a good family and she has an impeccable reputation, that will also go a long way in restoring your family's name and honor. A girl making her come-out, one who is sweet and charming, would be best, I believe. Get her with child as soon as possible and show society you are a devoted husband and loving father. That will cause any gossip to cease."

Hart wanted to tell her that *she* was the one he wanted for his duchess. That he wanted to see her belly swell with his child. He wanted Olivia by his side—and in his bed.

But he remained silent. If he spoke now, she would come up with a thousand arguments why she wouldn't be suitable for him.

No, he would bide his time and when it was right, he would make his feelings known. Lady Olivia would have no choice. If a duke offered for her, she would have to accept him. Her father would make certain of that, the only time the man would ever prove to be useful.

Hart only wished the Season was already over and done so he could slip a ring on her finger and claim her as his duchess.

CHAPTER THIRTEEN

OLIVIA ENTERED THE church she had set foot in so many times in the past, its warm familiarity filling her. Several people nodded respectfully to her. She saw Uncle Theo's coffin at the front of the chapel and swallowed hard, tears threatening to spill down her cheeks.

The Duke of Mansfield led her up the aisle and seated her in what was the ducal pew. She recalled that it had remained empty every Sunday and each holiday for the five years she had resided in Rumsford. The duke took the seat next to her. Her father and Higbee sat to his right.

They had stopped at Deerfield Park before coming to the church. Mansfield suggested they freshen up before heading into the village for the funeral. Olivia had never seen the house since it was a few miles outside Rumsford and sat at least a mile or beyond the road running past it. She was awed by the home's beauty and sheer size. Owning one house such as this would be overwhelming but the duke mentioned that while this was his country seat, he also owned seven more estates scattered about England. The thought of such staggering wealth was incomprehensible.

She watched as the new vicar entered and greeted the congregation. Her heart grew heavy, thinking how Uncle Theo had been replaced. Still, she hoped this clergyman had a good heart and would do his best for the people of Rumsford and beyond.

Tears began to slide down her cheeks and Olivia fumbled with her reticule, trying to open it.

Suddenly, a handkerchief appeared and she took it.

"Thank you," she whispered to the duke.

He smelled of sandalwood today. His left side touched her right, his warmth bringing her comfort. She wiped her tears and clutched the handkerchief in her left hand, ready to use it again if needed. She would make sure it was laundered and returned to him.

Even if she wished to keep it.

It was wrong of her to think of her attraction to this man during her uncle's funeral but Olivia couldn't help it. The duke had been kind to her from the moment they had met in that alleyway. He was impossibly handsome and knew how to put others at ease, drawing them into conversation without any seeming effort. It was very easy to like him—and dangerous to do so. She was a nobody, a girl past her first youth. One with a reputation for having failed miserably during her only Season. It was foolish to think a man such as the Duke of Mansfield could ever be interested in someone like her. She should merely be grateful that he had included her today, allowing her to say her goodbyes to Uncle Theo in person instead of from afar.

Olivia turned her attention to the new vicar. The duke had said the clergyman's name was Reverend Smallwood and that he had a wife and three children.

"I wish I had known Theodore Knight as most of you did," the vicar told those gathered. "I met him when Mrs. Smallwood and I arrived in Rumsford and visited him at Mrs. Feldham's home. We spoke twice and, both times, I was the one who left comforted when I had intended to bring comfort to a dying man. Reverend Knight loved God Almighty and the people of this parish. Most of all, he loved his wife, whom he lost a year ago, and his beloved niece, Lady Olivia, who is here with us today."

She trembled at Smallwood's words, feeling the sorrow of her loss deeply. Then the duke placed his hand over hers. It was so large, hers disappeared. It not only warmed her but brought her solace.

"Since this congregation knew Reverend Knight, I would like to ask if anyone wishes to speak about him to us all. I invite you to do so now." He stepped to the side, away from his pulpit.

Olivia waited, hoping someone would go forward and share something about Uncle Theo. When no one did, a wave a sadness filled her.

"Go," urged the duke, whispering in her ear.

She turned, her eyes wide. "I cannot. I am a woman."

"Then I will."

Mansfield rose and moved to the front of the chapel.

"I have never been in this church," he began. "My parents were rarely at Deerfield Park and when they were, my father was not the kind of man who sought religious comfort. I am sorry because I would have known Reverend Knight if I had been allowed to come and worship here. As it is, I only recently made his acquaintance when I inherited the dukedom and returned from war. I visited with him on two separate occasions."

He smiled. "And I have never met a more likeable man in my life."

She felt those gathered relaxing.

"We had very good conversations. Reverend Knight was witty and probably the most intelligent man I have met. He had more love in his heart for his congregation than I thought possible. He wasn't merely resigned to dying. He looked forward to it because he would be with his Lord and Savior and reunited with his wonderful wife."

The duke looked out at those in the chapel. "He spoke of his niece during both my visits to him. How she had been the child he and Mrs. Knight had never had. How she had brought light and love into their lives."

Mansfield now turned to her. "I have now met Lady Olivia and see why her uncle thought so highly of her. She is a reflection of all that he taught her. The best in him is now present in her.

Though I may not have known Theodore Knight for long, I am more than happy to be acquainted with his niece. I hope, as the Duke of Mansfield, that I might bring the same consideration to and care for others that both Reverend Knight and Lady Olivia do. If I can emulate their examples, I will be a better man than I ever thought I could."

The duke bowed his head for a moment and then returned to the pew.

Olivia leaned close and whispered, "Thank you."

Mansfield's brief but heartfelt speech opened the floodgates and several of the village's citizens made their way to the front, one by one. Some speeches were brief and halting, due to the emotions of the speaker, while others were warm and witty, recollecting many good times in Uncle Theo's life. By the time Reverend Smallwood concluded the service, Olivia felt uplifted instead of disheartened.

The congregation filed from the chapel and the vicar came to them.

"It is a delight to meet you, my lady, although I am sorry it is under such sad circumstances. Your uncle didn't think you would be able to come to today's funeral. I know he and your aunt are smiling down from heaven."

"It was thanks to His Grace that I was able to journey from London." She smiled up at the duke.

Her father cleared his throat and she introduced both him and Higbee. Reverend Smallwood looked a bit puzzled at meeting them and she supposed he wondered why neither man had taken the opportunity to speak about their relationship with the deceased when given the opportunity.

"I know the burial is private but you should go and speak to those who came to the service," the vicar suggested to her. "I will have the coffin placed in the wagon and taken to its burial site next to your aunt."

"We will meet you there, Reverend," Olivia promised and then allowed the duke to escort her outside, her relatives trailing behind them.

She was welcomed by those she hadn't seen since January, happy to speak with many of them a final time since she had been given no warning that she was leaving Rumsford. All wished her well and many had kind words for the duke, thanking him for speaking on Reverend Knight's behalf.

"I was happy to do so," he told each of them.

The four returned to the ducal carriage and the coachman drove them as close as he could to the grave before stopping. The duke descended first and helped her out. Her father and Higbee followed, a sour expression upon both their faces.

They made their way to where her uncle would be laid to rest and Olivia paused beside her aunt's grave, kissing her fingers and touching Aunt Beryl's headstone.

"He is with you now," she said softly.

Reverend Smallwood offered a few words and then a lengthy prayer on her uncle's behalf.

"If there is anything I can do for you, my lady, please let me know."

"You have been most kind, Vicar. I hope you and your family will enjoy living in the parsonage and being at Rumsford."

The clergyman said goodbye to the others and left.

Her father also turned to go and the duke said, "Do you not wish for some private time with your brother?"

The earl harumphed. "I don't need it. We were never close. In fact, I almost didn't come today."

Left unsaid was he most likely did so to be in the presence of a duke.

"I would like a few moments if you don't mind, Your Grace," she said.

Her father glared at her and then said, "Come along, Higbee."

The two returned to the carriage. Mansfield whistled low.

"They are quite the pair. It is a good thing Wynter asked you to move to her and Donovan's. Those two are not to be trusted."

She shook her head. "We cannot choose our relatives."

"No," he said, trying to keep the bitterness from his tone. "My father was cruel and ignored me all my life. He sent me away for something Reginald did. My older brother wasn't man enough to own up to what he had done."

Seeing his vehemence, Olivia couldn't help but ask, "What did he do?"

"He murdered my younger brother."

She sucked in a quick breath. "Hart?" she asked. "Are you all right?"

He closed his eyes and took several deep breaths before opening them. "I am now. For a long time, I carried hate in my heart until I saw it did no good. I only wish I had been the one to shoot Reginald and not Garner."

Without thinking, she reached for his hand. Their fingers entwined. Their gazes locked.

Something passed between them. Something undefinable. Indescribable. Yet tangible.

Mansfield turned back to Uncle Theo's grave. "It seems your uncle was well-loved by those of Rumsford."

"He was the happiest man I have ever known, meeting each day with joy."

He squeezed her fingers. "Might we stop by my family's plot for a moment?"

"Of course."

Olivia knew exactly where it was because it held the largest monuments in the cemetery. When Hart had told her of his brother's death by dueling and his father's passing on the same day, she had recalled the double service and burial performed by her uncle last summer. She had not attended it since she had never met the duke or the marquess. Aunt Beryl had died only the week before and Olivia had not wanted to attend another funeral so soon. Her uncle had not mentioned how the pair had died, only that both had passed away in London and their bodies had been brought back to Rumsford for burial.

She followed the duke now, their fingers still joined, and they came to stand before the grave of a boy named Percy. She could see he was only six when he died. Or was murdered. The thought of one brother killing another horrified her. And to think the marquess actually blamed his brother for it. Hart appeared to be in his mid-twenties, which meant he would have been no more than ten or so when accused of Percy's death.

Hart knelt at the grave, still holding on to her hand, as his other touched the grass.

"I think of you every day, little brother. Know you are missed and always loved."

He rose and tugged on her, taking her a few plots away. Olivia saw this was the grave of Ada Martin, who also had died at age six. Again, he knelt, resting his hand upon the earth.

"I love you, Ada. I wish I could have known you. I know Percy is caring for you now."

Her throat tightened with unshed tears.

The duke—whom she could only think of as Hart now—smiled sadly at her.

"My father sent me away. Everyone was told Percy's drowning was accidental. I was never allowed to come home again. Mother and Ada were away at the time so I never got to say goodbye to either of them."

"You never came home?" she asked, her heart heavy.

"No. I remained at Turner Academy year-round, along with my fellow Terrors. You see, the academy was for troubled boys. Boys who had done terrible things. I soon learned that my new friends had been accused of wrongdoing, the same as I—and that they were all innocent. We bonded together over our mutual dismissal by our families. The Terrors are my brothers now."

Olivia squeezed his fingers, wanting to reassure him.

"Thank you," he said softly. "For being here. I have never told anyone else beyond the Terrors of Percy's deliberate drowning by Reginald."

"Thank you for confiding in me. I will never speak of it to anyone."

Hart gazed at her a long time. Once again, she felt something connecting them.

"Come. We must return to London."

He held her hand until they reached the carriage and then he helped her into the vehicle. She took the seat opposite him again. Her father tried to strike up a conversation with the duke but Hart shook his head and turned to gaze out the window pensively. Nothing was said until they reached the Haverhills' townhouse in London.

She bid her father and cousin farewell and Hart accompanied her to the door.

Before he knocked, he took her hand again and lifted it to his lips, kissing it tenderly.

"Thank you. May I call upon you tomorrow?"

"Yes," she said breathlessly, wondering why he wished to do so.

"Would you like to return to Gunter's?" he asked. "Neither of us got to sample one of their ices."

Olivia smiled, understanding now that he wished to take her to the tea shop. "I would like that. Very much."

"Then I will call for you at two o'clock tomorrow afternoon."

He released her hand and knocked on the door. The butler admitted her and she turned and watched Hart return to the carriage as the door closed.

"The duchess is waiting for you in the winter parlor," the butler said. "I will take you to her now."

"Thank you," Olivia said, wondering how—and why—her relationship with the Duke of Mansfield had subtly changed.

CHAPTER FOURTEEN

OLIVIA JOINED WYNTER in the morning room the next afternoon.

"I hope you will utilize this room as your own," her friend said. "I come here to read. Write letters. Think."

"I wouldn't want to interrupt you and infringe upon your privacy," she protested.

"You won't." Wynter chuckled. "Frankly, I am not in here as often as I would like. I also have a sitting room off my bedchamber so I can always retreat there if I require privacy. Are you finding everything to your liking?"

"Very much so. Thank you for the flowers in my bedchamber. They brightened the room. It is so light and airy. I do appreciate your invitation to stay here, Wynter."

"Your father seems dreadful. I don't much like the looks of your cousin, either. I met him last year and he did not make a favorable impression upon me. He runs with a fast crowd."

"Father is encouraging Higbee to take a bride this Season," Olivia shared. "It is one of the reasons I was brought to London. It seems as if there has been some gossip about me since I made my come-out and then never returned."

"Well, your mother passed," Wynter noted. "Polite Society should understand that."

"For a year of mourning. But I never appeared at another Season. Father says the rumors abounded as to why I remained in the country. He considered Uncle Theo's illness good timing, having his brother conveniently die so I would have nowhere to go and be forced to come to London." She sighed. "It seems the *ton* believes everything from my family is ashamed of me to thinking I am disowned or even dead."

"What?" Wynter exclaimed.

"I think it foolish nonsense but Father is afraid unless I make an appearance this Season, it will harm Higbee's chances of making a good match."

Her friend sniffed. "I don't think your cousin is ready to settle into marriage. As I said, his friends are some of the most notorious rogues in the *ton*."

She shuddered. "Higbee has offered to introduce me to them. He made it sound like he would be doing me a favor."

"I would steer clear of the lot of them, Olivia. They are rakes and gamblers. If you have a good-sized dowry, some of them would try to wed you strictly for that and never be faithful."

"I am looking for fidelity," she said, her thoughts turning to Hart. She should tell Wynter that she and the duke had planned an outing this afternoon.

The door opened and Haverhill entered, toting his son in his good arm.

"Hello, ladies. I come bearing a gift." He brushed his lips upon his wife's cheek and handed the baby to her.

Wynter cooed at her son. "What is my good boy doing to-day?"

"Crawling faster than I can move," Haverhill said, laughing. "I've been in the nursery the past hour. Sam is faster than my speediest thoroughbred. I do have some business to attend to but I will return in time for tea."

They bid the duke goodbye and then Wynter asked, "Would you care to hold Sam?"

Olivia nodded and took the baby. He wanted to stand so she let his feet rest on her thighs and held him by the waist. Sam studied her with interest and then touched his hands to her face.

"Cheek," she said. "Cheek."

Sam grinned and touched her nose.

"Nose." Olivia took his hand and brought it to his own nose. "Nose." She then returned it to hers. "Nose." She repeated the action. "Your nose. My nose."

Sam laughed and warbled something.

"I am going to say my son is brilliant and saying *nose* right now," Wynter said. "Donovan and I are competing, trying to be the first to have him utter *Mama* or *Papa*. He's taken with his Auntie Olivia, though."

She nibbled playfully on his fingers. "Olivia is a mouthful for anyone. Perhaps I should be Auntie O."

Sam laughed again and rested his small, chubby fingers on her face.

"Face," she told him. "Auntie O's face."

He began wriggling, bored with the game.

"Put him down. He loves to crawl."

Olivia did so and saw just how fast Sam moved. Wynter retrieved a small basket filled with toys and sat on the floor, pulling one out and handing it to her son. Oliva joined them and they spent half an hour playing with the baby.

"Oh, he's a Terror in the making," Wynter said.

"Will he go to Turner Academy?" she asked.

Her friend cocked her head. "You know of it?"

"Hart—that is, His Grace—mentioned it to me."

"I see. Yes, I believe Turner Academy would be a good place for the next generation of Terrors but that is far into the future. Right now, I cannot imagine letting Sam go and sending him off to school." Wynter paused. "I am surprised Hart told you about the academy."

"It was yesterday."

Wynter took Olivia's hand. "I know yesterday was hard for you."

"Actually, it wasn't. I had been told I would not be allowed to attend Uncle Theo's funeral. Getting to do so and seeing the people of Rumsford eased my mind. I was not given a chance to say goodbye to any of them before I was brought to London."

Olivia lifted Sam to her lap and held up a rattle. The baby took it and shook it with delight.

"Donovan says of the four Terrors that went to war, Hart was most affected by it. He was there the longest and though he hides his feelings from the world, he had wearied of war."

"He doesn't smile often," she said.

"He does around you," Wynter pointed out.

She felt her cheeks heat. "He has been kind to me. First, helping with Midnight. Then, by inviting me to travel to Rumsford with him." She eased Sam from her lap and then said, "He asked me to go with him to Gunter's today since neither of us got to try their ices."

Wynter's eyes lit up. "That is marvelous."

"He will be here soon. I should let my maid know so she can accompany us."

"That won't be necessary. Gunter's is the one place in London Hart may escort you to without society frowning."

"Truly?" She thought a moment. "But we must get there. I cannot be alone with him in his carriage."

"Walk," Wynter suggested. "It has turned into a most pleasant day."

The door opened and the butler said, "His Grace, the Duke of Mansfield, is here."

Hart rounded the corner and entered the room. "Ah, my favorite person," he declared.

Embarrassment filled Olivia until she realized he meant Sam. The duke went straight to the baby and scooped him up.

"Have you missed me, little one?" he asked, tossing Sam into the air and catching him.

The baby squealed in delight. Hart raised Sam high in his arms and then quickly lowered him before lifting him back up. Joy filled both of their faces, causing Olivia's heart to warm. It was apparent the duke loved children.

"Shall we take you to Gunter's with us?" Hart asked the baby.

"No," Wynter said emphatically. "Sam is much too young to be trying ices. Besides, it is almost time for his afternoon nap." She stood and took the baby. "I will take him to the nursery."

"I will go upstairs with you," Olivia said. "I must retrieve my bonnet and reticule. I won't be long," she promised.

"I will be cleaning up the toys," Hart said. "Terrors can make a terrible mess."

They left him picking up the scattered toys and went up the stairs. The nursery governess met them and took Sam. Wynter accompanied Olivia to her bedchamber.

"I hope you will give Hart every consideration."

Olivia shook her head. "He is merely being kind to me, Wynter. He dislikes my father and Higbee more than you do. He knows I feel liberated leaving their household. Our going to Gunter's means nothing."

Wynter took Olivia's hands in hers. "Perhaps. Perhaps not. I do know that Hart is lonely. He has no blood relatives left. Yes, the Terrors function as his brothers, but they have encouraged him to find a bride." She paused. "You could be that bride, Olivia."

"A duke can do far better than me. I am—"

"Beautiful and smart and generous," Wynter supplied. "Hart sees that. Just be open to the idea. Don't push him away."

She nodded, emotion filling her, and tied her bonnet under her chin.

Wynter hugged her. "I will see you later. Enjoy yourselves."

Olivia returned downstairs and found Hart waiting in the foyer. They left the townhouse and she said, "Might we walk to Berkeley Square? It isn't far."

He nodded knowingly. "We wouldn't want to break any rules." He called out to his driver, "We are going to walk. I will return later."

The driver tipped his cap to them and they started off, Hart tucking her hand into the crook of his arm.

"Do you enjoy walking?" he asked.

"Very much so. I find it the best exercise. After all, I have spent the last five years in the country. Walking is common there. It is hard to understand why more people in London don't do so. I find it ridiculous to board a carriage merely to travel three blocks. Why, with the congested streets, people could walk to their destinations and back home again long before their carriages could get them to where they are going."

Hart laughed, rich and deep, and Olivia found she very much liked the sound of it.

"Practical. I shall add that to the list."

"List?"

"Yes, my Olivia list."

"Why do you have a list? And what is on it?"

"Ah, curiosity. Another trait you possess. Let me see, what is on the list currently? You are intelligent. Interesting. Kindhearted. And now practical and curious go on the list, as well." He grinned. "What would be on your Hart list?" he asked cheekily.

"I have no list, Your Grace," she told him, her heart beginning to thump wildly.

"Hart," he reminded her. "We are alone so it is safe to be a rule-breaker and use my given name."

"Actually, your nickname, Aaron."

He pretended to stab himself in the heart. "You wound me, Olivia. I never like hearing that name. I found it above the bed I was to occupy at Turner Academy and quickly had them change it. Finch did the same. He is William Finchley but has always been Finch."

"The others do not use nicknames?" she asked.

"No. They are Miles, Wyatt, and Donovan. I suppose I could bestow nicknames upon them. Probably their wives have already done so—but I doubt those names are for delicate ears."

Olivia found herself blushing profusely. "Do you always say outrageous things?"

"Actually, no. I was always more serious. Not as grave as

Miles, but Donovan and Wyatt were the ones who always did the flirting."

"You . . . are flirting with me?"

He glanced down at her. "I suppose I am. It is what a single gentleman does when in the company of a pretty girl."

"I am no girl. Cousin Higbee says I am on the shelf."

"Cousin Higbee is an arse."

She giggled. "We do agree on that."

"He seems to always be in your father's company."

"Higbee has lived with us since he was twelve. He lost his parents and since Mama never produced an heir, my father has always focused all his attention upon Higbee."

"I have seen him at White's. Now that he has been introduced to me and we have actually shared a carriage, he will want to become my closest friend."

Olivia chuckled. "Snub him. You are a duke. Your closest friends are all dukes. Tell him so."

He placed his hand over hers. "Excellent advice."

They arrived in Berkeley Square and crossed it toward Gunter's. She saw a man emerge from the shop carrying a tray. He raced across to a parked carriage and the door opened. A hand from inside claimed an ice and then took the other one perched on the tray.

"Are they . . . eating in their carriage?" she asked.

"You didn't know? That is what most people do when they come to Gunter's. A waiter comes out and writes down their request and then returns with the item. It is quite the fashionable thing to take an ice from your carriage at Gunter's. During the height of the Season, this area will be jammed with phaetons and curricles. Everyone wants to have their ice and be seen."

She shuddered. "Then I am glad we are coming now. I dislike crowds and avoid them when I can."

They entered the shop and were seated quickly. A man brought them two large cards.

"Take your time and then let me know what you wish to

have," he said cheerfully.

Olivia perused the writing. "There are so many choices," she declared. "I will have a hard time deciding."

"Not me," Hart proclaimed, pushing aside the card. "I see chocolate listed. For me, that means there *is* no other choice."

She laughed. "Well, then I must get something else." She perused the list thoughtfully. "I think I will go with maple."

Hart signaled the waiter. "Two ices. Maple for the lady and chocolate for me."

"Yes, Your Grace."

As the waiter scurried away, he asked, "How did he know I was a duke?"

Olivia gave him a knowing smile. "I told you. You are a newly-minted, unwed duke. Everyone in London knows who you are."

"I suppose I should add blunt to my list of your qualities," he teased. "You do not mince words with me." Hart gave her an admiring glance. "And I like that. Honesty, I believe, will be lacking in abundance when I begin to forge my way through Polite Society."

"The Hart list should include you being self-important," she teased back. "Dukes are snobbish, easily bored, and think highly of themselves."

A shadow crossed his face. "I wish I weren't a duke," he said wistfully.

Her heart went out to him. "You are new at it, just as you were once new at Turner Academy and new to war. You became well-versed once you got your bearings. Being a duke will be the same. You will find your own way, Hart, and it will be a good one. You have the Terrors to lean upon for advice but it will be your heart which will lead the way."

He gazed at her a long moment. "Thank you."

The waiter returned with a tray bearing their ices and placed them on the table. "Anything else, Your Grace?"

"No, thank you."

Olivia dipped her spoon into the ice and lifted it to her mouth in anticipation. It was sweet and cold and utterly satisfying.

"I could eat one of these every day," she said.

He nodded as he spooned the chocolate concoction into his mouth. "Delicious. Would you like to try a bite of mine?"

Hart gathered a small bite onto his spoon and held it toward her. Before she accepted it, she saw the two women seated at the table next to theirs. One frowned in disapproval while the other looked on eagerly, waiting to see what Olivia would choose to do.

"No, thank you," she said, averting her head.

"Oh."

He sounded hurt and she quietly said, "That is too intimate a gesture, Your Grace. Others were too interested in our actions."

He glanced to his left and smiled at the two women. "Lovely weather we're having."

"Yes, Your Grace," both replied in unison and then gaped openly at him.

Olivia concentrated on eating her ice but the moment had spoiled their fun. They finished eating in silence, the carefree conversation from before now gone. She could not afford any mistakes.

And thinking she could possibly have a future with the Duke of Mansfield was definitely a mistake.

CHAPTER FIFTEEN

Hart sat silently as Lawson, his valet, finished tying his cravat. Nerves filled him.

Tonight was the opening of the Season.

He dreaded it.

His London tailor had seen that Hart had the right clothes for each invitation issued to him. He had replied affirmatively to all events during the first two weeks, not knowing which ones Olivia might be attending. Word had passed among the *ton* that Lady Olivia Knight was staying with the Duke and Duchess of Haverhill, her dear friends, so Hart assumed she had received her fair share of invitations. He would have asked her—if he had ever seen her long enough to speak with her.

Ever since their outing to Gunter's, Olivia had made herself scarce. He hated that those two judgmental women had forced her to retreat like a turtle into its shell. At least where he was concerned. From what he gathered, she did go on various outings with her friends, which relieved him. When he came to tea, however, she seemed to have a letter to write or some other excuse to leave. He received a polite smile from her and then she retreated from the room.

Once, he had slipped away from tea and found her in the nursery playing with Sam. He had stood in the doorway, a lump in his throat, seeing how right she looked with a babe in her arms. Clearing his throat, he told the nursery governess he had come up to take a quick peek at Sam. Olivia had smiled graciously and handed the baby over—and then left the room. Hart couldn't even enjoy his time with Sam because he longed to talk with her.

Would she try to avoid him tonight?

"There, Your Grace," said Lawson, nodding his approval.

"Thank you," he said. Glancing in the full-length mirror, he added, "I am glad you know how to put the right items together to make me look this good. As an army officer, I never had to worry about what to put on. It was my uniform every single day."

"England is grateful for your service, Your Grace," said the valet. "I hope you have a fine time tonight."

"That remains to be seen," he grumbled.

"Oh, Your Grace, you most certainly will. You are a duke of the realm and the most eligible bachelor of this Season."

Hart frowned. "How do you know so much about the Season?"

Lawson smiled. "The network of servants who trade in gossip is vast. If you have need of knowing anything about any young lady you might be interested in, merely ask me. I can have that information for you within a day or two. If you find a lady physically attractive, I can ascertain for you if she is amiable and kind, either with her peers or her servants. Frankly, Your Grace, I believe the way a member of Polite Society treats her servants says a great deal about her. Especially if she is suitable to be your duchess."

Hart thought Lawson quite bold for a servant but he agreed and said, "What do you know of Lady Olivia Knight? Her father is Lord Rivers and her cousin a Mr. Rivers."

"I can ask about the gentlemen but I already know of Lady Olivia from the Duke of Haverhill's servants. They are quite fond of her. She is undemanding and gracious."

He could have guessed Olivia would treat servants as well as she did others. It made him worry how she might treat her many suitors.

"I am off," he announced, leaving his ducal suite and heading downstairs.

Bomer handed him his hat and an umbrella. "It looks as if it might rain, Your Grace. It is important to be prepared."

A footman called from the door, "His Grace's carriage is here."

Miles had asked Hart to go with him and Emery to the opening ball at Lord and Lady Roxbury's townhouse.

"Have a pleasant evening, Your Grace," his butler told him.

Hart strode toward the carriage and climbed inside, sitting across from his friends.

"You look very elegant in your new evening clothes," Emery complimented. "It is the first time I have seen you in them."

"It won't be the last," joked Miles. He lifted his wife's hand and kissed it. "Fortunately, Emery says we only have to stay in town until mid-June."

"That allows us to enjoy the Season and London before the heat gets to be too much," she explained.

"I say why come at all but my wife enjoys being in town and with her friends."

"Speaking of friends, how is Lady Olivia doing?" Hart inquired.

"She brought Midnight to us yesterday," Emery shared. "She and Wynter waited until they learned Lord Rivers was at his club and they went and collected Midnight from the stables. Oh, she is a beautiful kitten. So sweet and affectionate."

"I worried that Ben would chase after her as he does the dogs," Miles said. "He did the complete opposite. He stroked the kitten gently. Even dragged a piece of string around and let Midnight chase it. The creature spent half the day curled up in Ben's lap once he tired her out."

"He begged to sleep with her last night," Emery added. "Miles said no and placed Midnight in a basket beside Ben's bed." She smiled. "This morning, though, his nursery governess found boy and kitten curled up together, fast asleep."

"It is good to hear Ben is so good with her," Hart said. "I would like to come see Midnight for myself. Hopefully, her paws and tail have healed nicely."

"They have," she said and then her eyes widened. "Miles!" she cried suddenly.

His friend bent and retrieved something from the floor of the coach. He held the receptacle just under his wife's chin and she vomited into it before sitting back, her eyes closed. Miles dabbed a handkerchief to her lips.

"If you are ill, we must turn the carriage around," Hart said. "There is no need for you to attend a ball in your condition."

Emery opened her amber eyes. "I am not ill, Hart, but I am in a certain way."

Her meaning was clear. "When will the next little Notley arrive?"

"Toward the end of November, I believe. I have only been sick twice now. We have yet to tell anyone since it is so early."

"Your secret is safe with me but I do offer you my heartiest congratulations. Ben will make for an excellent older brother."

She smiled. "I think so, too."

"So, I understand there will be a receiving line we must go through. Olivia told me about it."

"She did?" Miles asked.

"Yes. I had no idea what the Season involved and so I had her explain some of it to me, especially the balls. I know ladies will have programmes and that if I wish to dance with them, I must sign my name to a particular number."

"Once," Emery said emphatically.

"Beg pardon?"

"Olivia must not have mentioned that practice to you. Only dance once with a lady, Hart. If you dance twice with her, it shows you are most interested in her."

"It is publicly staking your claim to her," Miles added. "And never dance thrice with her in a single evening."

"Why not?"

"That would ruin her reputation," Emery said.

"So, I can only ask . . ." His voice trailed off.

She looked at him encouragingly. "Is there someone special you wish to ask to dance?"

He shrugged. "Perhaps."

"You are too transparent," Miles warned. "It is Olivia, isn't it?"

"Yes," Hart admitted. "But I will only dance with her once."

She frowned. "But if you are interested in her, asking her twice would let the *ton* know so. A duke always has the upper hand when two men are vying for the same lady."

"I can't let her know I'm interested in her," he complained.

"Why not?" Miles asked.

"Olivia was miserable during her first Season. Even now, she doesn't seem to feel she is good enough to be a member of the *ton*. Her father has her believing she is unworthy. She lacks in confidence. I want her to shine this Season. To be absolutely brilliant and let others see how remarkable she is. I must give her that opportunity. Only then will I press my suit."

Emery frowned. "I do know how horrible her come-out was but you walk a fine line, Hart. If you wait too long, others will swoop and could very well sweep Olivia off her feet."

His jaw set stubbornly. "Then that is a chance I must risk. She must be allowed to have other men court her. Compliment her. Make her feel she is of value. I don't think she would believe it if only I did so. I want others to see that Olivia is a diamond of the first water—and I want her to believe that, as well."

"Have you told anyone else this?" Miles asked.

"No. You are the first. The other Terrors and wives should know, too. We all need to keep an eye on her."

"I hope she will shine as you wish her to do," Emery said. "I think you would be good for each other."

They arrived and disembarked, being swept up in the swell entering the Roxburys' townhouse. Fortunately, they were earlier than most and it did not take long to go through the receiving line. Hart entered the ballroom with his friends and gazed about.

"She's not here yet," he said anxiously.

Emery touched his arm. "She will be. Be sure to greet her as soon as she does. If you sign her dance card, others will. Polite Society always follows whatever a duke does. Dancing with Olivia will make a statement. Miles, you might want to ask her to dance, as well."

"Let us see how it goes, my love. If gentlemen follow Hart's lead, Olivia will not want an old, married man to fill a spot on her programme."

Secretly, Hart hoped Miles would ask Olivia to dance because it would mean one less potential suitor dancing with her.

He spied Wyatt and Meadow and motioned them over. Briefly, he told them what he had shared with Miles and Emery.

"I thought you and Olivia would be an excellent match," Meadow said with certainty. "But I do understand how you want to lift her up and allow her to feel special."

"There she is," Wyatt said, nudging him.

Hart looked and saw her entering with Donovan and Wynter. A footman offered Olivia a programme, which Wynter helped her attach to her wrist.

"Ask for the supper dance," Wyatt recommended. "Once you dance it, you are then to escort your partner in to supper. We can all dine together. It will do her reputation good to be seen dining with four dukes and three duchesses."

"All right," he said, nerves again fraying his edges.

Donovan saw them and steered Wynter and Olivia their way. Hart swallowed hard, trying to push his nerves down.

They arrived and the group exchanged greetings. Then he noticed how the others deliberately began speaking with each other, leaving the two of them to engage in conversation.

"You look lovely tonight, Olivia," he said softly.

It was true. She wore a gown the color of a summer lake, making her eyes more blue than gray tonight. Her blond hair was swept back into a simple chignon. She wore no jewelry and he cursed inwardly, thinking her father should have provided her with some. When they wed, he would shower her with jewels.

"Thank you," she said shyly and then glanced around.

"Would you agree to a dance between us tonight?" he asked.

She turned back to him, her lips slightly parted. "You don't have to ask me to dance."

"I think I do. Think practically, my lady. If a duke asks to sign your dance card, others will take note."

Understanding lit her eyes. "Oh, you wish to try and help me find suitors. That is kind of you." She paused, her eyes brimming with tears. "You are always so kind to me."

He lifted her card and scrawled his name next to the supper dance.

"I heard you delivered Midnight to Ben yesterday."

"Yes. Emery sent a note to me this morning, telling me how taken they are with one another." She smiled and it made Hart want to burst out in song.

Movement appeared at their elbows and they both turned.

"Ah, Cousin."

Mr. Knight stood there, with three of his friends in tow. All the men were quite handsome and gazed at Olivia with hungry eyes.

Hart wanted to punch every one of them in the mouth.

"Your Grace, may I present my friends—Lord Bell, Lord Cooperton, and Lord Waltham. Gentlemen, His Grace, the Duke of Mansfield."

He nodded curtly, not offering his hand.

"And gentlemen, this is Lady Olivia Knight, my uncle's daughter."

Cooperton stepped forward. "Lady Olivia. It is a genuine pleasure." He bowed over her hand and kissed it too long for Hart's taste.

The other two followed suit and each begged for a dance from her. She agreed and her dance card was passed around.

Though he didn't want to leave her side, Donovan tugged on

his arm. "I have a few people I would like you to meet. We will see you at supper, Lady Olivia."

They moved away and Donovan said, "Miles shared your plan regarding Lady Olivia. I caution you, my friend. She will be quite popular. Do not wait too late to make your move."

"I won't," Hart replied, already seething, knowing Olivia would be dancing with others. "Just long enough for her to be convinced of her worth."

Donovan introduced him to several people, including two young ladies making their come-out. One, doe-eyed and pretty, gazed at him in wonder.

"I have never met a duke," she told him, nervously wringing her hands together.

"Haverhill is also a duke," Hart said.

"Oh, he is Papa's friend. I don't really know him."

"May I request a dance, my lady?"

She beamed.

Hart looked at the second girl, who gazed at him boldly, unlike the first.

"Your Grace, it is wonderful having you here in London for the Season."

"Better here than a battlefield," he quipped.

"Oh, you were a soldier?"

"Yes. Until recently."

Giving him a come-hither smile, she said, "I would love to hear all about your . . . experience. At war, of course."

He knew a vixen when he saw one but still signed her programme anyway. Anything to keep his mind off Olivia.

Hart danced with the two debutantes, both very different from one another. The naive doe fairly trembled in his arms. He told her to relax and enjoy her come-out, noting she would be attending many events and making the acquaintance of dozens of gentlemen.

The other danced incredibly well but her eyes seemed far older than her years. At the end of their dance, as he escorted her back to her mother, she said, "I still would like to share in your experiences, Your Grace." She whispered her address to him and added, "I will wait up until dawn."

He stopped and glared at her. "You may wait all you like, my lady. I will be sleeping in my own bed every night."

"You are free to sleep in your bed, Your Grace. I am merely asking you to share mine for a while. I think we could have a most memorable time."

Hart figured either the girl was a slut or invited him to her bed so that her dear mama might enter and accidentally find them together, forcing him to do the honorable thing and offer for the girl.

"Look for another, pet," he told her. "I am not your man."

She gave him a pretty pout. "You cannot blame me for trying, Your Grace." She paused. "If you change your mind, you know where to find me."

He doubted her bed would remain empty for long.

Finally, the supper dance arrived. Hart made his way toward Olivia, who had just been escorted off the dance floor by Viscount Waltham. The two men nodded at one another and then he turned his attention to his partner.

"Shall we?" he asked, offering his arm to her.

Hart had watched her the entire evening. Olivia had danced with Knight's three friends and a stream of other men. He feared she would become too popular and he wouldn't have a chance at all with her.

Still, as he placed his arm about her, his palm resting against the small of her back as his other hand took hers in his, their gazes met.

He knew he had to have this woman as his duchess.

No other one would do.

CHAPTER SIXTEEN

OLIVIA HAD LOOKED forward all evening to partnering with Hart. She had danced many times already with no empty spaces on her programme. The fact that Hart had signed her dance card had seemingly encouraged others to do so. Not one of her partners seemed to know her from before or if they did, they were too polite to mention it to her.

She knew, though, the supper dance with Hart was to be a waltz. The dance was much different from any others danced, in that it was intimate. She would spend the entirety of it in his arms.

The musicians struck the first note and she found herself whirled away. An array of colors passed by as Hart twirled her about the dance floor with ease, making Olivia feel light on her feet and graceful. Her belly seemed to explode with a mass of fluttering butterflies, leaving her breathless and eager.

"For a woman who said she danced not at all during her come-out, you are a remarkable dancer, my lady."

"I did attend the local assemblies several times a year in Rumsford so I was able to remain in practice. However, I did not know how to waltz. Fortunately, Wynter thought of that and so this past week, both Winslow and Amesbury practiced with me. Haverhill encouraged them to do so, saying I shouldn't have to dance with a one-armed man."

"Donovan makes light of his injury," Hart noted.

"Did he lose his arm during the war?"

"No. He was a lucky man, dashing into battle at the head of his men. Never got a scratch on him. It was a carriage accident once he returned to England that took his lower arm and hand and caused the scar on Wynter's cheek."

"He seems so adept at everything, even without it," she said. "He is forever toting Sam about the house with ease."

"Donovan is one of the most determined men I have ever known. If he puts his mind to something, nothing is impossible. He still rides regularly." Hart glanced across the room. "And I see he still waltzes with Wynter."

Olivia turned and saw the couple gliding effortlessly across the dance floor and smiled.

"Have you enjoyed this evening?"

"Very much so. It is different from five years ago."

"Has anyone mentioned your come-out?"

"No. I doubt anyone remembers me beyond the women who adore gossip. I think Father was foolish in thinking people still talked about me all these years later. Frankly, I am unrecognizable from how I appeared then."

They finished the dance and Hart said, "Are you ready to go into supper?"

She nodded and placed her hand on his forearm, knowing she had the privilege of dining with the most handsome man at tonight's ball. She saw Higbee with Lady Lydia and hoped the young girl was enjoying tonight's ball held in her honor.

They followed the crowd into supper and he took her to a table at the front where Lord and Lady Roxbury sat along with Wynter, Emery, and Meadow.

Once Hart seated her, he said, "I will go through the buffet for you. Anything particular you might wish for?"

"I am easy to please. I will trust your judgment."

Olivia listened politely to the conversation as the others spoke, looking across the ballroom. She saw her father with a few of his friends and assumed they had been in the card room the entire evening. Her gaze met Lord Bell's and he nodded to her. He was one of Higbee's friends she had danced with but she hadn't really spoken to any of them much because of the nature of the lively dances. All three, however, had asked permission to call upon her tomorrow. She didn't know if it was because her cousin had encouraged them to do so or if they truly wished to get to know her better.

Or if they were interested in her dowry.

Haverhill had called her into his study this afternoon, informing her that her father had paid a visit that morning. He had told the duke how much Olivia's dowry consisted of, which was a surprisingly large amount. The earl had urged Haverhill to help watch for fortune hunters, stating his daughter must be protected from them. Haverhill told her he had assured Lord Rivers that Olivia was in good hands and they would take care to assess the character of her suitors.

Talk of money had embarrassed her but Haverhill said it was a necessary evil as far as the Marriage Mart went. He told her to trust her gut and that it and her heart would guide her decision. She still had doubts that any gentleman would offer for her, having received not a single proposal during her come-out Season. Tonight, though, had been somewhat encouraging. Perhaps she would find a husband after all.

Just not Hart.

She had seen how the women present—wed or unwed—had followed him with their eyes as he moved through the ballroom. She had also overheard a few conversations that assessed everything from his looks to the number of properties he held. It seemed so mercenary. Olivia knew, however, that this was the way of Polite Society. Hart, as a duke, would be expected to marry from the highest echelons of the *ton*, most likely another duke's daughter. Two were making their come-outs this Season and she had noticed he danced with both of them earlier.

The men returned with plates full of appetizing foods and soon the table was merry as they ate their fill.

"Lady Lydia looks quite lovely tonight," Wynter told their hostess.

"It took over two hundred hours to sew the rosettes onto her gown," Lady Roxbury shared.

The women launched into a discussion of fashion and what would prove to be popular this Season, based upon the gowns worn this evening. Lady Roxbury beamed throughout the conversation, a hostess who claimed three duchesses and four dukes at her table, obviously the envy of everyone in the room.

Then a footman appeared and whispered into Lord Roxbury's ear. He blanched and nodded. The servant scurried away and the earl said something privately to his wife. The color drained from her face and she sprang to her feet.

"Excuse us," Lord Roxbury said and the couple hurried from the table.

"I wonder what is wrong," Olivia said.

"Plenty," Winslow replied. "Only two disasters strike at a ball. One involves something wrong with the buffet, which we can all attest is not the problem."

"The other would be that Lady Lydia has been caught in a compromising position at her own ball," Amesbury continued.

The pit of her belly grew cold. She had last seen Lady Lydia with her cousin. Remembering what Wynter said about Higbee running with a fast crowd, she wondered if he had amassed gambling debts—which Lady Lydia's dowry could repay.

Hart slipped his hand around hers and squeezed her fingers. "It might not be what you think," he said softly.

She realized he, too, had seen Higbee with the earl's daughter.

"What will happen if she has been compromised?" Olivia asked the table.

"It depends," Haverhill said. "If it were a mere kiss she engaged in, then a betrothal will be announced shortly. Marriage contracts will be drawn up. An announcement will be placed in the newspapers. The banns will be read." He shrugged. "If it is more serious, then it would not surprise me if an announcement is made before supper ends and a special license is purchased, followed by a hasty wedding."

Dread filled her. Instinct told her it had been Higbee who had taken advantage of Lady Lydia.

The conversation continued until she saw Lord and Lady Roxbury enter the supper room again. Close behind them was their daughter—and Cousin Higbee, a smirk upon his face.

Olivia watched as Higbee found her father and nodded. Lord Rivers returned the nod. Then she saw Lord Cooperton and Lord Waltham slip into the room and take their seats. They must be the witnesses who saw poor Lady Lydia's ruination.

The four came toward their table and Olivia's companions fell silent. Higbee stood off to the side, while Lady Roxbury slipped her arm about her daughter's waist. Lady Lydia had two spots of color on her cheeks and a wild look in her eyes, as if she were trapped. In effect, she had been. Olivia believed her cousin had been hunting for a fortune and he had landed one this evening.

Footmen appeared with trays of champagne and began distributing the flutes throughout the crowd. The toast that would have been in Lady Lydia's honor would now become one toasting to her and her groom's future. A sick feeling washed over Olivia, knowing how Higbee had laid a trap for the innocent girl.

Lord Roxbury accepted a flute and tapped a knife against it. The sound could be heard above the din and the crowd quietened. She saw people looking about and beginning to nod with understanding.

"Lady Roxbury and I wish to thank you for coming tonight to this first wonderful ball of a new Season. I would ask that you raise a glass tonight in my daughter's honor." He swallowed. "And to help us celebrate her betrothal to Mr. Knight."

Hart squeezed her hand again. "Perhaps it won't be as bad as we think."

"It will be worse," she said quietly. "I pity her. She has been confined to a prison of someone else's making, from which there will be no escape." Olivia tugged her hand from his. "This is what happens when rules are broken. There is always a price to be paid. And it seems women are those who pay it for a lifetime."

Lord and Lady Roxbury returned to their seats and two more were brought to accommodate the newly affianced couple. She found herself next to Higbee, who smiled broadly at her.

"So, what do you say, Cousin Olivia? Aren't you going to congratulate me?"

"Why should I? You trapped that poor, naive girl into marriage because you wanted her dowry."

He assessed her with new eyes. "My, you are already learning the ways of the *ton*. Who knows? The same may happen to you."

"I know the rules, Higbee. They are unspoken but ring loud and clear. I will not find myself compromised as Lady Lydia did. Especially with one of your friends."

He gave her a knowing smile. "We'll see." He turned away.

Olivia glanced to Hart. "Would you please excuse me? I wish to go to the retiring room."

Emery heard her and said, "I am headed there myself. In fact, I think Miles and I will be leaving now that supper has ended. We don't want to infringe upon your fun, though, Hart."

"Hart can ride with us after the ball ends," Haverhill said.

"Miles, I will meet you in the foyer. Would you have them bring the carriage around?" Emery asked.

"Of course," her husband said.

Olivia rose and accompanied Emery to the retiring room. Her friend told not to wait for her since Olivia needed to return to the ballroom for the next set, which would be beginning soon.

"Perhaps you can come tomorrow and see how Midnight is adjusting to her new home," Emery suggested. "Oh, no. That won't do."

"Why not?"

"You will be expected to be at home to receive your callers. I am certain at least a few gentlemen have asked to visit you tomorrow."

"A few," she admitted, though knowing three of them were her cousin's friends now set her teeth on edge.

"How about tea then?" Emery suggested. "Can you free yourself for it?"

"I would be happy to come for tea."

They separated, each going behind one of the provided curtains. Olivia then washed her hands and took one of the towels a maid provided. She left the retiring room and started toward the ballroom when two women close to her age stepped out, blocking her way.

"Excuse me," she said, trying to go around the pair, but one latched on to her forearm.

"You think you can reenter Polite Society with ease?" the blond woman asked. "We remember who you are, my lady. You were the laughingstock of your Season. People didn't speak behind your back but talked openly about how pitiful you were."

"I want to know how you came to be friends with those duchesses," the brunette said. "I have been introduced to each of them and they didn't care a fig for me. What makes you so special?" Her gripped tightened on Olivia's arm.

Olivia kept silent, knowing to spar verbally with these two would only lead to trouble. She couldn't recall their names but remembered they had been a part of her come-out group and treated her terribly.

"You were boring and obese then. Not a gentleman one would dance with you, despite your dowry. And I have heard your father increased it in order for someone to take you off his hands." The blond smiled triumphantly.

"You won't land the husband you think you will. The Duke of Mansfield can do much better than the likes of you. You may have slimmed down but you are still the dull, humorless chit you were back then. Besides, no man worth his salt wants a bluestocking for a wife."

She jerked her arm from the woman's hold and walked away,

her head held high as she heard them titter with laughter.

Despite her moderate success tonight, Olivia suddenly felt the worst of failures. She didn't want to continue with the Season. She didn't want to wed just any man.

She only wanted Hart as her husband. And that would never come to pass. Those two might be terrible gossips but they only voiced what others were thinking. She wasn't good enough for a duke, much less one such as Hart.

A voice in her head told her to ignore what the women had said. She supposed it was Uncle Theo trying to bolster her spirits as she returned to the ballroom. Olivia squared her shoulders. She did not want to return to her father's household and endure living there for a single day. She certainly didn't want him to wind up choosing her husband for her. She desperately wanted children now that she had been around Ben, Leah, and Sam.

She would do her best to find a man she could trust. One who would care for her and protect her from vipers such as those women who verbally attacked her.

Olivia consulted her programme to see who might be her next partner and pasted a smile upon her face as she stepped into the ballroom. Within minutes, she was dancing as she pretended to have the time of her life.

CHAPTER SEVENTEEN

"I THINK YOU should wear the rose gown this afternoon," Wynter suggested.

Olivia nodded at Mary, who placed the chosen gown across the bed and then helped Olivia from the gown she wore into the new one.

"Mary, pull a few wisps of Lady Olivia's hair along her temples so they help frame her face."

The servant did as requested and Wynter nodded with satisfaction.

"That will be all, Mary," Olivia said, dismissing the maid.

After Mary left, Wynter asked, "Are you nervous?"

"More than I should be," she admitted. "I know three of Higbee's friends are coming to call. A few others, as well, but for the life of me I cannot remember any of their names. Last night's ball and all the introductions seem a blur to me."

"Well, they will know yours and you do look lovely," her friend said. "Besides, each caller will be announced by name so that will refresh your memory."

"What if no one comes?" she whispered.

Wynter laughed. "Oh, that will not happen."

"I have never had anyone call on me, other than when you and the others came to my father's house for tea."

"I do remember we were uninvited. It must have been a surprise to see all of us in one place but we did want to show you that you are supported."

Olivia smiled. "I thought it a lovely gesture. One which I will never forget."

Wynter slipped her arm through Olivia's and said, "Shall we go to the drawing room?"

As they made their way downstairs, Wynter asked, "Will Hart be coming this afternoon?"

"No. He did not ask to call."

She had hoped he would ask to do so but a part of her knew he would most likely be visiting one or both of the duke's daughters he'd danced with at last night's ball.

"Have you received word from your father or cousin today?"

"You mean about Higbee's sudden betrothal? No, I haven't. I dread attending the wedding. My heart goes out to poor Lady Lydia, being stuck with Higbee. I still cannot believe he compromised her in her own parents' home on the opening night of the Season. I saw two of his friends enter the ballroom after the incident occurred so I would guess they were the two who stumbled across and discovered the couple." She shuddered. "They are both coming to call today."

"I can refuse them entrance," Wynter said, her mouth tight with disapproval.

"No, I don't want to seem ungracious. I simply won't be home to them in the future. I will make certain they understand that before they leave today so that they will never call again."

"Hmm. We should work out a system between us, Olivia. There will be gentlemen that you do not want to encourage and would like to see leave." Wynter grinned. "And then there will be a few you will wish to kiss."

"Kiss? But that would ruin me," she protested.

"Only if you are caught at it," Wynter said, her eyes bright with amusement. "I wouldn't do so at any social engagement but if I know you are interested in a certain caller, I can manage to give you an opportunity to be alone with him briefly. I highly recommend that you kiss a few men. It will help determine which you should choose as your husband."

Olivia stopped. "I have never kissed anyone."

Her friend said, "Then it is high time you start. Tug on your ear if you are interested in kissing a man."

"And if I want to get rid of one?" She thought a moment. "I know. If I tug on my left earlobe, I want them to leave. Left. Leave. If I pull on my right?" Olivia grinned. "Then it might be right to try for a kiss."

"You are so clever. That will be easy for me to remember."

"Will His Grace be joining us this afternoon?" she asked.

"Some days but not today. Come along."

They arrived at the drawing room and Olivia was astounded because the room was filled with flowers.

"Why, it looks as if a garden has sprung up in here," she exclaimed.

"These bouquets are all for you," Wynter revealed. "Gentlemen who are coming to call sent them, as well as a few you may not have invited to do so. I have saved all the cards for you so you can peruse them later and see who else is interested in you but did not call today."

"I never expected anything like this."

Wynter placed her hands on Olivia's shoulders and looked her squarely in the eyes. "You are a wonderful woman and one of the prized catches of this Season, my sweet friend."

"That is hard for me to believe," she said, remembering the gossips from last night and how they had ruined the evening for her.

"The gentlemen who come will assure you of that fact. Come, let us sit. The first will be arriving any minute now."

Wynter was right because, seconds later, the butler opened the door and announced Higbee's three friends. They entered and gave her numerous compliments. She doubted Lord Cooperton or Lord Waltham meant them. They were the two she suspected played a role in Higbee's seduction of Lady Lydia.

Viscount Bell, though, had been present in the supper room

the entire time. He was the one who asked her several interesting questions and truly seemed to regard her answers. It didn't hurt that he was handsome, with fair hair and sky blue eyes. She thanked him for the bouquet he had sent, assuming he had done so.

Olivia did spend a few minutes speaking with the other two men after the viscount left and thanked them for their flowers.

"No bouquet could match your beauty, Lady Olivia," Cooperton said.

"Actually, all of them do. I appreciate your interest in me but it is not reciprocated. I hope you will both find other eligible young ladies to call upon."

"You're giving us the boot?" Lord Waltham said, his shock evident. "Why?"

"Because both of you helped my cousin trap Lady Lydia into their betrothal. That speaks very poorly of your character."

Waltham sniffed. "There are far more fish in the sea than you, my lady." He strode off.

Cooperton remained. "You are far more clever than I gave you credit for. That is intriguing."

"As intriguing as my large dowry?" she countered.

The earl laughed. "Your tongue is sharper than a knife, my lady. How I would like mine to tangle with it."

Heat filled her cheeks at the bold remark. "Good day, my lord. Please do not return."

"I will see you at tonight's ball," he said and strolled away.

Another half-dozen suitors arrived after that. Olivia slowly began to distinguish one from another. She found herself liking two viscounts, a baron, and a marquess above the others. Gradually, they began saying their goodbyes, all stating they would look for her this evening.

The marquess hung back, making sure he was the last to leave.

"Thank you for coming, Lord Braithwaite," she said, admiring how broad his shoulders were.

"I enjoyed the little time I spent with you, Lady Olivia." He hesitated and then asked, "Might you care to drive in the park with me at five o'clock today?"

She remembered from her come-out that was the fashionable hour for the *ton* to be seen.

"I regret I cannot, my lord. I have plans to go to tea at four o'clock at the Duchess of Winslow's residence. In fact, I must leave soon so that I will not be late."

He eagerly asked, "Do you think Her Grace would mind if I escorted you there—and stayed for tea?"

Wynter, who stood nearby, answered, "She wouldn't mind in the least, my lord. It would be lovely if you would escort us there."

"My carriage is out front. We could use it if you'd like."

"That would be lovely," Wynter said. "Give us a moment to collect our hats and reticules."

They left the drawing room and Olivia asked, "Are you sure Emery won't mind?"

"She will be pleased. Lord Braithwaite seems nice."

Soon, they were riding in the marquess' carriage. He was easy to converse with and she was glad to be able to spend a little extra time with him.

"Are you good friends with Her Grace?" he asked.

"We are new friends but have quickly grown close," Olivia replied. "Today, we are going to see a kitten that I gave to her son."

The carriage pulled up to the Winslow townhouse and the marquess helped both her and Wynter from it. The butler announced them and Emery greeted the trio with a gracious smile.

"I hope I am not imposing, Your Grace," Lord Braithwaite said with a most pleasant smile. "I had called upon Lady Olivia and since my carriage was already waiting, I offered to accompany her and Her Grace to tea. I do not wish to intrude, however."

"Nonsense, my lord," Emery said. "You are most welcome to

stay."

"What about me?" a voice called.

Turning, Olivia saw Hart crossing toward them. Her heart began to race.

"A Terror is always welcomed," Emery said. "Have you met Lord Braithwaite?"

The two men exchanged greetings and Olivia saw Hart glance briefly at her before turning his attention back to the marquess.

"Please have a seat," their hostess said. "The teacart will be along shortly."

"How is Midnight?" Hart asked.

"He is why Olivia came to call today."

"I also wanted to see the kitten," Hart said. "Is she with Ben now?"

"They are napping together," Emery informed them. "Why don't the two of you sneak up to the nursery before tea comes? You can see Midnight and then return. You know the way."

Olivia felt odd leaving Lord Braithwaite since she was the one to have brought him.

"Go on," Emery urged. "Wynter and I will entertain his lord-ship."

"All right." She stood and Hart did the same. They exited the drawing room and headed for the staircase.

"Did you have many callers today?" he asked. "I assume Braithwaite was one of them and he tagged along to tea."

"He asked me to go driving in the park with him but I was already committed to tea with Emery."

"I see."

They reached the nursery and Hart opened the door. The nursery governess sat in a rocker working on her needlepoint. She nodded at the pair.

"Lord Ben's fast asleep," she said quietly.

Olivia tiptoed to the bed and found Ben and Midnight curled up together. She reached out to brush his hair back from his brow.

"He looks like an angel as he sleeps," she said softly.

"And a devil when he is awake. Ben has all the makings of a Terror."

She stroked Midnight's silky fur.

"Her paws looked healed," Hart noted.

"I would not have brought her to Ben otherwise."

They gazed at the boy and kitten another minute and then she turned. "We should rejoin the others."

She nodded at the nursery governess and they stepped into the corridor again.

"You didn't answer me before. Did you have many callers?"

"Some. Higbee's friends among them. Two of which I told not to bother to return. I believe they aided him in his scheme to entrap Lady Lydia."

"Did they take that well?"

"Lord Waltham pouted. Lord Cooperton may give me a bit of trouble. Nothing I cannot handle, however."

"If he tries to kiss you, don't let him," Hart warned.

Annoyance filled her. "I have no intention of kissing Lord Cooperton. I do plan to kiss a few gentlemen, though," she said, wanting to see his reaction. "Wynter suggested it. She said I shouldn't make up my mind to marry anyone unless I have first kissed them."

"Is that so?" His gaze held hers. "Have you decided to kiss Lord Braithwaite?"

"Not yet. Not that it is any of your business. I have to approach this slowly. I have never kissed anyone before."

"You haven't?" His sapphire blue eyes glowed.

"No one was ever interested."

"I can teach you how to kiss," he volunteered.

Her face grew hot. "That isn't necessary."

"No—but it might help you to see what a kiss should feel like."

Hart lowered his head until his mouth touched hers. Slowly,

his lips brushed against her own, bringing a tingling sensation. His hand wrapped around her nape, holding her steady as he pressed his mouth to hers. Her body seem to wake from a long slumber. Her palm flattened against his chest. He increased the pressure slightly and then pulled away, nipping her bottom lip, surprising her. Then his tongue licked where he had done so and he rose to his full height.

"That's a start," he told her. "I will return to the drawing room. Take your time."

She realized that her face must be bright red as she watched him saunter down the corridor to the staircase. When he was gone from sight, she brought her fingertips to her lips and touched them.

Hart had kissed her.

And it had been wonderful.

Olivia heard a door open and looked over her shoulder, seeing the nursery governess with Ben in her arms. The small boy held Midnight.

"Are you taking him downstairs?"

"Yes, Her Grace had asked for him when he awoke from his nap."

"Let me take him for you." She smiled at Ben. "You want to come with me?"

"O," he said, grinning at her.

She chuckled as she took boy and kitten from the servant. Her suggestion of having Sam try to call her Auntie O had been received with delight by her friends. Emery had told Ben to call Olivia Auntie O. He was only saying a few words at this point and auntie seemed beyond him. He did call her O, though.

"O go?" he asked.

"Yes. O and Ben and Midnight. We're going to the drawing room."

"Biscuit?"

She laughed aloud. "I see you have mastered the most important word to a boy, Ben."

He grinned again.

She entered the drawing room and Ben saw Emery.

"Mammamma!" he cried.

Olivia placed him on his feet and he set Midnight down before he ran to Emery. His mother scooped him up and smothered his face with kisses.

"There's my good boy."

"Biscuit?" Ben asked.

"Of course, my love." She took one from the teacart and gave it to him, settling him in her lap.

Olivia picked up Midnight and joined them.

"Her Graces were telling me about your daring rescue of the kitten," Lord Braithwaite said, giving her an admiring glance.

"It wasn't much. The kitten is safe now."

"And much beloved by Ben," Emery said. "They are already inseparable. She seems to have a calming effect on him."

"Then I must think about getting Sam a kitten when he is a bit older," Wynter said. She looked to the marquess. "My son is eight months now and already all boy."

Olivia enjoyed tea. Lord Braithwaite was very charming. She noticed, though, that Hart said very little.

"We should be going," Wynter announced. "Olivia and I will need to prepare for this evening's ball."

"Thank you, Your Grace, for being so accommodating and allowing me to invite myself to tea," the marquess said.

"It was delightful meeting you, my lord," Emery replied. "I look forward to introducing you to my husband this evening."

"I will walk out with you," Hart said.

Lord Braithwaite offered his arm to Olivia and she took it, conscious of Hart behind them as they returned to the carriage.

"I will see you later," he said, going to his carriage as they entered Lord Braithwaite's.

"Forgive me for being so bold, Lady Olivia," the marquess began, "but I would like to request a dance from you this evening. Before anyone else can sign your programme."

She pinkened with pleasure, looking to Wynter, who nodded approvingly. "Of course, my lord."

"Would you reserve the supper dance for me? I would appreciate getting to spend more time with you and furthering this afternoon's conversation."

"I will reserve it for you, my lord," she said demurely.

They arrived at Wynter's and the marquess helped both ladies from the coach.

"Thank you again for letting me call upon Lady Olivia at your home, Your Grace."

"You are most welcomed any time, Lord Braithwaite." Wynter went inside, leaving them alone on the pavement.

"Do you have plans for tea tomorrow?" he asked Olivia.

"No," she said faintly.

"Then I will ask again. Would you care to drive with me tomorrow afternoon in the park?"

"I would like that very much," she told him. "Why don't you come for tea and we can leave after it is served?"

He beamed. "Thank you for the invitation." Braithwaite took her hand and kissed it. "Until this evening."

He returned to his carriage and gave her a jaunty wave as the vehicle drove off. Olivia entered the townhouse and found Wynter waiting for her in the foyer.

"Well?"

"I invited him for tea tomorrow. We will go driving in the park afterward."

Her friend nodded. "I like him."

Olivia nodded. "I like him, too."

CHAPTER EIGHTEEN

H ART DIDN'T LIKE the Marquess of Braithwaite one bit. He stewed about the man as he sat in his bath. As Lawson shaved him. As he dressed. As he made his way downstairs. As he entered Wyatt's carriage.

Immediately, Wyatt asked, "Who put a bee in your bonnet? I have never seen you make a more sour face."

Before Hart could reply, Meadow leaned over and patted Hart's knee.

"What was that for?" he asked suspiciously.

"I assume that Olivia had several suitors visit her today and you are jealous."

His jaw dropped. "How did you know?"

She shrugged. "It was easy. You have made known to us your intentions toward her—though you refuse to tell her. Today was the first day suitors would call. As sweet and kind and beautiful as Olivia is, I am sure there were a sea of gentlemen in Wynter's drawing room today and you were lost among them."

"I did not call on Olivia," he said stiffly.

"Oh?" she asked. "Did you learn from your valet the number of men who courted her today?"

"I ran into her with one of them," Hart said grumpily.

Wyatt burst into laughter. "Perhaps that will get you moving in the right direction. So, tell us where you were and who this lord is?"

"I went to tea at Emery's and she and Wynter showed up with a Lord Braithwaite in tow. Blast him! He wasn't even invited. He merely invited himself and went along. Emery, of course, was gracious and accepted his presence."

"Braithwaite is very charming," Wyatt said.

"How do you know?" he accused. "Are you friends with him?"

"Don't glare at me as if I've broken some sacred trust with you. I am your friend, Hart. I merely have met Braithwaite at the club. He's a genial sort. The kind that makes a good impression wherever he goes."

"I'm afraid he's going to kiss her," Hart blurted out.

He thought back to the brief kiss he had shared with Olivia.

Her first kiss.

Hart had wanted to prolong the kiss. He longed to explore her. Time, though, hadn't been on their side. He had merely gained a taste of her and could think of nothing else since then.

Except for his dislike of Braithwaite. His immense dislike of Braithwaite.

"Remember, Hart, that you wanted men to pay attention to Olivia," Meadow reminded him. "A man of Braithwaite's reputation and looks will certainly boost her spirits and confidence."

"But what if he tries to kiss her?" he demanded. "What if she *likes* his kiss?"

"Then you need to make certain you kiss her, as well," Wyatt said.

"That may prove difficult. She is skittish now. Especially after her cousin ensnared Lady Lydia last night. Olivia is very conscious of the rules of Polite Society and does not want to break them. She is afraid of being forced to wed a man she detests."

"If she were caught in an embrace with you, I don't think that would be the case," Meadow said encouragingly.

"No, I don't want her hand forced," he insisted. "I want her to come to me willingly. To want to build a life together. Otherwise, she might always have doubts that I only offered for her to save her reputation."

"I suppose Wyatt and I can help you," she offered.

"How?"

"If you are a guest in our home, I can make certain that an opportunity arises for the two of you to share a kiss."

Guilt filled him, having already done so today but he wasn't going to kiss and tell. And if Meadow was willing to help him further his suit, Hart would certainly take advantage of the opportunity.

"What do you suggest?"

"Let me think," she replied.

They arrived at Lord and Lady Powell's townhouse and he went through the receiving line with Wyatt and Meadow, itching to see Olivia. He hadn't determined if he would ask her to dance or not. Perhaps he should back off for a bit and give her the chance to truly stretch her wings without him hovering about.

Entering the ballroom, he spied her. She stood with Donovan and Wynter but he only saw her. She wore her blond hair piled high on her head. Her gown was the color of daffodils in the spring. Hart wanted to drag her from the room and kiss her senseless.

Instead, he joined them and smiled. "Good evening. I hope everyone is well."

They exchanged pleasantries and Hart said to Olivia, "You are looking very lovely this evening."

She moved her shoulders as if uncomfortable. "Thank you."

"What is wrong?"

Olivia glanced around and then leaned toward him. "I feel I am showing entirely too much bosom."

He couldn't help but drop his gaze. Her breasts did look lovely, full and round, the tops peeking enticingly from the neckline of her gown.

"Madame La Renn tells me this is the fashion but I don't like having so much of myself on display."

"I wouldn't worry about it. Other women will be dressed similarly. It would seem odd if you covered up your natural beauty."

She crinkled her nose. "You think a bosom is beautiful?"

"Yours is," he said with a smile, causing her to blush to her roots.

"Ah, Cousin Olivia, there you are."

Hart tore his eyes from said bosom and saw Mr. Knight approaching with Lady Lydia on his arm. Last night, the girl had looked thunderstruck. Now, though, she oozed contained rage.

"And Your Grace," Mr. Knight said fawningly. "This is the Duke of Mansfield. Your Grace, my betrothed."

He bowed over her hand and saw anger simmering in her eyes.

"This is my cousin, Lady Olivia Knight," Knight continued.

The women exchanged a few words and then Lady Lydia said, "Would you please fetch me some punch?"

"I suppose I can do so. I will return shortly." Knight smiled as a predator might. "Why don't you tell His Grace and my cousin about our upcoming wedding?" Knight strolled off.

Through gritted teeth, Lady Lydia said, "There is not going to *be* any wedding."

Olivia took one of the woman's hands. "He compromised you on purpose, didn't he? And Lord Cooperton and Lord Waltham were a part of it, weren't they?"

"How did you know?"

"I saw the two of them slip into the ballroom after you and Higbee arrived there with your parents. I have met both men and they are the antithesis of a gentleman."

Panic filled the young woman's eyes. "I cannot marry him. I cannot be tied to someone I loathe because of a lie."

"Knight lied?" Hart asked sharply.

Lady Lydia nodded. "He managed to steer me away from joining the others at supper. He is quite handsome and I had only just met him. He asked about a certain book in my father's library and I didn't think it would harm anything to show it to him. Once we were there, though, he tried to kiss me. I slapped him."

"Good," Olivia said. "He needed that. Higbee was terrible to me when we were children and just as loathsome now."

"His friends showed up and he told them it was done. They were to find my father. I had no idea what was going on. Mr. Knight wouldn't allow me to leave the library for some minutes. He stood in front of the closed door, blocking my way. The next thing I knew, Mama and Papa were there." She swallowed hard. "And then Mr. Knight told a most vicious lie."

Lady Lydia's mouth trembled. "He said—and his friends attested to it—that we had been swept away by passion. That he had pushed my gown from my shoulders and it was down about my waist as he . . . as he . . ." She winced. "As he kissed my breasts."

Olivia gasped. "Oh, I knew he was a blighter but this is unspeakable."

"It never happened," Lady Lydia said. "I would never engage in such rash behavior, especially with a man I had only met minutes earlier. But the two lords backed up Knight's story. Suddenly, I found myself in the ballroom in front of all those guests, hearing Papa announce my betrothal." Her eyes welled with tears.

"You were Knight's focus from the beginning," Hart said. "Do you have a large dowry?"

Lady Lydia nodded.

"He could want you for it in order to cover gambling debts," he told her. "Have the marriage contracts been signed yet?"

"No. Papa and his solicitor met with Mr. Knight and his man this afternoon. They did not come to an agreement as of yet. Mr. Knight says, though, that they will soon and that the banns will be read starting this Sunday." She looked at Hart and Olivia. "I refuse to marry such a liar. I don't care if all of Polite Society looks down their nose at me. I won't do it."

Olivia said, "You do realize if you are the one known to break the betrothal that will happen. The gentleman is never the one the *ton* blames."

Lady Lydia nodded. "I do. I spoke to Mama today about what happened once I had my wits about me. She told me I should go through with the marriage. That Mr. Knight was most handsome and he was to be an earl one day." She bit her lip. "I had hoped for her support."

"Have you told your father the truth?" Hart asked.

"No. I am embarrassed to say such things in front of him." She dropped her gaze. "I don't know why I told the two of you. You are strangers to me."

"I know exactly what Higbee is like," Olivia said. "We need to right this wrong somehow." She paused as she caught sight of her cousin. "He is coming."

"Please. Don't tell him I told you anything," Lady Lydia pleaded.

"We won't," Hart assured the girl.

Knight handed his fiancée a cup of punch. "I hope you enjoyed chatting with my cousin. We grew up together, you know."

"We did," Olivia said, her gaze steady on her cousin.

"Come, Lady Lydia," Knight urged. "We should circulate. I am sure there are many who wish to offer us felicitations."

"Wait," Hart said. "Might I request a dance with you, my lady?"

Lady Lydia looked stunned by the request but Knight smiled and said, "Go ahead, my dear. Dancing with a duke is an honor."

Hart lifted her dance card. "I see the first number is open." He wrote his name next to it. "I will see you shortly, my lady."

Once they left, he turned to Olivia. "We must help that girl. You can see how miserable and angry she is."

"But how? The betrothal has been announced publicly. If she were to break it, she would be ostracized. You don't understand how terrible it would be for her, Hart."

"What if it were made known what your cousin did to secure that betrothal?"

She shook her head. "I don't know. The gossip would be fierce."

"Better gossip endured for a short while versus a lifetime in that man's company," he replied. "I will think on it. You do the same. Perhaps, together, we can come up with a plan to save Lady Lydia from a lifetime of misery."

CHAPTER NINETEEN

O LIVIA FOUND HERSELF surrounded by a group of gentlemen, all demanding her dance card. She watched Hart slip away and realized that he was not going to ask her to dance this evening. She supposed he only had last night to get others to do so. Now that she seemed to have attracted enough partners, she doubted he would dance with her again. Regret washed over her, knowing she would never be in his arms again.

Yet he had kissed her this afternoon. She had thought of nothing else since it had occurred. Hart even offered to teach her how to kiss. That first lesson had been a teasing one, opening her eyes to what might happen between a man and a woman. Olivia knew nothing about kissing, only that Wynter had suggested she try it with the men she was interested in.

Viscount Bell asked for her programme next and she gave it to him.

"I am disappointed that the supper dance has already been claimed," he said. "I will choose another one, though. And I wish to call upon you again tomorrow if I may do so."

"Only if you come alone and not in the presence of your other friends," she replied tartly.

"I see." He scrawled his name across the page and returned it to her. "I will do so."

A few others asked to sign and then she found herself face to face with Lord Cooperton.

"Good evening, Lady Olivia," he said, his eyes dropping to her chest.

"My lord," she said curtly.

"Might I—"

"You may not."

He sniffed. "I have yet to ask—"

"And I told you that I wanted nothing to do with you," she said firmly.

Two gentlemen stepping up to her stopped abruptly.

"My lady—"

"I made myself perfectly clear, Lord Cooperton. I do not wish to dance with you. I do not want you to call upon me. I do not want to be seen in your company. I cannot be any clearer."

"My lady," he said brusquely, bobbing his head and hurrying away.

The two newcomers moved toward her and one said, "It is about time that swine was put in his place. Good for you, Lady Olivia. Might I claim a dance?"

After both of them signed, she had no empty spots left. She was glad she had remembered to place Lord Braithwaite's name on her card when she'd first received it. She looked forward to speaking more with him.

The evening passed quickly. The only time Olivia felt sad was when she saw Hart glide by, his partner one of the pretty girls whose father was a duke. The couple looked perfect together, Hart in his black evening wear, lithe and lean as he danced, his chestnut hair gleaming in the candlelight of the ballroom. She hoped his partner knew what a good man she was gaining, recalling how incensed Hart was at Higbee having lied in order to bring about a betrothal between him and Lady Lydia. Olivia doubted they would be able to do anything to stop the ceremony but she thought it sweet of Hart to want to try.

Lord Braithwaite claimed her, looking quite dashing in his evening wear, the black contrasting with his light brown hair. She had noticed his eyes were hazel and seemed to change color.

Tonight, they were lively, with more green in them than brown.

"I have been looking forward to this moment all evening," the marquess told her as he led her onto the dance floor.

"I have, as well," she replied.

As Braithwaite slipped an arm about her waist and took her hand in his for the upcoming waltz, he said, "I am not used to such honesty."

"Why shouldn't I say so?" she asked.

"I like that you do not play games, Lady Olivia."

The music began and he moved her about the ballroom with ease. They did not speak during the dance. She supposed he knew they had time for that once supper began.

When the last chord sounded, he held her for a moment longer, smiling down at her. Olivia grew warm under his gaze but did not pull away.

The marquess released her and placed her hand atop his forearm, leading her into the room designated for supper this evening and to a table in a corner for only two.

"Do you mind if we sit here?" he asked. "I am feeling selfish and would like you all to myself."

She glowed at his words. "I would like that very much."

He snapped his fingers and a footman rushed over. "See that no one else takes this spot," he ordered.

"Yes, my lord," the footman replied.

"Let's go look at the offerings from the buffet," he told her.

Braithwaite led her to where a long line of tables began and Olivia's eyes widened at the amount of food upon them. She had not gone to the buffet last night. Hart had brought back food for her. The staggering number of serving platters boggled her mind. She thought back on the times she had stuffed herself with food, hoping to find comfort in it and still feeling empty with loneliness after she had done so.

As they went through the line, the marquess asked her about her likes and dislikes and helped her fill her plate. When they finished, he took her back to the small table and seated her, asking the footman to bring them some champagne.

"Do you always order other people's servants about so much?" she teased.

"I know Lord Powell from our school days," he said. "Not that it makes a difference."

"Where did you attend school and university?" she asked.

He told her and shared a few tales of his adventures at school, none featuring Lord Powell. Olivia asked about that.

"Powell was too high-strung for my tastes. He worried over every little thing and went out of his mind on examination days."

"And you were more cavalier?" she asked, a little disappointed that it seemed as if he didn't take his studies seriously.

"No. My scores were always important to me," he revealed. "I am a scholar at heart. I was never nervous because I was always so well-prepared when the time came. Students such as Powell played most of the time, not bothering to read all the selections or failing to practice conjugating verbs or making translations."

"You did all those things?"

He nodded sheepishly. "I adored everything about school and my studies. If I had my druthers, I would be a university don and teach other young men. Or perhaps travel to the Far East and be a part of excavations."

"That would be quite exciting."

"Being a don—or traveling halfway around the globe?"

"Either. I, too, adore learning. Though I have been told not to bring that up with the gentlemen of Polite Society."

Braithwaite frowned. "Balderdash. Never hide your intelligence, my lady. There are actually some gentlemen who find that most attractive."

His eyes glowed at her and Olivia realized Braithwaite was one of those men.

"What are some of the subjects you found fascinating, then or now?" he asked.

They began discussing geography and history and moved on

to literature and politics. Supper flew by. She didn't recall eating anything on her plate but she must have done so because it was half-empty by the time others started returning to the ballroom.

"This has been a most enlightening discussion," the marquess told her. "I am looking forward to our drive through Hyde Park tomorrow afternoon."

He rose and helped her from her seat.

"Don't forget you are coming for tea beforehand," she reminded, eager to chat more with him.

"I haven't." He lifted her hand and touched his lips to her gloved fingers. "Until tomorrow."

OLIVIA AND WYNTER saw the last of their visitors out as Wynter's husband entered the drawing room.

"More bachelors. More flowers," he complained good-naturedly. "If I would have known my household would be turned upside down, I might have had you go stay at Wyatt's or Miles' place."

Wynter punched him in his shoulder. "Oh, do be quiet and let Olivia bask in her popularity." She looked to her friend. "You did enjoy yourself this afternoon, didn't you?"

She nodded. "Very much so. I still cannot believe there are those who wish to visit with me. And the flowers they send. Why, I cannot imagine the bills florists must be sending out if this is happening all across London."

"Lord Braithwaite will arrive soon. Why don't you go and freshen up?" Wynter suggested. "I will share with Donovan what we spoke about earlier."

Olivia left the room and returned to her bedchamber. Before her callers had arrived this afternoon, she had told Wynter of her conversation with Lady Lydia and how Higbee had orchestrated the entire incident, even down to having his friends lie about what they had seen. She had begged Wynter to think about how they could help the poor girl. The Terrors—and their wives—were all intelligent. If anyone could stop this wedding from happening, they could.

She returned to the drawing room and found Lord Braithwaite already there. He stood and greeted her.

"I apologize for being early, my lady. I am usually punctual but I was eager to see you."

She thought that rather sweet and told him so.

"See, you are always honest to a fault with me. It is one of your best qualities."

"Ah, here is the teacart," Wynter announced. "I do believe we will have several items here to tempt you, my lord."

Braithwaite turned to Olivia and quietly said, "Not as much as you."

She felt the color rise on her cheeks and looked away.

Wynter poured out and the four of them enjoyed a splendid hour together. At its end, the nursery governess appeared with Sam. Immediately, the duke went and claimed his son, bringing Sam back and bouncing him on his knee. Olivia watched the marquess look upon them with curiosity.

"You seem quite comfortable, Your Grace," he said. "I do not see many men playing with their children."

"Then you need to find better company," Haverhill said. "I and my friends are quite involved in our children's lives."

"You are close with the Dukes of Amesbury and Winslow, I believe," Braithwaite said.

"And the Duke of Mansfield," Haverhill added. "We were all at school together and then fought on the Peninsula before coming back and laying claim to our titles."

"I envy you," the marquess said. "I lost both of my good friends to the war. Though I am friendly with several gentlemen at my club, no one has replaced them in my heart."

"The next time you see us at White's, I hope you will join us," Haverhill said.

Olivia could have hugged the duke for that.

"You'd best make for the park," Wynter suggested. "Otherwise, it will be so crowded you'll see nothing of it."

"Thank you for a lovely tea, Your Grace," Lord Braithwaite told his hostess.

Olivia rose. "I have already brought my things down so you wouldn't have to wait."

His eyes glowed with appreciation. "You are as thoughtful as you are beautiful, my lady."

The marquess escorted her outside to his waiting curricle and helped her into it. They were only a few blocks from the park. The afternoon proved warm for this time of April and she closed her eyes, enjoying the feel of the sun upon her face.

"Do you enjoy driving your curricle?" she asked, opening her eyes.

"Yes. It is a bit more challenging than controlling a horse you ride, especially when the London streets are crowded, but I do like it."

They chatted about several things, passing a few others who had arrived a bit early. Then the marquess turned to the right.

"This is a circular path. It will lead us back to the main thoroughfare," he told her.

Olivia thought how peaceful it was as they drove in companionable silence. She wondered if this man might be the one for her. He wasn't put off by her intelligence. He was affable and kind. She would definitely have to think about kissing him at some point.

They rounded a bend and a large grove of trees appeared on their left. After a moment, Braithwaite slowed the carriage and then brought it to a halt.

Turning, he asked, "May I kiss you, Lady Olivia?"

She was taken aback by the abruptness and quickly sucked in a breath.

"If it is too soon, I will understand. I can be patient."

She thought a moment and then said, "Yes. Please do so,"

knowing she shouldn't pass up this opportunity.

Closing her eyes, she waited and felt him draw near. One hand cupped her cheek as he pressed his mouth to hers for a moment. Then he broke the kiss. He gazed at her intently. His thumb stroked her cheek before it fell and he took up the reins again, clicking his tongue so the horse would start up again.

Braithwaite did not refer to the kiss. He began talking about an upcoming exhibit at the British Museum that he was interested in attending and wondered if she might like to accompany him to it.

"Yes, I would enjoying seeing it," she told him.

They passed several other couples, nodding politely at them, and then the marquess returned her to the Haverhill doorstep.

"Thank you for coming to the park with me today," he told her. "And thank you for the kiss."

"You are most welcome."

"Will you be at the musicale tonight?"

"Yes."

"I look forward to seeing you there."

He rapped on the door and the butler admitted her. Olivia returned to her bedchamber and sat in the chair by the window.

The kiss had been sweet. Brief. Full of potential. But she had felt nothing like she had in those few seconds when Hart had kissed her. Then, her body had sprung to life. This time, it was as if she waited for . . . something. Something she couldn't pinpoint.

Was Lord Braithwaite the one for her? She didn't think she could tell by one kiss. Perhaps they would have to try it again for a longer spell.

She did like him quite a bit, though. She could see where he would make a good husband.

Would Hart make good on his promise and teach her more about kissing? If he did, perhaps she could try whatever she learned with Lord Braithwaite.

Olivia pondered on things until Mary arrived to help her dress for the evening.

CHAPTER TWENTY

I N THE CARRIAGE Wynter asked, "Did you enjoy your drive through the park with Lord Braithwaite?"

"Yes," Olivia replied.

"Was it crowded?" Haverhill asked. "I loathe crowds."

"It wasn't when we first arrived. I believe we were among the earliest arrivals. By the time we left, however, I saw carriages everywhere."

"Lord Braithwaite has paid you special attention," Wynter said. "He seems to like you quite a bit. Is the feeling returned?"

"He is extremely nice," she said.

But he wasn't Hart.

"Hah! Nice," muttered Haverhill.

"Pay no attention to Donovan," her friend urged. "Nice in a gentleman goes a long way with me."

"With me, as well," she agreed. "I just feel it is too soon to make any kind of commitment to a single person."

"Don't rush things," Haverhill advised. "It is only the first week of the Season."

"I realize that, Your Grace, but I do feel pressured by my father to find a husband. He has made clear that I must wed this year. I can only hope I will receive an offer by Season's end from a man I can respect and hopefully get along with."

The duke gazed at her steadily. "You don't have to do anything you don't wish to do. If you find yourself at Season's end with no offers or offers you do not wish to accept, then know you will always have a home with us. Don't let the threat of Lord Rivers turning you out into the cold cause you to make a hasty decision. Marriage is for life. You want to spend that life with the right person."

He took his wife's hand and kissed it tenderly as tears welled in Olivia's eyes.

"Thank you, Your Grace."

Haverhill snorted. "Don't you think it is high time you started calling me Donovan? After all, Wynter looks upon you as a sister. I can be your protective older brother."

She smiled through watery eyes. "I would like that very much."

Wynter told her what to expect at tonight's musicale. "I have heard it is an Italian soprano and that she is most remarkable."

"I have never been exposed to much music other than hymns at church," Olivia admitted. "I hope I will be able to appreciate tonight's performance."

They arrived and she was glad to find no receiving line to go through. Entering the room designated for the evening's entertainment, she soon found herself surrounded by three gentlemen. Two had called upon her previously and she had liked them. The third was new to her and introduced by his friend.

Then Viscount Bell joined them, followed by Lord Braithwaite. Gradually, the others peeled away, leaving her in a lively conversation with the two lords.

"Ah, it looks as if others are taking their seats," Lord Bell said. "Shall we do the same?"

She followed him to a row. He entered and sat to her right, with Lord Braithwaite taking a spot on her left. Olivia glanced around the room and did not see Hart anywhere. She knew tonight's affair to be an exclusive one but she thought, as a duke, Hart would have been invited to it. Perhaps he had been or he had chosen to attend another event. She chastised herself for thinking of him when she had two handsome, eligible men seated on either side of her.

The soprano came to the front and they all applauded her. Olivia had never been to the opera or the theater though she had longed to do so. Her father didn't care for the fine arts and did not keep a box anywhere. No one had asked her to a performance during her come-out. Hopefully, she would be able to attend one or both during this Season.

She was grateful for Donovan's offer. It eased the pressure she felt to choose a husband quickly. She continued to be lost in her thoughts until she heard applause and joined in.

"You looked as though you have been woolgathering, my lady," Lord Braithwaite said.

"Perhaps a little," she admitted. "The Season is so busy. It seems I never have a moment to myself." Making a quick decision, she added, "I have decided that I will not be receiving callers tomorrow afternoon for that very reason. I need some time to myself, even if it's just to read or sit and think."

Disappointment crossed his face. "I am sorry to hear that. I hope you will attend tomorrow night's ball."

"Yes," Lord Bell chimed in. "It would be a shame for you to miss it."

"I will be there," she promised.

"Might I fetch you some ratafia?" the viscount asked.

"Yes, please. If you will excuse me for a few minutes."

She rose and retreated to the retiring room. Inside, she heard someone being sick and waited outside the curtain to see if the woman would be all right. Much to her surprise, Emery emerged, looking pale.

"You should not be here," she told her friend. "You are ill. I will find—"

"I am fine," Emery assured her, smiling. "This happens when you are enceinte."

Olivia broke out in a smile. "Oh, that is wonderful news, Emery!" she exclaimed.

"I have meant to tell you but things have been so busy. It is hard to get a private moment during the Season."

"I totally agree. I know you must be thrilled. And Ben will be a big brother now."

"Yes, come late fall. Most likely the end of November."

"Are you certain you are all right?"

Emery nodded. "I am now."

"Good. I will see you later."

Her friend left and Olivia took care of her own needs. She left the retiring room and as she made her way back to her companions, she was startled when someone latched on to her elbow and yanked her into a dim alcove.

"Good evening, Lady Olivia," Lord Cooperton said, smiling.

"Release me," she demanded, tugging on her arm.

He did not. Her mouth grew dry. If anyone saw them in here together, they would think the worst. Olivia would be compromised.

And forced to wed this cad.

"Your father favors my suit, you know," he told her. "I have been friends with Knight for a long while and Lord Rivers looks upon me as a second son."

Olivia did not know this. She had no intention of marrying this man, however.

"Let me go," she said again, more insistently, but his fingers only tightened.

"Knight told me you would be attending this Season. Begged me to consider you for a wife." He laughed softly. "I remember you from your come-out. Not many do. You were a fat, pitiful chit. Plain and even worse—a bluestocking. No one was interested in you. I told Knight I would dance with you that first evening merely because of our longstanding friendship. Little did I know the ugly duckling had become a beautiful swan." He smiled again. "With an even larger dowry than before."

His free hand came to her cheek, his fingers brushing it. His touch made her flesh shrink.

"You have pushed me away, my lady, but that won't do. You

will dance with me at tomorrow night's ball."

Then Cooperton jerked her toward him. His mouth came down on hers, grinding against it. She pushed hard on his chest but didn't make any progress in escaping so she endured the despicable kiss.

Finally, he released her. "Until tomorrow, Lady Olivia."

He sauntered from the alcove and she held her breath, listening to see if he spoke to anyone. After waiting a few minutes, she emerged, looking both ways and grateful she saw no one.

Returning to her seat, she saw the concerned look on both her companions' faces.

Lord Bell handed her the ratafia and she thanked him, hoping her hands didn't shake as she drank it.

Lord Braithwaite leaned over and said, "If you need anything, my lady, you have but to ask."

She gave him a grateful smile and then turned her attention to the front of the room as the soprano took the stage again. Her thoughts were muddled, worried about Lord Cooperton and what he might do at tomorrow night's ball. She didn't want to cause a scene but she was not going to be bullied by the man. She had allowed Higbee to do so for far too long and she had promised herself never again.

The evening ended and she thanked her seatmates for taking good care of her before she made her way to the foyer. Spying Meadow, she went to stand with her friend.

"You look out of sorts," Meadow said.

"Is it that obvious?"

"To me. What can I do? Is the Season already overwhelming you?"

Olivia nodded. "Somewhat. In fact, I have decided not to be home tomorrow to callers. I need time to myself."

"Why don't you come for a visit with me? I know Leah would love to see her Auntie O."

"That would be lovely."

"Come around three and then you can stay for tea."

She hugged Meadow. "Thank you."

Olivia joined Wynter and Donovan and they went outside and into their waiting carriage.

"I am taking tomorrow afternoon for myself," she announced. "I need a respite from all the callers."

"Good," Donovan said. "I get my drawing room back for an afternoon."

Wynter laughed. "When do you even come to the drawing room during the day? Besides, I am sure it will be filled with flowers for Olivia. You might as well stay in your study."

"I will," he agreed. To Olivia, he said, "If you need somewhere to hide in the townhouse, I can show you a few places."

"Thank you. I think I will read some and then I am going to visit Meadow and Leah," she informed him, thinking of how Emery was now with child.

And hoping that if she found a husband, she would also have a child of her own.

⟫⟫⟪⟪

HART SPENT ALL morning disgruntled. He had gone into the musicale last night and the first thing he had seen was Olivia surrounded by suitors. Jealousy raged within him and he found himself turning around and leaving immediately. His head told him he was doing the right thing in allowing her to enjoy the company of other men.

His heart, though, was begging him to voice his feelings for her.

A knock sounded on the door and his butler brought him a note on a silver tray. Hart thanked him and opened it.

And finally smiled.

It was from Meadow. She had promised to help him find a way to be alone with Olivia and it seemed today was that day. Olivia would be at tea this afternoon and Hart was instructed to come, as well. He supposed Meadow would make some excuse and leave them alone.

Hart planned to kiss Olivia. He had told her he was willing to give her a few lessons. He hoped his actions would let her know how he felt about her. That her response to his kiss would tell her they were meant to be together.

He immersed himself in business and was happy to find the day passed quickly now that he was in better spirits. When the time came, he didn't bother to call for his carriage and walked the two blocks to Wyatt's townhouse. Gaining admittance, he saw Wyatt lingering in the foyer.

"I have been waiting for you. We have been at the club. I invited you back for tea. That is our story, according to my wife."

"Then I will stick to it," Hart said, chuckling. "Meadow has thought of everything. How am I to be left alone with Olivia?"

"That will be up to Meadow," his friend said. "I am merely to follow her lead."

The two men entered the drawing room. Hart saw Olivia look up in surprise.

Wyatt went and kissed his wife's cheek. "I tried to leave Hart at the club but he followed me home, knowing it was teatime."

Hart greeted Meadow, who told him, "You are always welcome. Olivia and I have been enjoying our visit. Please come and join us."

He nodded, seating himself beside her. "Good afternoon, Olivia. It is nice to see you. Did you attend last night's musicale?"

"I did. You were not there."

"No. I made other plans," he lied.

Tea arrived and the four enjoyed pleasant conversation. Hart kept thinking it could always be like this.

If he told Olivia how he felt.

Emotions warred within him. He would wait and let their next kiss decide his course of action.

The nursery governess appeared with Lady Leah. Olivia took the girl first and Hart thought how right she looked with a babe in her arms.

Wyatt finally demanded a turn with his daughter and, once again, it surprised Hart how much his wild friends had taken to being husbands and fathers.

Then Leah began fussing and Meadow said, "I am afraid she is cutting another tooth. Feel her, Wyatt. Is she warm?"

"A bit. She ran fever the last time one erupted."

"We should go put her down," Meadow suggested. "She always seems to want us to do so when she is out of sorts." She stood. "If you were truly guests, I would worry about leaving you alone. You are more family, though, so I know you understand our need to soothe Leah."

"Of course," Hart said smoothly. "Leah's needs are your priority. We have plenty of cakes to keep us occupied. Go," he urged.

"We won't be gone a quarter-hour," Wyatt said. "Thank you for understanding."

The couple left with the fussy baby and Hart tried to calm himself. Already, his insides raced at the thought of kissing Olivia again.

He faced her and all thought of being cavalier went out the window.

Placing his hands on her shoulders, he said, "I was going to offer to continue our kissing lessons."

Her eyes widened. "You have changed your mind?" she asked.

"Yes. I was at the musicale last night, Olivia. I left, however."

"Why?" she asked, clearly confused by his confession.

"Because I hated seeing you in the company of other men."

He tightened his fingers. "I have wanted you from the beginning but I wanted more for you. I wanted you to see your worth in the eyes of others. I wanted you to enjoy a full Season, with men paying you compliments and bringing you flowers. I thought if you saw yourself through the eyes of others, it would enhance your confidence.

"I can't do it anymore. I envy every man who steals a smile from you. I am in a constant state of worry that you might fall in love with one of them." He paused and then said, "I want you for myself, Olivia. No other woman will do as my duchess."

His mouth came down on hers. Hart had wanted the kiss to be tender but need surged through him. He wanted to brand her as his. To devour her. He kissed her with all the yearning that had filled him, easing her mouth opening and thrusting his tongue inside. She startled and he remembered she had little experience in kissing. He gentled the kiss a bit, pulling back, leisurely exploring her, tasting her, enjoying her.

Slowly, Olivia began to participate in the kiss, her tongue mating with his. Again, desire exploded in him and his arms went about her, bringing her to him. Hart kissed her with everything he had. Everything he felt. He had wanted this woman—and now she would be his.

Forever.

He broke the kiss, his lips trailing along her jaw and to her pulse. He licked there, feeling it jump. Slowly, his mouth traveled lower as he released her shoulders and cupped the perfect globes, kneading them. Touch wasn't enough.

He needed to taste them.

His fingers skimmed the swell of her breasts, dipping inside, reaching down and tweaking her nipples. Olivia gasped. He pushed her gown and chemise down, capturing one breast in his mouth, his tongue laving the nipple. Sweet noises came from her as she squirmed against him. He had been right to do this. To tell her how he felt.

As much as Hart wanted to continue his explorations, he had no idea how much time had passed and knew Wyatt and Meadow wouldn't be gone forever. He raised his head and repaired her gown, slipping her clothing back into place. A dazed expression was fixed on her beautiful face and, once more, he kissed her thoroughly.

Breaking the kiss, he rested his brow against hers and said, "I love you."

She stilled.

Hart hadn't meant to say those words. He didn't even know if he did love her.

He raised his head. "At least I think I love you," he amended. "I have never loved a woman before so I am quite new at this." He hesitated and then added, "But if it means that every waking moment I think of you and long to be with you, then I suppose it is love. I do think of you all the time, Olivia. I want to be with you. Talk to you. Touch you. Kiss you. I want to go to sleep with you gathered in my arms and awake with you by my side."

Her radiant smile was worth the wait.

"I love you, too," she said. "I do know what love is. I witnessed it between Uncle Theo and Aunt Beryl. I think they fell more in love with each passing day. That it deepened throughout the years they were married. I never knew I could have a chance at it." She blinked, tears cascading down her cheeks. "Until I met you."

Hart kissed her again, gently this time, as if sealing a promise between them.

"I will go to your father tomorrow morning and tell him my intentions. You should go, as well. You are a part of this."

She frowned. "I was told by Lord Cooperton last night that my father favors his suit."

He laughed. "That is where being a duke has its advantages, love. Your father may have thought Cooperton was good enough for you. He will quickly change his mind when a duke tells him that he wants you."

"You do truly want me?" she asked uncertainly.

He smoothed her hair. "I do. Very much. Let us keep this between us for now, though. At least until I have your father's permission. Then we can announce our betrothal."

"Whatever you say."

"No, I want your say to be included. Your voice is as important as mine. I think of the two of us, you are far more intelligent than I am."

"I doubt that."

"I don't," he said. "All I know is I want you to be my friend. My lover. My duchess." He kissed her fingers. "I didn't really ask you, though. I can remedy that now."

Hart dropped to his knees and clasped her hands. "Will you do me the honor of becoming my wife?"

"Yes!" she cried joyfully, this time kissing him.

They were still kissing when Wyatt and Meadow returned. Hart heard someone clearing his throat and broke the kiss, He grinned at Olivia and then turned to their friends.

"Olivia has agreed to marry me," he said, beaming.

She laughed. "I thought we were not going to tell anyone yet."

"That is already proving to be difficult. I want to shout it to the heavens."

Wyatt and Meadow came over and embraced them.

"We are so happy for you, my brother," Wyatt said.

"You are perfect together," Meadow added.

"We will not announce our betrothal until after I have spoken with Olivia's father tomorrow. I plan to call upon him and make my intentions known."

"So, when is the wedding?" Wyatt asked.

Hart looked to his bride-to-be. "Are you going to make me wait? Or can I purchase a special license?"

Olivia smiled. "We have already wasted enough time, Hart. I say we should wed as quickly as possible."

"Yes!" he said, laughing.

And then kissed her again for good measure.

CHAPTER TWENTY-ONE

HART SAT QUIETLY as Lawson filled him in on *ton* gossip. It amazed him how vast the valet's knowledge was regrading movements of the Polite Society.

"You had mentioned Lady Olivia previously," Lawson said. "She went for a carriage ride with Lord Braithwaite in Hyde Park."

"That won't be occurring in the future," he informed his valet.

Lawson's brows arched. "Is there something you wish to inform me of, Your Grace?"

"I would—but then half of London would know about it by tomorrow morning. I am not ready for that."

Lawson frowned. "I would never share anything outside this household that you wished to be kept secret, Your Grace. Even outside this chamber, for that matter."

Hart thought the valet trustworthy and said, "Very well. Lady Olivia has agreed to be my duchess."

The valet smiled broadly. "That will be news well received. When it can be shared," he added before Hart could object. "Among your friends' servants, Lady Olivia is highly thought of. She is polite and considerate. The Haverhill servants have adored having her stay with them. When might Your Grace decide to make knowledge of the betrothal public?"

"Soon. Lady Olivia only agreed to my proposal this afternoon. I plan on visiting Lord Rivers, her father, first thing in the morning."

"He is often in the card room at events," Lawson said helpfully. "As is his nephew, Mr. Knight." A look of distaste crossed the valet's face. "A bad business about his betrothal."

"I agree. Do you know if Knight is in debt?"

"Apparently, he is heavily in debt and that is why he is seeking to wed this Season. Lady Lydia's dowry should see his debts paid. But Lord Rivers is in excellent health. It could be many years before Mr. Knight becomes the next Lord Rivers."

Hart silently agreed. He had been thinking about how to help Lady Lydia but had come up with no solution to her problem. A woman in Polite Society had little control over her own destiny. The fact Knight and his friends lied about Lady Lydia's behavior didn't sit well with Hart. It might be something he brought up with Lord Rivers after discussing the upcoming betrothal to Olivia.

Lawson finished tying Hart's cravat and then held out his coat. He slipped into it and glanced into the mirror.

"Lady Olivia is a very lucky woman," the valet said.

"No, Lawson. I am the fortunate one," he replied.

He went downstairs and Mrs. Bomer handed him an umbrella. "You'll need this tonight, Your Grace. I can smell rain in the air."

"Thank you," he told his housekeeper.

"His Grace's carriage just pulled up, Your Grace," his butler informed him.

"Thank you, Bomer."

Hart left his townhouse and climbed into Donovan's carriage. His friend had sent a note around saying they would call for him. He supposed Olivia had shared their news with Donovan and Wynter. He couldn't blame her. They would need to pull Miles and Emery aside tonight and clue them in as to what had occurred.

"Good evening," he said, taking a seat next to Olivia. "You

smell and look divine," he told her.

"It is the same floral scent I usually wear."

"Keep wearing it," he urged.

"I hear congratulations are in order," Donovan said, smiling broadly.

"Thank you," Hart replied. "We are not making this public knowledge. Only Terrors—and honorary Terrors—are to know," he said, smiling at Wynter.

"Having given birth to a Terror, I would hope I would be included in the group," she replied.

"Sam is a sweet boy," Donovan protested, as if classifying his son as a Terror was a bad thing.

"He is," his wife agreed. "But a Terror all the same."

They spoke of inconsequential things until just before they arrived, when Olivia said, "Would you please keep an eye out for Lord Cooperton tonight? I have a feeling he would like to cause some trouble for me."

"I will gladly drag him outside and give him a thorough pounding," Donovan said. "Unless you would rather do so, Hart."

"No thrashing will be necessary," he said. "I don't want any hint of scandal surrounding Olivia. I already have my brother's duel being whispered about. I overheard two matrons discussing it the other night. When I passed them and said hello, I thought they would faint dead away."

"A duel?" Wynter asked. "Why haven't I heard of this?"

"Reginald was my good-for-nothing older brother who died in the duel, killed by a cuckolded husband," Hart told her. "I had worried others would bring it up but, so far, I have only seen a few give me surreptitious glances. Beyond the aforementioned matrons."

"That is all you'll get," Donovan assured. "They never speak the gossip directly to a duke's face. Marrying Olivia and settling down from bachelor to happy husband will allow any rumors regarding Reginald to die."

"I hope so," Hart said.

They exited the carriage and Hart felt right with Olivia on his arm as they entered the townhouse. For once, he didn't grumble wading through the receiving line because he had the most beautiful woman in the world on his arm and her undivided attention.

They entered the ballroom and he told her, "Dance with others tonight. I don't want anyone to be aware of our betrothal. I do, though, plan to claim two dances. I am told that will signal to the *ton* that I am interested in pursuing you with a passion."

A footman handed her a programme and Hart tied it onto her wrist for her.

"Which dances do you wish to claim?" she asked, her color high.

"Definitely the supper dance. I don't think I could stomach a single bite if I had to watch you dining with another man. It was horrible watching Braithwaite take you to that out of the way table."

Hart took her card and signed his name beside the supper dance. "I think the last one, as well. It will achieve the impact I want and we can leave directly after we are done with it."

He signed his name again to the last number. "I am staying by your side. I dare Cooperton to come near you."

She squeezed his arm. "Thank you for looking out for me."

Other gentlemen approached her, all a little wary, seeing Hart standing next to her. Olivia was genial with all and, soon, her programme was filled.

"See? No Cooperton in sight. Even if he did want a dance, none are to be had," he assured her.

"I am slightly relieved. I spotted him. He is standing across the room."

Hart glanced around the ballroom, locating Cooperton, who stood with Knight. He nodded at Knight, who returned the nod.

"I am thinking of saying something to your father regarding your cousin's ungentlemanly behavior with Lady Lydia."

She sniffed. "Lady Lydia brings a large dowry and her father has an impeccable reputation. My father won't care what Higbee did." She sighed. "Oh, how I wish we could help Lady Lydia. I am afraid that will be impossible."

"Don't despair. The Terrors are still working on coming up with a solution."

"It looks as if the dancing is about to commence," Olivia said. "I see Lord Bell headed my way."

Hart took her hand and kissed it tenderly. "I will see you later, my lady."

He had no interest in dancing with anyone other than Olivia. He went to the card room and located Lord Rivers. At first, he thought to speak with Olivia's father and ask to call upon him tomorrow. Instead, he decided the element of surprise would be in his favor and he would merely show up tomorrow morning, throwing the earl off-balance. Hart didn't think Rivers would object too strenuously by having a duke marry into his family. For his part, however, he would insist he and Olivia keep a polite distance from her father. The man had never treated her properly and Hart saw no reason for them to waste time in the earl's presence.

After playing several hands and winning all but one, he returned to the ballroom and waited another set before it was time to claim Olivia for the supper dance. He did so, enjoying every moment he held her in his arms. Pride swelled within him, knowing this woman would soon be legally his. He couldn't wait to make love to her. Since they were going to wed by special license, he might even do so before the wedding took place. They would marry soon anyway. If a child resulted from that first coupling, no one would be the wiser.

It might also be nice to have already made love together before their wedding night. He knew Olivia would be nervous, having never done so before. He wanted her to enjoy their wedding and not be worried about what came after the ceremony.

The dance concluded and they joined Miles and Emery in leaving the ballroom. Hart asked them to hold back a moment and they shared their good news with their friends before they entered the supper room.

Emery threw her arms about Olivia and then Hart, saying, "I am glad you told us in private. I would probably have squealed with delight in front of everyone at supper."

"We should be announcing the betrothal soon," Hart said. "I plan to visit with Lord Rivers tomorrow morning and will leave directly after that to purchase the special license in Doctors' Commons."

"Could we host the wedding and breakfast?" Miles asked.

"Meadow offered to do so," Olivia told the pair as they moved toward the supper hall. "But thank you for the offer."

"Do you have an idea when you will wed?" Miles asked.

Hart looked to Olivia. "Hopefully, next week. I don't know how long it takes for a woman to ready herself."

She smiled at him, love in her eyes. "I will be ready whatever day you wish."

"Just be certain Meadow knows," Emery said.

"We will tell her once I have spoken with Lord Rivers," Hart said.

They joined the Haverhills and Amesburys for supper. Hart saw Lord Braithwaite gazing at Olivia and knew the marquess would be saddened to hear he had lost out at a chance with her.

Once supper finished, the women retreated to the retiring room. Miles and Wyatt returned to the card room. Donovan asked Hart to stay for a glass of port.

"Have you thought of asking Finch to officiate?" his old friend asked.

"No, but that is a good idea. I had written him earlier, filling him in on what has been happening in my life. I did mention Olivia but Finch will probably be surprised to learn I am ready to wed so soon."

Donovan chuckled. "If you bothered to mention Olivia, Finch

will already know your intentions. He can easily read between the lines."

"I worry about him," Hart said. "I hate that he is away from the rest of us. I miss seeing him, even more so because I see the three of you all the time."

"He had little choice in life," Donovan said. "His family wasn't willing to purchase an army commission for him. Lord Marksby offering Finch the living in Marbury allowed him to settle down."

"But does he have any friends?"

"He never mentions any to me in his letters," Donovan said. "I think Finch knows he is lucky to have a profession and a roof over his head."

"Do you ever wonder what he was accused of?" Hart asked. "Why he was sent to Turner Academy? He never shared his story with any of us."

"I have over the years," Donovan admitted. "It must be a heavy burden he carries, not to even let his fellow Terrors lighten the load."

"Do you think he is guilty of whatever his family accused him of doing?"

"If he is, it changed him. Finch is a good man. Of that, I am certain."

"I will write to him after I meet with Lord Rivers. It would be right to have all the Terrors united for the wedding."

"He has performed the first three. He would be hurt if he wasn't asked to do the same for you and Olivia."

"She will adore him," Hart said.

They finished their port in companionable silence and eventually returned to the ballroom. Hart claimed Olivia as his partner for the final dance of the evening. As he led her to the center of the dance floor, he noticed the looks tossed their way.

"People are noticing this is our second time to dance together," he said.

"Yes," she said breathlessly, her eyes shining up at him.

Hart slipped his arms about her. "I have something to ask you once the waltz is done."

The music began and he enjoyed twirling her about the ballroom. He knew many envied him for being Olivia's partner and he was delighted that she had blossomed in such a short time.

When the music faded, he took her arm and bent to her ear. Whispering into it, he said, "I don't want to wait until our wedding night to claim you. May I come to your bed tonight?"

CHAPTER TWENTY-TWO

O LIVA PACED HER bedchamber nervously. Mary had un-dressed her and she had sent the maid to bed.

Now, she waited for Hart.

At first, his request had surprised her. Then she had seen the wisdom in it. Hart must know how anxious she would be come their wedding night. What better way to allay her nerves than to couple before their wedding occurred? That way, she would not spend the days leading up to the ceremony and the entire day itself besieged by fright.

In truth, she wanted him to come to her bed. Ever since that first kiss, she had known. He was The One. Her body responded to Hart in a way it never had. She wanted to give all of herself to him.

Tonight, she would.

Olivia had already sneaked downstairs and unlatched the French doors in Donovan's study. Hart would enter through them and then make his way to her bedchamber. He assured her he would not be caught. If he were, what would happen? They would wed quickly, which they already planned to do.

Still, agitation filled her. Not so much about Hart being found in her bed but what she was to do with him in that bed. She had no experience and figured he had plenty. If she didn't please him, he would never tell her so. He would be a gentleman and marry her anyway.

She felt a slight breeze and wheeled, seeing he had entered her bedchamber and now closed the door quietly. Her heart began pounding twice as fast as he turned and came toward her.

He placed his hands on her shoulders. He wore no gloves. Olivia could feel the heat of his fingers burn through her thin wrapper and night rail.

"Have you changed your mind?" he asked softly.

"No. Only I worry that—"

He kissed her before she could finish the sentence. Quickly. Then he raised his head.

"That is why we are doing this now. To alleviate any fears you have."

"I am afraid I won't please you," she said, her voice small.

His hands framed her face. "You will. Just as I will please you."

She blinked. "I hadn't thought of that."

Hart smiled, his thumbs caressing her cheeks. "A good deal of my pleasure will result if I please you. I hope I can. We have a lot to learn about one another. We won't figure it all out in a single night. But tonight should take the edge off the unknown for you. I want to make you happy, Olivia. Happier than you have ever been." He hesitated and then asked, "Do you know what is involved in lovemaking?"

"No," she whispered.

"Good. Some people come in with preconceived notions. You and I are a blank slate. We will write our love story upon it. It will be ours alone. Whatever we do together, we do for one another. No judgment. Just what feels right to us. There are no rights or wrongs. Only the love we share. It will be manifested in ways pleasing only to us."

"You mean how you . . . when you . . ." She couldn't complete the sentence.

Hart tipped her lowered chin up and met her gaze. "Don't ever be embarrassed, love."

Olivia swallowed. "When you kissed my breast," she said

bravely.

"Yes. Did you like that?"

She nodded. "Very much."

"I enjoyed it, too. I will make certain tonight that both your magnificent breasts receive my full attention. I will kiss them and many other places on you, Olivia. You will tell me what you like. What is enjoyable."

"All right," she agreed, hoping she could do as he asked.

Hart kissed her again, deep and slow, taking his time. Her blood heated. Her arms went about his neck. She pressed her body to his, wanting to feel his hardness against her softness. She felt them moving and opened her eyes, finding they were now in the chair, Hart sitting in it with her on his lap.

He grinned. And kissed her again.

She gave over to the kiss, opening to him, allowing him to explore every nook and cranny of her mouth. In return, she did the same to him, until they both panted, desire filling them. The place between her legs throbbed. Not painfully. Just insistently. She had never really been aware of it before. Until now. With Hart.

He carried her to the bed, which Mary had already turned back, and placed her upon it. She watched as he slowly undressed, each layer coming off until he stood bare. His leanness was hardened by muscle and she itched to run her fingers over his body. He pulled her to her feet and into his arms, kissing her again, hard and insistent. Something stirred below them and she broke the kiss, looking down.

His manhood jutted out from a nest of curls similar to her own, standing at attention. She touched it. He sucked in a quick breath.

"Is it all right that I touch it?" she asked timidly.

"It is more than all right," he assured her. "I like that very much."

Olivia wrapped her fingers around the head. It felt hard in her hand. Her thumb rubbed the tip, which felt soft as velvet. Hart stood with eyes closed, breathing heavily, as she continued her explorations. Then he placed his hand atop hers.

"I will explode at any moment. I need to see to your needs first. Then you may touch me all you wish."

She didn't quite know how he would explode or why she should be attended to first, but he was the expert so she merely nodded.

"May I undress you?" he asked.

"Yes."

Hart untied the belt of the wrapper and pushed it from her shoulders. He ran his hands up and down her bare arms. Olivia could feel her nipples coming to attention, straining against her night rail.

"So beautiful," he murmured, kissing her throat as he slid the night rail down. It fell to her waist and his hands caressed her breasts even as he kissed her senseless. Then he tugged the night rail over her hips. It pooled on the ground and he lifted her to the bed.

He worshipped her in a way Olivia had never known, touching her reverently, causing her insides to go molten and her bones to dissolve into nothingness. He kissed her breasts as before, giving each one equal attention as his hands roamed her body. She heated, as if she had a fever—only the fever was Hart. As he kissed her, his hand glided up her bare thigh and then touched her core. She could feel the dampness and wondered why it was there.

"Ah, you are wet for me," he said approvingly. "It shows you desire me."

"I do," she agreed, growing bolder.

He stroked up and down the seam of her sex, parting her folds, plunging a finger deep within her. She whimpered and then began to moan as that finger moved in exquisite ways, turning her mindless. Another joined it and Hart continued the rhythm. Something built within Olivia and then without warning, it erupted. She saw a multitude of stars as the heat spread throughout her and waves of unimaginable pleasure rolled through her.

It had barely ended, leaving her limp, when Hart kissed his way down her body and parted her thighs. Suddenly, his tongue pierced her core, moving in a similar rhythm to his fingers. This had to be wrong yet it felt so incredibly right. This must be what he had spoken of. How things would occur between the two of them and as long as they wanted it, it was fine.

Olivia certainly wanted this.

She moved against him, her fingers pushed into his hair, the pressure building and then erupting as before, only longer and stronger. Hart kissed his way up her belly, all the way to her mouth, his tongue plunging inside. She strained against him. Wanting more. Needing more.

Then he rose above her, still kissing her, and pushed against her core. He entered her quickly, a brief moment of pain erupting, and then none. He filled her completely.

"I'm going to move now. It will be like the waltz only it's a dance just for the two of us. Sometimes, we dance it slowly. Other times, it will be hard and fast."

She nodded.

And so it began. She caught his rhythm and begin rising to meet him, each thrust filling her, causing her to think only of him. Olivia smelled him. Tasted him. Touched him.

Then he thrust a final time, crying out softly as she felt the pleasure wash over her anew. Hart collapsed atop her, burying his face against her throat. She wrapped her arms about him, never wanting to let go.

"You are wonderful," he murmured against her neck.

"It was all right?" she asked, still worried.

He lifted his head, gazing into her eyes. "You, my sweet Olivia, were spectacular. The best it has ever been. And it will only get better. I promise."

She giggled. "If it does, I might die from pleasure."

Hart withdrew from her, lying on his side, turning her so she faced him.

"The French call it *la petite mort*," he told her.

"The little death."

"Yes."

Olivia snuggled against him and then asked, "When can we die again?"

Hart laughed.

⋙✕⋘

HART HAD TOLD Olivia to come to her father's house at eleven o'clock. He would now meet her outside. He hadn't wanted them to come together unchaperoned. Not yet. He wanted all to be above board until he had Lord Rivers' approval.

His carriage pulled up and he disembarked, walking to Donovan's carriage and helping her do the same.

"Are you ready?" he asked.

Her eyes danced with mischief. "Now that I know what the marriage bed is all about? Of course, I am ready."

"You little minx," he said, wishing he could pull her into his arms for an extended kiss.

Instead, he took her arm and escorted her to the door.

Olivia greeted the butler who opened it and asked if her father was at home.

"He is in his study, my lady. With Mr. Knight and Lord Cooperton."

Hart presented his card to the butler. "I wish to see him. Without the others present."

"Of course, Your Grace. Might you wish to wait in the winter parlor?"

"Here is fine because I won't be waiting long."

The butler retreated and Olivia rested her head against his shoulder a moment. "It is hard to believe this is happening," she said.

"I will leave here and head straight to Doctors' Commons."

He paused. "I wrote my friend Finch this morning. I have asked him to come to London in order to perform the ceremony. I know I should have checked with you first but I was hoping you would agree."

"I know of Finch," she said. "Wynter and I had a long talk this morning after breakfast. She told me about him. He is the only Terror I do not know. She said Finch has officiated at the previous three ceremonies. I was going to ask you if he could do the same at ours."

Hart grinned. "See? We already think so much alike." He bent and gave her a sweet kiss. "The next kiss you receive will be from your betrothed."

Knight and Cooperton appeared in the foyer, both with a suspicious look on their faces. The butler followed them and said, "His lordship will receive you now, Your Grace."

"Thank you."

Without a word to the pair, he brushed past them, bringing Olivia with him. The butler paused a moment and then entered the room, announcing him.

Hart gave her a reassuring smile and they stepped into the lion's den.

CHAPTER TWENTY-THREE

HART WATCHED LORD Rivers rise to greet them. A puzzled expression crossed his face as he saw Olivia accompanied his visitor.

"Your Grace," the earl said, bowing and then offering his hand. "This is such a pleasure."

Hart shook Rivers' hand and then indicated Olivia beside him. "Surely you wish to greet your daughter, my lord."

Rivers frowned and then said, "Olivia," his tone clipped. He turned back to Hart. "Please, have a seat, Your Grace."

Hart led Olivia to a group of four chairs. The earl joined them.

"While I am delighted to see you, Your Grace, I do wonder why you are here, much less with my daughter."

"I have come to seek your permission to marry Lady Olivia."

Rivers' jaw dropped. It took him a moment to recover and then he sputtered, "*Marry* the chit?"

"Careful," warned Hart, offended by the earl's tone and choice of words.

"Let me get this straight. You wish to wed my daughter. How is that even possible?"

"I do," he said firmly. "I am in love with Olivia and plan to make her my duchess."

Rivers sat back in his chair, clearly flabbergasted by the notion. Then a pleased look entered his eyes.

"I would welcome an alliance between our families. I am merely surprised by this sudden turn of events."

"Because you gave Lord Cooperton permission to court me?" asked Olivia.

Rivers appeared startled. "Why, yes. I look upon Cooperton fondly. He has been a good friend to my dear nephew. Cooperton indicated his interest in you. I thought no one else would care to woo you and so I told him to go ahead. In fact, he was just here asking for your hand in marriage, which I readily agreed to." He paused. "Of course, circumstances have changed. I cannot refuse a duke." The earl smiled ingratiatingly.

"Send for your solicitor," Hart said. "Mine will be here shortly. I wish to sign the marriage contracts immediately."

"Immediately?" the earl questioned. "Why so?"

"Once I leave here, I will obtain a special license. Lady Olivia and I will be married within the week."

The earl frowned and looked to his daughter. "Surely, you would rather wed in a smart town wedding at St. James' instead of some private ceremony. Why, we could ask all our friends. It would be a grand occasion."

Hart knew the earl wanted to trade upon the new relationship with his future son-in-law. Before he could respond, Olivia did.

"We don't want a large wedding, Father. A wedding at St. James' would largely be made up of your friends. Mansfield and I prefer a more intimate, private affair. With our friends."

Disappointment filled Rivers' face. "Of course. I understand. When and where will the wedding take place?"

"The Duke and Duchess of Amesbury have agreed to host," Olivia said. "We haven't set the exact date yet."

"Then let me send for my solicitor," the earl said.

"Send for your nephew, as well," Hart said. "There is a matter I wish to discuss with him present."

"What matter?" Rivers asked, suspicion crossing his face.

"The matter of his betrothal to Lady Lydia."

A pleased looked settled upon Rivers' face. "Ah, yes. They

will wed in little less than a month. I suppose it will be good that your weddings will not conflict with one another."

"Knight will not be marrying Lady Lydia," Hart stated.

"What?"

"Your nephew gained his fiancée through a falsehood," he said. "He—and his two wicked friends—lied in order to trap her into a betrothal, most likely because she has a hefty dowry and Knight's gambling debts are tremendous."

"It doesn't matter how the betrothal came to be," Rivers said flatly. "It will go through as planned."

"It won't," Hart countered. "Or I will ruin you and your nephew. I am a duke of the realm, my lord, and I have powerful friends in Polite Society. The Duke of Winslow. The Duke of Amesbury. The Duke of Haverhill. We are all in agreement that what Knight and his friends did was immoral and must be set to rights—or else you and he will pay."

"That's outrageous!" Rivers proclaimed.

"I doubt your nephew is clever enough to have hatched such a scheme, which means responsibility for this lies at your door. Lady Lydia was a young girl with a spotless reputation. You cannot tell me that she met Knight, danced once with him, and then became a wanton, full of uncontrolled passion."

Rivers blanched. "How do you want the betrothal to be broken?" he asked dejectedly.

"Publicly," Hart said. "Your nephew is to admit he lied regarding the incident and, as a gentleman, realizes that he is honor-bound to release Lady Lydia from the betrothal with no consequences."

"What? You want Higbee to confess in front of the *ton* that he lied? He will never find another bride after doing so."

"If he does as I request, I will pay Knight's gambling debts, down to the last farthing."

Hart had already put that into motion. He had visited with his solicitor early this morning, stating what he wished to be drawn up in the marriage settlements and asked for every marker connected to Higbee Knight to be purchased immediately.

"Send for your solicitor and nephew," he said.

"I will let you know when they are here," Rivers said and departed the room.

Half an hour later, the earl returned, having left Hart and Olivia alone the entire time. They hadn't missed his toxic presence and had enjoyed the brief respite.

Rivers stiffly said, "The others have gathered in the library, Your Grace. They are awaiting your presence."

He stood and offered Olivia his arm.

"She is not invited," the earl said.

"The dealings concern Lady Olivia. She will attend," Hart said, narrowing his eyes. "Is that understood?"

The earl nodded curtly and exited the room. They followed and found two solicitors, their clerks, and Higbee Knight in the library. At first, Hart had not wanted Knight present during the discussion and signing of the marriage settlements but then he decided it would be good for Olivia's cousin to know just how well she would be taken care of by her husband and the new family they would create.

"Mr. Griffin, have you prepared the copies I requested?"

"Yes, Your Grace," his solicitor replied, distributing one to the earl and a second one to Rivers' solicitor.

Rivers handed it back. "I don't read things such as this. Barton will inform me of anything important."

"Give me a few minutes, my lord," Barton said, indicating for Griffin to pass the second copy to Barton's clerk.

The two men read for some minutes, Barton nodding occasionally, his face giving nothing away. Finally, he placed the pages onto the table.

"Your daughter will be looked after incredibly well, Lord Rivers. His Grace has been most generous."

"Give me the gist of the contracts, Barton, and don't bore me," the earl replied.

"You are to present His Grace with Lady Olivia's dowry. Once the marriage ceremony has been performed, His Grace is gifting Her Grace with the entirety of it."

"Wait," Rivers said, clearly confused. "You are telling me that *she* is the one who will have sole access to her dowry?"

"Yes, my lord," Barton said. "No strings are attached. Her Grace may spend the dowry in whatever manner she wishes."

"That is outrageous!" Knight declared. "Olivia will have a husband. A wealthy one, at that. What does she need with all that money? It would merely go to waste."

"Your opinion is not being sought, Knight," Hart said. "Do keep quiet."

Spots of color dotted Knight's cheeks but he remained silent.

"Lady Olivia will also be given two unentailed properties," Barton continued. "There are a few other items but those are the most significant portions of the settlements."

"If you have no objection, Lord Rivers, I would like the contracts signed now," he said. "I will be leaving here to purchase the special license."

The earl sighed. "I have no objections. Where do I sign?"

Barton and Griffin oversaw the signing of every copy, with one being given to Olivia. She hadn't spoken during the proceedings but her eyes shined brightly as Griffin awarded her a copy.

"Thank you," she told Hart.

"Mr. Barton and his clerk may leave," he said.

Rivers dismissed the pair and Hart asked Griffin, "Have you obtained what I asked for?"

"Of course, Your Grace," the solicitor said, withdrawing a new set of papers from his satchel.

"What's this?" Knight asked, his suspicion evident.

"These concern you," he told the arrogant young man. "You will not be marrying Lady Lydia, after all."

Knight sprang to his feet. "You cannot—"

"Sit!" commanded Rivers. "His Grace has made it clear that the marriage is not to take place."

"What business is it of his?" Knight demanded.

Hart glared at Higbee as he said, "I have made it my business. You took an innocent young girl and deliberately lied about her, besmirching her reputation. You will now correct that mistake.

You will announce in front of the entire *ton* that you are breaking the betrothal because it was agreed to by nefarious means."

Knight looked appalled. "You expect me to get up in front of everyone and admit that I lied? That I forced Lord Roxbury to agree to the betrothal under false pretenses?" Knight's eyes narrowed. "I will not be humiliated by you or anyone else, Mansfield."

"That is exactly what I am saying. Else I will ruin you and your uncle. I have the means and plenty of motive."

Knight pointed at Olivia. "*She* is the one who has spoken poison in your ear, Your Grace. Ever since we were children, she has always lied."

"If you confess your sins publicly, I will tear up your markers."

Knight froze. "You possess them now?"

Hart glanced to Griffin, who nodded, and said, "I do."

"You told me you would pay off his gambling debts," Lord Rivers objected. "Not that you had bought Higebee's markers. Even if he tries to atone publicly, you could still call in the markers and demand payment in full at any time."

Hart looked steadily at Knight. "I am a man of my word. Once you have spoken at this evening's ball, I will tear up the markers. Burn them. I will even give them to you and allow you to do so. If you don't?" He let the question hang in the air a moment. "I will call them in and you will rot in debtors' prison."

Knight's eyes flew to Lord Rivers. "Uncle?" he pleaded.

The earl shook his head. "There is nothing I can do. You have made your bed, Higbee. You must deal with the consequences. I haven't the coin to extricate you from this mess. You know that."

Knight's face reddened, in anger or embarrassment. Then Hart saw resignation as the man's shoulders slumped.

"I will do as you ask," he said.

"Good. Lady Lydia will be made aware of the situation. It will be up to her whether or not to attend tonight's ball," Hart said. "You do not have to name the friends who supported your story but you must acknowledge their role in the deceit."

Without a word, Knight left the library. Hart accepted the markers held by Griffin. The solicitor and his clerk said farewell and left the room.

"You will get your pound of flesh, Your Grace," Lord Rivers said, bitterness lacing his words.

"Come," Hart said to Olivia but she held up a hand.

"Do not expect to receive an invitation to our wedding," she told her father. "Those in attendance will be the ones who love and support us. Mansfield has more love for me in his smallest finger than you have ever shown me in my lifetime. You have never been a father to me and I don't expect you to start now."

She drew in a long breath and exhaled it. "We will be polite when we see you at *ton* affairs but you will never be received in our home. And if I hear even a hint of gossip—that you have disparaged us to anyone in Polite Society—then I will give my husband permission to destroy you. So walk the straight and narrow, Father. Hold your tongue. Be gracious. Or suffer the consequences," Olivia warned.

Pride filled Hart in seeing Olivia finally stand up to her brute of a father. He gave her a smile. "Ready?"

She took the arm he offered and they left the townhouse.

"What now?" she asked.

"I am off to Doctors' Commons. I think it best you call upon Lady Lydia and explain to her what will unfold this evening."

"That is a good idea. I would also like to extend to her my friendship. Even with what Higbee will admit to and him breaking their betrothal, many in Polite Society will find it hard to accept her. I want her to know she has friends. In fact, I will see if Wynter, Emery, and Meadow wish to accompany me."

Hart brushed a kiss upon her cheek. "You are an amazing woman, Olivia Knight."

"Soon to be Olivia Hartfield, Duchess of Mansfield," she added with a grin. "With the best husband to be found in all of England."

CHAPTER TWENTY-FOUR

TWO HOURS LATER, Olivia stood in front of Lord and Lady Roxbury's townhouse, her three friends in tow. They presented their calling cards to the butler and were escorted into the drawing room. It pained her to see no beautiful bouquets and no eligible bachelors present. Higbee's betrothal and the scandal of him being caught with Lady Lydia had chased away all the gentlemen who might have vied for Lady Lydia's hand.

The earl and countess rose, a questioning look on both their faces at the arrival of the four women. Lady Lydia stepped forward.

"It is so good to see you again, Lady Olivia." She took Olivia's hands in hers and squeezed them.

"It is a pleasure to see you again, Lady Lydia. You as well, Lord Roxbury. Lady Roxbury. I know you must remember my good friends. We supped together at your ball."

Lord Roxbury nodded. "I do remember you." A shadow crossed his face as he must have recalled the circumstances of how that supper had turned out.

"Won't you please have a seat, Your Graces? Lady Olivia?" the countess asked. "I can ring for tea."

"No, that is not necessary," Olivia said. "We won't stay long. We just wanted to come and inform you of something that will occur tonight at the ball which Lord and Lady Kendall are hosting."

She turned and smiled at Lady Lydia. "It is very good news."

The girl looked hopeful as she said, "Have you and His Grace come up with a plan?"

"His Grace?" the earl asked.

Lady Lydia faced her parents. "Lady Olivia is Mr. Knight's cousin."

A look of distaste crossed both the Roxburys' faces at the mention of their daughter's fiancé.

"Lady Olivia and the Duke of Mansfield showed interest in my plight. I . . ." Her voice faded and then she squared her shoulders and continued. "I asked for their help."

Lord Roxbury shook his head. "Lydia, you know how sorry I am but you simply must wed Mr. Knight. If not, your reputation will be ruined."

Lady Roxbury's eyes filled with tears. "You know, my darling, how much we love you. But we cannot see you destroyed."

Lady Lydia's eyes blazed with anger. "Marrying that man would destroy me, Mama. You know that."

"Lady Lydia will not be forced to wed my cousin," Olivia told them. "The Duke of Mansfield and I spoke with my father, Lord Rivers, and Higbee just a few hours ago."

"Mr. Knight is breaking the betrothal?" Lady Lydia asked, hope evident on her face.

"What business is this of yours, my lady?" Lord Roxbury demanded.

"I learned how unhappy Lady Lydia was at the betrothal. How my cousin—and his friends—lied about the events in order to ensnare her into a marriage. Higbee has massive gambling debts and was looking for a girl with a considerable dowry so that he might pay them off."

"If Mr. Knight ends their betrothal, it will be as good as ruining Lydia for life," Lady Roxbury wailed.

"Please," Olivia asked. "You should consider your daughter's happiness above all else, my lady. I grew up with my cousin. I know what a snake in the grass he is. She would be miserable with him."

"At least she would still be received in Polite Society," said the countess. "If he ends the betrothal, the scandal will only affect our daughter."

"Higbee will end their engagement at tonight's ball," Olivia confirmed. "He will also own up to how he orchestrated the betrothal. That he and his witnesses deliberately lied regarding the circumstances and that nothing untoward occurred."

Lady Lydia gasped. "In front of everyone? Mr. Knight will admit to his wrongdoing?"

"He will," she assured the girl. "*He* will be the one who becomes a pariah in Polite Society. As for you, my lady, you will be standing with your friends when this announcement is made."

"Who?" she asked, bewildered. "My friends all know what a scoundrel Knight is. They have fled. I have no one but my parents' support at this point."

"You have us," Emery said.

"All of us," Wynter added.

"Three duchesses standing by you," Meadow confirmed. She glanced to Olivia. "And a soon-to-be fourth."

Lady Lydia turned to Olivia. "You and His Grace are engaged?"

"Yes," Olivia confirmed. "If we four and the four dukes are standing with you, it will make a tremendous statement to the *ton*. We will make known how we feel you were wronged. My friends have all agreed to host events this Season and make certain you are invited. Others will follow suit. Soon, I believe this drawing room will be filled with gentlemen wishing to woo you."

Lady Lydia burst into tears. She threw herself into her mother's arms and the countess comforted her.

Lord Roxbury shook his head. "I do not know what to say, my lady. What you are doing for my child. I can never repay the debt I owe you."

"The Duke of Mansfield is merely trying to right a wrong,"

she said. "My fiancé is the best man I know. He was very moved by your daughter's plight and wanted to do everything in his power to see her reputation restored."

Lady Lydia hugged Olivia. "You and the duke are angels. I truly saw no way out of this situation."

"Not everyone will be agreeable," she warned the girl. "There will be a few who might shun you though nothing is your fault. I believe, however, that the majority of the *ton* will embrace you again." She paused. "So, will you attend tonight's ball, my lady? If you do, we will be there for you."

Lady Lydia smiled through her tears. "Of course, I will be there. I wouldn't miss seeing this for the world. Thank you, my lady." She looked to the three duchesses. "Thanks to all of you."

"I think it best that we all be seen together in public soon after tonight's ball," Olivia said. "What if we went shopping together tomorrow? Or to a bookshop?" She looked to her friends.

"Why not both?" Emery suggested. "I am always in need of a new hat. We could go to Mrs. Hamlin's establishment and then browse for books afterward."

"Mrs. Hamlin's?" Lady Roxbury asked. "She is very exclusive. We have not received an invitation to shop with her."

"We have," Meadow said. "Lady Lydia will be welcome if she is in our company."

"Mrs. Hamlin is an astute businesswoman," Wynter added. "She will know the hat she provides to you will be the talk of town—because Lady Lydia will be. For her to be seen in a Hamlin original makes good business sense."

"Shall we say tomorrow at ten?" Olivia asked. "I would suggest the afternoon but I have a feeling Lady Lydia will need to be at home in order to receive callers."

"Callers?" The girl's eyes lit up. "Oh, do you truly think a few gentlemen might call on me?"

"They will. Tomorrow and in the weeks to come," Olivia said. She rose and her friends followed suit. "We shall see you at the Kendalls' ball tonight."

➤➤➤✦◀◀◀

Hart climbed from his carriage and went to the door himself. Upon knocking, the butler admitted him.

"I will let them know you are here, Your Grace."

Donovan was the first to join him in the foyer.

"How does it feel to be an engaged man?" his friend asked. "Did you get the special license?"

"I did. The marriage contracts have been signed. I also had sent a groom from my stables with a letter to Finch. He returned just before I left. Finch replied that he is happy to perform the ceremony and that next Tuesday would be convenient for him. I will send my carriage for him that morning. I am hoping he will stay at least a day or two."

"That's very good news. It will be good to see him."

Olivia and Wynter descended the stairs. Hart's eyes went to his fiancée and again pride swelled within him, knowing she was to be his.

"Shall we?" he asked and they went to the carriage.

Once they were settled, Hart asked, "How did things go with Lady Lydia and her parents?"

"Very well," Olivia told him, sharing the conversation and how thrilled Lady Lydia was to escape being shackled to Higbee for life.

"Do you truly believe Knight will admit to all his misdeeds in front of the *ton*?" Donovan asked.

Hart withdrew a sheaf of papers from his coat. "These markers are reminder enough. If he does as he promised, I will hand them over."

"I wish you would have merely kept them, instead of being such a gentleman," Oliva complained. "If you had them, it would give you power over him. It might have made him walk a more straight and narrow path."

He lifted her hand and kissed it. "Who knew you could be so vindictive? I shall be the one who walks that path so that I never find myself on your bad side," he teased.

They arrived at the ball and the four went through the receiving line, greeting Lord and Lady Kendall.

"Might I ask a favor of you?" Hart said to the earl.

"Anything, Your Grace. I am at your service."

"Two announcements need to be made during supper tonight. The first will come from me. I wish to announce my betrothal to Lady Olivia."

Lord Kendall's eyes gleamed with excitement. "It would be an honor to allow you to make that announcement, Your Grace. And the second?"

"It will come from Mr. Higbee Knight. Believe me when I tell you that your ball, Lord Kendall, will be the most talked-about of the Season."

"I see. What will Mr. Knight be sharing?"

"I believe that should be a surprise. If you could see that my friends and I are seated at your table for supper I would appreciate it. There will be eleven of us."

"I will see to it at once, Your Grace."

They entered the ballroom and found Lord and Lady Roxbury. Lady Lydia beamed up at him.

"First, I must say congratulations, Your Grace. Lady Olivia will make for an outstanding duchess."

He smiled at the young woman. "Thank you. I believe she will."

"I also would like to offer my gratitude," she continued. "You have arrived at a solution I thought to be impossible. I appreciate your efforts on my behalf more than I can ever say."

He glanced to Olivia, who nodded at him. "Lady Olivia and I will be marrying by special license this coming Tuesday. We would like to invite you and your parents to our wedding."

"Thank you, Your Grace," Lady Lydia said. "If you were not a duke and we were not in a public ballroom, I do believe I might embrace you."

"You may do so at our wedding." He paused and then looked to the earl and the countess. "I have already spoken with Lord Kendall. He knows an announcement is to be made during supper. I ask that the three of you join us at the head table."

"We are happy to do so, Your Grace," the earl said. "I know my daughter has expressed her gratitude but I want you to know how very much this means to Lady Roxbury and me. If there is anything I can ever do for you, name it."

Olivia tugged on his arm. "Higbee is here. With Lord Waltham and Lord Cooperton."

Hart spied the trio. "Stay here. I will return shortly."

He made his way to where the three men stood and without greeting them, said, "I have informed Lord Kendall that two announcements are to be made during supper. I will make the first and then yield the floor to you."

Knight's eyes bored into him. "And the markers?"

He patted his coat. "Safe and sound. Do what you have been told to do and they are yours. If not, I will call for full repayment tomorrow morning."

Hart returned to Olivia and said, "He knows when he is to speak."

"I still have doubts whether he will go through with it or not. It would take a courageous man to address the *ton* and admit to such callous actions. Higbee is anything but brave."

"He will. He knows I will call his markers in first thing tomorrow if he doesn't. Your cousin is soft. He knows he would never survive in debtors' prison."

"I hope you are right."

"I am, love. Let's enjoy the ball. Might you have a few dances for your betrothed?"

She arched an eyebrow. "A few? Two is all you are getting, Your Grace."

"Then make them both before supper. We may be besieged

after it and wish to escape."

"Very well." She handed him her programme. "Which would you prefer?"

"The opening number and the supper dance," he told her, writing his name beside both.

They danced the first number together, a lively reel, and then parted. He kept a constant eye on Higbee Knight. Though he had assured Olivia her cousin would comply, Hart still worried that the man might try to weasel out of things. He didn't trust Knight or his two companions.

Finally, the supper dance arrived and he claimed his betrothed.

As they danced, he said, "Last chance to cry off from our betrothal before anyone learns of it."

"Cry off?" she asked. "If I did, what gentleman would warm my bed tonight?"

She batted her lashes at him and Hart laughed.

"You are a minx. My minx," he told her, gazing down upon her. "Am I allowed into your bed tonight?"

"Only if you tell me that you love me. And mean it."

He stopped dancing and said, "I love you more than words could ever say, Olivia. I have always been a man of action. I will let my body speak to yours."

With that, he swept her up into the dance again.

CHAPTER TWENTY-FIVE

HART ACCOMPANIED OLIVIA into the supper room, Miles and Emery next to them. He led them to the head table, where Lord and Lady Roxbury and their daughter awaited them with their hosts.

Lord Kendall smiled. "Welcome, Your Graces. As you see, I have had the table expanded so that we might fit your entire party."

"Thank you for being so accommodating, Lord Kendall. I won't forget your generosity," he said.

Wyatt, Meadow, Donovan, and Wynter joined them. Hart found himself seated next to Lady Kendall.

The countess said, "I hear you will announce your engagement to Lady Olivia this evening. My congratulations to you, Your Grace."

"Thank you, my lady. I appreciate your husband's willingness to allow the announcement to be made tonight."

"And the other one?" she asked.

"That is to be a surprise." He chuckled. "But you will be known for having hosted a most memorable ball."

When supper was over halfway through, Hart caught Lord Kendall's eye. The earl nodded and signaled to a footman.

"Champagne is being brought out for the occasion, Your Grace," Kendall said.

"That is most thoughtful, my lord."

Once the champagne had arrived and was being distributed, the earl asked, "Would you like to make the announcement? I can introduce you beforehand."

Hart realized his host wanted in on a little of the attention.

"If you would be so kind as to introduce me, my lord, Lady Olivia and I would be grateful."

"Very well." Lord Kendall rose.

The gathering fell silent. Hart knew their table had been the talk of the evening and had caught many people looking their way in anticipation.

"I want to thank all of you for coming tonight. Lady Kendall worked extremely hard and I believe the decorations and food for tonight's ball have surpassed that of any event held this Season."

Polite applause sounded and the earl continued.

"I would ask my friend, the Duke of Mansfield, to come and join me. His Grace has an announcement to make."

A hush filled the room as Hart rose from his chair. He helped Olivia from her seat and they joined Lord Kendall.

"Thank you, my lord, for hosting such a magnificent ball this evening." He gazed out across the crowd, who studied him with interest. Reaching down, he took Olivia's hand and raised it to his lips for a tender kiss. A few gasps echoed through the room.

Then facing those gathered, Hart said, "I am delighted to inform you that Lady Olivia Knight has accepted my offer of marriage."

Thunderous applause erupted and they smiled at one another. He turned and picked up his champagne glass and added, "I ask that each of you drink a toast to celebrate my good fortune. To Lady Olivia."

"To Lady Oliva!" the room echoed.

Hart took a sip of the cold champagne and then offered her some. She sipped it and gazed up at him, love shining in her eyes.

"I love you," he said simply. "I cannot wait to be your husband."

Then stunning the crowd, he bent and pressed his lips to hers for a brief kiss. The hall erupted as everyone buzzed about the public kiss.

"You certainly surprised this crowd," she said.

He grinned at her. "I hope to surprise you even more tonight in bed."

She blushed. "You are very wicked, Your Grace."

"You bring it out in me. Go and take your seat."

She did as he requested and the buzz died as Hart spoke again.

"There is another announcement of importance to be made this evening."

He knew where Knight stood in the back. Olivia's cousin had not taken a seat at supper with anyone. His two friends seemed to have deserted him. Lord Rivers hadn't bothered to put in an appearance and Hart wondered if the earl would cut ties with his nephew and heir apparent.

"Mr. Knight wishes to say a few words."

Hart returned to his seat as Higbee Knight made his way to the front. Withdrawing the markers from his pocket, he made sure Knight saw them placed upon the table.

Knight faced him and quietly whispered, "Bastard." Then he turned to face the guests.

"I will not mince words," he began. "I did a terrible thing. I wanted a bride who came with a fortune and learned the first night of the Season that Lord Roxbury's daughter fulfilled that requirement. I acted rashly and claimed events which did not take place had occurred. Two of my friends falsely supported my claim."

Knight paused. "I did not compromise Lady Lydia. I lied, as did my friends. There was no need for us to become betrothed. She is innocent in this matter. Since the marriage settlements have yet to be signed. I am withdrawing my offer of marriage to her."

Knight turned to Lady Lydia. "I am sorry if I caused you any embarrassment."

He whirled and snatched the markers from the table and then walked across the room, his steps echoing in the silence. Only after Knight exited the room did it erupt.

Hart turned to Lady Lydia. "Your reputation is restored. Stand and let them see we are your friends."

She did so, along with her parents. Hart and Olivia were the first to speak with them. Olivia embraced Lady Lydia, while Hart bent and kissed her cheek. They moved away and the remaining dukes and duchesses at their table all came forward, each saying a few words, taking her hand, and offering smiles.

Standing to the side, Olivia said, "You have worked a miracle, Hart."

"I always had a strong sense of right and wrong. Lady Lydia had been terribly wronged by your cousin. Hopefully, tonight will see her back on the path she was meant to traverse." He gazed down at her. "Are you ready to leave?"

She smiled, mischief in her eyes. "I have been ready ever since I knew what we would be doing after we left. I already told Wynter we were scheduled for an early departure. She and Donovan agreed."

The couple joined them and Donovan said, "I hear we are to make a break for it now."

Hart laughed. "You heard correctly."

The four tried to slip unnoticed from the room but were stopped numerous times so that Hart and Olivia could receive congratulations on their betrothal. Donovan told them he would summon the carriage and after twenty minutes, they finally escaped.

Once inside the vehicle, Hart slipped his arm about Olivia. Looking at his friends, he said, "If you don't mind, I believe I will kiss my fiancée the entire way home."

Donovan guffawed. "Suit yourself. It gives me time with Wynter." He pulled his wife into an embrace.

Hart turned back to Olivia. "I believe it was St. Ambrose who said something about *'when in Rome'*.

"It was," she said. "Hurry up and kiss me."

Hart did.

OLIVIA AWOKE, A little tired but happy to be so. Hart had made love to her twice last night before slipping from her bed and sneaking out of the townhouse. She rolled to her side and buried her nose in the pillow, inhaling deeply and catching a whiff of his scent. She couldn't wait until they could wake up together each morning. That would be next Tuesday, the day of their wedding, when she would meet the last of the Turner Terrors. The Reverend William Finchley was scheduled to arrive then. Hart was sending his carriage to Marbury to bring his friend back to London and hoped Finch would remain a day or so in order for Olivia to get to know him.

Hart warned her that Finch was somewhat of an enigma, the only Terror who had never revealed why he had been sent to Turner Academy. He also was the only one who had not gone to war. Hart told Olivia he believed a war raged within Finch and that, one day, it would erupt. The Terrors and their wives would need to be there for Finch when it finally did.

She rang for Mary and dressed carefully, knowing those out and about today would be interested in what the bride-to-be of the Duke of Mansfield wore. She knew Lady Lydia would also undergo the same scrutiny during their outing to Mrs. Hamlin's shop.

Oliva passed Donovan as she reached the foyer.

The duke smiled at her. "How is the almost duchess this morning?"

She did her best to look regal as she replied, "She is in excellent spirts, Your Grace." Then she smiled. "Actually, I am blissfully happy."

"I don't see how, seeing as you will be stuck with Hart for the rest of your life," he teased.

"You Terrors." Olivia laughed. "I feel I am gaining not only a husband but a coterie of brothers."

"We are family," Donovan agreed. "I am off now. Business to attend to. Enjoy your shopping expedition."

She entered the breakfast room and greeted Wynter.

"You seem in unusually good spirits," her friend said. "Being betrothed suits you well." She paused. "I believe you have a certain glow about you."

Olivia felt her cheeks heating and wondered if Wynter knew that Hart had been a late-night visitor.

A footman brought her tea and as they ate, they talked about the events of the previous evening.

"I do hope Lady Lydia will be received well by others," Wynter said. "There will be some who judge her for Knight's wrongdoings but today's outing should go a long way in helping restore her reputation."

"I agree. Thank you for participating."

A maid entered the room. "Your Grace? Lord Sam has a fever. The nanny sent me to fetch you. You seem to soothe him better than anyone."

"Oh, my poor little love," Wynter said. "Teething can be awful. If you will excuse me."

Olivia finished her breakfast and decided to go to the nursery afterward to see how Sam fared. When she entered, she saw the baby in Wynter's arms as her friend rocked him.

"How is he?" she asked.

"I don't think it's teething," Wynter told her. "He is warmer than usual and not tugging on his ear, which he has been doing when a tooth erupts. Would you mind terribly if I stayed home with him?"

"Of course not. Sam should always be your priority."

"It's just that we wanted to make a statement with this morning's outing."

"Wynter, I believe that two duchesses and an almost duchess

will be quite enough for Lady Lydia. Don't worry about it."

"Thank you for understanding. I feel better staying. If the fever increases, I will send for the doctor. Give everyone my love."

"I will." Olivia bent and brushed her lips against Sam's brow, feeling the heat.

She returned to her room for a bit and then made her way downstairs when it was time to depart. They had decided to go in a single carriage and Emery had volunteered to pick up the group.

When Olivia got into the carriage, Meadow was already there.

"Wynter won't be joining us. Sam has a fever and she is a bit worried about him."

"Teething?" both Emery and Meadow asked in unison.

"Wynter didn't think so. She will have a doctor come if the fever rises."

Lady Lydia joined them and Olivia explained why Wynter was missing.

As they journeyed the few blocks to the milliner's shop, Emery said, "I know we had discussed the possibility of going to a bookshop afterward but I forgot that Miles and I have an appointment with our solicitor."

"Oh, you shouldn't have come at all," said Lady Lydia.

"No, I have plenty of time for hat shopping," Emery said. "We can plan another day to look at books."

They arrived at Mrs. Hamlin's and the four entered the shop. Two women, noted gossips of the *ton*, were inside. It pleased Olivia to see them. They greeted the pair and turned away.

"I am so glad you could accompany us today, Lady Lydia," Meadow said. "You have such a keen sense of fashion. I know you will help me in choosing the perfect hat for my new gown."

Mrs. Hamlin came toward them and said to Emery, "Thank you for your note, Your Grace."

Olivia supposed Emery had dashed off a note to inform the milliner they were coming this morning and bringing a new customer along.

Mrs. Hamlin turned to Lady Lydia. "I think I have a wonderful addition to your wardrobe, my lady. Come and see what you think."

She watched the gossips as Mrs. Hamlin and Lady Lydia went to a far corner and looked at several hats. The two whispered a moment and then left the shop.

"How fortuitous that those two were the first ladies we saw," Meadow said. "It will spread like wildfire that Lady Lydia was not only in our company but favored by Mrs. Hamlin."

They stayed another hour, each woman trying on several hats and bonnets as four more groups of shoppers came through the store. By the end of their excursion, Lady Lydia had purchased three new hats and had commissioned two others.

"Thank you for taking me on, Mrs. Hamlin," the grateful young woman said. "I know how exclusive your clientele is."

The milliner smiled warmly. "You have lovely friends, Lady Lydia. They are good customers of mine. I hope you, too, will become a good customer." She looked to the rest, now the only ones inside the shop. "I will see all your purchases delivered by late this afternoon."

The group thanked her and went outside.

"Mrs. Hamlin is simply wonderful," Lady Lydia said. "I only dreamed of stepping inside her establishment."

"You will become a favorite of hers, I am certain," Meadow predicted. "And a good number of people saw you there. I think you are off to an excellent start."

"I am only sorry to cut our shopping excursion short," Emery apologized.

Olivia looked to Lady Lydia. "The bookshop is but a couple of doors down and your parents' townhouse only a few blocks away. Would you like to go there and walk home?"

The young lady's face lit up. "I love to walk. I do quite a bit of it in the country."

"If you don't mind, I think I will let Emery drop me at home,"

Meadow said. "I feel a headache coming on and would like to lie down." She embraced Lady Lydia. "I will see you this evening at the ball."

They said their goodbyes and Olivia and her companion headed toward the bookshop. Before they reached it, none other than Lord Braithwaite rounded the corner.

Olivia paused and said, "His lordship was calling on me with regularity. I am glad to see him so that I may speak to him about my betrothal."

They continued along and stopped on the pavement as he approached them.

"Good day, ladies."

"Good day, Lord Braithwaite," Olivia said. "Have you met my friend, Lady Lydia?"

"I have not had the pleasure," he replied, tipping his hat to her. "I am sorry about your recent misfortune, being attached to Knight."

"Thank you, my lord. I know there will be gossip surrounding me but I would rather chance that than be in an unhappy marriage."

The marquess glanced to Olivia and then back to Lady Lydia. "Might you do me the honor of saving a dance for me this evening, my lady?"

The girl blushed. "That would be nice, my lord."

"Shall we make it the first dance?"

"I will be happy to place your name upon my card." She looked at Olivia. "I will see you inside."

Now alone, Olivia said, "That was most kind of you, my lord, choosing to ask her to dance. Especially the first dance. If a lord of your standing and good reputation chooses to dance with Lady Lydia, others will, as well."

"I felt bad for her. I know Knight is your cousin but he is known as a terrible scoundrel. If I can help in a small way, so be it." He smiled at her and she saw a wistful look in his eyes.

"I also wanted to thank you for the times we have shared

together. You saw me for myself."

"I appreciated not only your beauty but your intelligence, Lady Olivia." He paused. "I am not upset. My parents were a love match and I know these things happen. I had hoped it would for us but seeing how you and Mansfield look at one another, I realize I never had a chance."

"You are a remarkable man, Lord Braithwaite. I promise you that your countess is out there."

"I hope so. In the meantime, I hope we might remain cordial."

She smiled. "I would like that very much. I will introduce you to my fiancé. I think the two of you would get along splendidly."

"I have met him but don't really know him. I know he is close friends with the men he attended school with."

"He is—but that doesn't mean he would turn down a friendship with you. Look for us at tonight's ball."

"I will." He reached over and opened the door for her. "I am off to my tailor, who is right next door. Good day, my lady."

Olivia entered the bookshop and saw Lady Lydia hovered near the entrance. She joined her.

"Did you hear he asked me to dance?" her new friend said, giddy with excitement. "I didn't know if I would ever dance again."

"Lord Braithwaite is a most kind and amiable man," she said. "If he dances with you, others will follow suit. Come, let us go look at the novels."

They spent a good half-hour perusing the shelves, each choosing two books they wished to purchase. She turned to leave and saw her way blocked.

Higbee stood there.

With a pistol pointed at her.

"Don't say a word," he hissed, stepping deeper into the aisle so that he and the gun were hidden from view. "Put your books down, the both of you."

Olivia did as he ordered, the pit of her belly going cold.

"We are going to walk outside and have a little chat, ladies. Slip your arm through mine, Cousin."

She obeyed him, hoping her legs would work. If they were outside with others passing them on the pavement, Higbee wouldn't be able to brandish his pistol. It would provide an opportunity to escape.

His left arm held her firmly in place as he pushed the pistol in his right hand into her side. To anyone casually glancing their way, the small gun wouldn't be visible.

Over his shoulder, he said, "Follow us, you little bitch."

She sensed Lady Lydia behind them as they left the store. A carriage stood out front, along with Lord Cooperton. He opened the door.

"Come here," he said to Lady Lydia.

She moved in front of Olivia and Higbee and the earl lifted her by the waist, swinging her into the carriage. Quickly, Cooperton climbed in after her and turned in the doorway.

"Come," he ordered Olivia who glanced to her right and saw no one on the pavement nearby.

Higbee released his hold on her, the hand holding the pistol dropping to his side. She looked to her left as Cooperton's hands fastened about her waist.

Lord Braithwaite was stepping from his tailor's shop. For a moment, their gazes met and then Higbee pushed inside behind her, closing the door as the carriage set off immediately.

Olivia only hoped Braithwaite had seen who she was with— and that he would know to tell Hart.

CHAPTER TWENTY-SIX

Hart closed his newspaper and folded it, placing it on the table in front of him. He sat at White's with Wyatt and Miles, who were debating over a new horse Miles was thinking of purchasing.

Donovan entered the room and glanced about. Hart caught his friend's eye and waved him over.

"How was your business?" he asked.

Donovan shrugged. "Nothing too painful."

"I am about to leave for an appointment with my solicitor," Miles informed the group.

Wyatt laughed. "You mean you'll sit quietly while Emery and Mr. Fillmore debate matters."

Miles shrugged off his friend's teasing. "Emery always has a good grasp of business affairs. We talked things over last night so I know what she's wanting to do." He grinned. "Fillmore won't know what hit him."

"She has been a help to us all," Donovan said. "On behalf of the Terrors, we thank you for having the sense to wed a woman who knew more about estate management than any man."

"I will still be seeking her advice on my summer harvest," Hart said. "Once Olivia and I speak our vows, I am hoping to talk her into leaving London. She wasn't keen on the Season anyway and only attending it because her father wished her to find a husband." He puffed up a bit. "Now that she has done so, I hope we can leave and return to Deerfield Park. I still have so much to learn about it."

"At least you inherited a good steward in Patterson," Wyatt pointed out. "It allowed you to come to London. Look how that turned out." His friend smiled. "We are all very happy for you, Hart. Olivia is a lovely woman and will keep you in line."

He laughed. "I am not the wild one who needs to toe the line, Wyatt."

Wyatt smiled sheepishly. "I am not a wild one now. Meadow has tamed me considerably. And Leah. Having a daughter changes a man. I am already fiercely possessive of her and already dreading when she makes her come-out."

"That's years from now," Donovan said.

"It may be," Wyatt said, "but I am already worried about the rogues who might tempt her. Especially having been one myself."

"If Leah is anything like her mother, she will tame any rogue interested in her," Miles said. "They do say a reformed rogue makes for the best husband."

A servant appeared. "Your Grace, a note came for you."

Donovan took it from the proffered tray and opened it. He read it and said, "I must leave. Sam is running a fever."

"Teething," chimed Miles and Wyatt together.

"No, Wynter says it isn't that. That it is rising and she can't get it down. She has sent for the doctor." Donovan stood. "I will see you later."

"Let us know if you need anything," Hart called as Donovan hurried away.

Miles also stood. "Time for me to depart, as well. Emery is due outside at any moment with the carriage. I will see you both at tonight's ball."

After Miles left, Wyatt said, "I am grateful the four of us are together again. I only wish Finch could be here, as well. Do you think he enjoys being a vicar?"

"I haven't a clue," Hart admitted. "I write to him sporadically and receive brief notes in return. He mentions his parishioners and Lord and Lady Markham but rarely says anything personal."

He glanced up and saw Lord Braithwaite hurrying toward him. He knew of all Olivia's suitors that Braithwaite had been the sweetest on her. The marquess had a sterling reputation. Hart hoped Braithwaite was coming over to offer congratulations on the betrothal and not itching for a fight.

Rising, he started to speak but Braithwaite waved a hand to silence any greeting.

"Lady Olivia is in trouble."

"What?" Hart tamped down the panic that flooded him.

"Sit," the marquess said. "You don't want to draw attention to this."

Reluctantly, he took a seat again, as did Braithwaite.

Wyatt leaned in and quietly said, "Tell us everything."

"I came across Lady Olivia and Lady Lydia on the way to my tailor's," Braithwaite began. "We spoke briefly and they entered a bookshop, while I proceeded next door. I was inside for three-quarters of an hour and as I left, I saw the two leaving the bookshop and getting into a carriage."

Braithwaite paused, a grim look upon his face. "Lord Cooperton placed Lady Lydia inside. He reached down and brought Lady Olivia into the vehicle. Mr. Knight, who stood on the pavement, entered behind her." He looked at Hart. "I believe I caught a glimpse of a pistol in Knight's hand."

Cold fear pooled in Hart's belly.

"I hurried after the carriage but it took off quickly," continued Braithwaite. "Something was wrong. I knew I had to come and find you, Your Grace."

"Thank you," he said tersely. "I fear this is retribution for last night. I am the one responsible for forcing Knight to publicly own up to his ungentlemanly behavior. He may be trying to get back at me by using Olivia." He raked a hand through his hair. "You have no idea where the carriage headed?"

"No, Your Grace. Only northward from Mayfair."

"Didn't Cooperton wish to court Olivia?" Wyatt asked.

"He did," Hart said. "She was on to him from the beginning, knowing him to be a scoundrel merely after her dowry, and refused his suit. Why?"

Wyatt rubbed his chin in thought. "It is just that Cooperton sought Olivia's hand for money. Knight did the same with Lady Lydia."

"You don't think . . . Gretna Green?" Lord Braithwaite asked.

Wyatt nodded. "I fear so."

"What the bloody hell is Gretna Green?" Hart asked.

"It is a place just over the border. The first village in Scotland on the main post road from London," Braithwaite said.

"Eloping couples stop at the blacksmith's shop, one of the first buildings seen," Wyatt added. "No banns to be read. No special license to be obtained. Just a quick wedding over the anvil."

Hart was still baffled. "I don't understand."

Wyatt gripped his arm. "Knight and Cooperton have been humiliated. They lost their chance at marrying beautiful women with large dowries. They have taken matters into their own hands and are trying to change their fates."

"What?" he hissed. "You believe they will try and force a marriage?"

"Yes," Braithwaite said.

He shot to his feet. "That will never happen. I will catch up to them."

"Sit," Wyatt said, glancing around. He smiled affably and loudly said, "You are quite humorous, Your Grace." Then he repeated through gritted teeth, "Sit."

Hart did so, anger filling him. "Why are you making me sit when I need to go after them?"

"You must do so quietly," Wyatt cautioned. "Already, they are unwed ladies in the presence of bachelors."

"But Olivia is betrothed to me," he said, anguish filling him.

"Still, it is her reputation—and Lady Lydia's—that are now at stake. If others learn of the abduction, the gossip will fly faster than carrier pigeons. If you catch them in time, you can still wed Olivia but her reputation will be tarnished. As for Lady Lydia, no gentleman will ever think to offer for her with such a stain upon hers."

"If you think Gretna Green is their destination—and I believe that to be the case, Your Grace—then you must do this quietly," Braithwaite admonished. "For the both of them."

"I will kill those bastards," Hart said, his tone deadly. He forced himself to take a deep breath and then asked, "What do you suggest?"

"You and I will shake hands with Braithwaite and quietly leave. We will get a carriage I have that is plain. No ducal crest or markings of any kind. We will use my fastest horses and give chase. They aren't that far ahead of us, possibly a half-hour or slightly more. By the time we leave London, they'll be an hour or more ahead of us. I would put my horses up against any they have. It is over three hundred miles to the border from here. We will find them today. I promise."

Wyatt turned to the marquess. "Stay here another half-hour. Have a coffee. Browse the newspapers. Look bored and then leave. If you rush off, it will look suspicious. Go first to Lord Roxbury's and tell him privately what has occurred and that Hart and I are in pursuit. Caution him to tell no one." He paused. "I am certain Lady Lydia will have several callers today. Tell Lord Roxbury he is to say his daughter is indisposed. A terrible cold. She is feeling poorly and will take a few days to recover. That should buy some time until she returns and hopefully protect her reputation."

"All right, Your Grace," Braithwaite agreed. "I will do as you ask."

"Afterward, go to Winslow and Haverhill and share with them what has happened," Wyatt concluded. "They will want to know."

Braithwaite nodded. Then he smiled brilliantly and said, "I do wish you and Lady Olivia the very best, Your Grace."

He offered Hart his hand and they shook. "Thank you," he said sincerely.

"Shall we go?" he said, turning to Wyatt.

"I suppose so." His friend rose and also shook hands with Braithwaite.

They departed White's and caught a hansom cab back to Wyatt's. The moment the fare was paid and they hurried toward the townhouse, Wyatt said, "Go have my grooms ready the carriage I asked for and tell them my fastest horses. Make sure it is Blevins who is our coachman. Have the carriage out front."

"Will you tell Meadow what happened?" he asked.

"Of course. She is my wife. I will also fetch coins. And guns. I want to be prepared when we confront the pair."

Hart nodded and rushed to the stables. He asked for Blevins and the head groom, explaining that Amesbury wished for the unmarked carriage and his fastest horses to be prepared swiftly. The groom sprinted into action, apparently realizing the seriousness of the situation. To Blevins, Hart shared briefly what had occurred.

"My betrothed and her friend have been kidnapped by two scoundrels who want to spirit them away to Gretna Green and force a marriage. We need to find them and put a stop to their journey."

"I understand, Your Grace. You can count on me," the coachman said.

The carriage soon appeared with a set of beautiful, sleek horses, all coal black. Hart boarded the vehicle and Blevins drove it to the front of the townhouse.

Wyatt appeared moments later, rifles in hand, a small case tucked under his arm and a satchel hanging on his shoulder. Hart swung open the door and Wyatt boarded. The carriage took off.

"Blevins knows the destination," he said. "I assume he will take the roads Knight's driver will use."

"It is most likely Cooperton's carriage we chase since he is an earl. I doubt Knight has his own transportation. There are many small roads to Scotland but Knight and Cooperton will be confident no one saw them and if they did, no one will think it was a kidnapping with a destination of Gretna Green. Cooperton will have instructed his driver to take the main road used by most travelers. They will have to make stops, Hart. To change horses. To eat. I think we will easily catch up to them today, probably in the next few hours, thanks to my driver and team."

He handed Hart a rifle. "Until then, we prepare."

Opening the case, Wyatt withdrew a pair of pistols with pearl handles. He slipped the satchel from his shoulder and opened it. Hart saw it contained ammunition. The two prepared their weapons in silence. He pushed aside all panic. All fear. All rage.

Instead, Hart focused on his enemy and what was to come. His single goal was to safely retrieve Olivia and Lady Lydia.

Then he would exact retribution.

CHAPTER TWENTY-SEVEN

"WHAT ON EARTH are you doing, Higbee?" Olivia demanded as the carriage took off.

"Seeking my revenge," her cousin said tersely. "And redress for the wrongs done to me."

"To you?" She snorted. "Only you would believe you were wronged when you were the villain who perpetrated the injustice."

"I am no villain," he hissed.

"I am not going to be subjected to whatever you intend." She opened her mouth to scream as loudly as she could and hopefully attract the attention of some passerby brave enough to stop their vehicle.

"I wouldn't do that, my lady," Lord Cooperton said.

She glanced to the opposite seat and saw the earl held the tip of a knife to Lady Lydia's throat. All the air went out of her.

Lord Cooperton pressed the blade to the skin and a drop of blood appeared. Tears leaked from the young lady's eyes.

"Please, my lord. Lower it," Olivia begged.

He did so, removing his handkerchief and methodically wiping away the trace of blood from his weapon. As he did so, his gaze bored into hers and he said, "You will be quiet—or you will be restrained. I have brought rope to bind you and gags to silence you if you choose not to cooperate."

That was the last thing she wanted. It would be impossible to escape if they were immobile.

"I won't cause you any trouble," she said meekly. "Neither will Lady Lydia."

Higbee snorted. "Of course, she won't." He smiled at the crying young woman. "Come over here, my lady. Move to the other side, Cousin."

Though it was difficult with the carriage in motion, Olivia stood and wobbled as she and Lady Lydia tried to exchange seats. The coach hit a hole in the road and Olivia tumbled into Lord Cooperton's lap. His arms tightened about her, preventing her escape.

"Ah, this is more like it," he said, his voice as smooth as silk, his breath hot on her cheek.

She turned away and saw Higbee had wrapped an arm about Lady Lydia. The girl wept silently as Higbee forced her face into his chest.

"Stay," he commanded.

Not surprisingly, her cousin closed his eyes and within a minute she heard a soft snore come from him.

"He is a most boring companion on the road," Lord Cooperton said. "He sleeps at the drop of a hat."

"How long will we be on the road?" she asked, hoping to glean where they might be headed.

The earl studied her a moment. "You aren't as bright as I had given you credit for. I would have thought you understood."

"I understand that you have abducted me and Lady Lydia. Are we to be held for ransom? Is this how Higbee plans to make his money now that he has lost Lady Lydia's dowry?"

Cooperton clucked his tongue. "The plan is for the chit to still become his wife."

Realization struck her like a thunderbolt and she gasped.

"You are making for Gretna Green."

"Ah, that is more the Olivia I expected."

Hearing her name come from his cruel lips chilled her. She wriggled to escape his grasp but again he tightened his hold on her.

"An elopement to Gretna Green was our combined solution," the earl continued. "Knight will have his fat dowry, minus having to pay for his gambling debts, thanks to Mansfield surrendering the markers. And I will get the bride I desired."

Fury filled her. "I am already betrothed," she stated. "The contracts have been signed."

"It won't matter if we speak our vows first over the anvil," he countered.

"There will be no agreement on my part. You can't force me to say the words."

A gleam filled his eyes. "I believe I can. You see, Olivia, we will go first. Knight and the lady will be standing there, along with my coachman, who will act as our witness. When we reach the part for you to repeat your vows—and I have been guaranteed the ceremony is quite brief—you will do so.

"Or my driver will cut Lady Lydia's throat."

She gasped, her eyes turning to the opposite seat. The earl had been speaking quietly and Lady Lydia still wept, her face buried against Higbee's chest. At least she hadn't heard the diabolical scheme.

"So, you see, dear Olivia, it is up to you whether your friend lives—or dies."

"If your driver murders Lady Lydia, he will be wanted for murder. And Higbee would blame you for her demise."

He chuckled. "Do you think I really care what Knight thinks? He may be charming and handsome but he would never stand up to me about anything. He is weak. Spineless. I am not worried about him in the least. But I do worry about you. You seem to be a good person. How will you feel with Lady Lydia's death upon your conscience?"

She knew the earl would see the scheme through. He was telling her about it now so that she would have time to think and realize she had no choice.

But she did. Scotland had to be a good three hundred miles

away. It would take at least three days for them to reach the border. Surely, along the way, there would be an opportunity to escape. As usual, her reticule was stuffed with coins. She never left the house without ample money. It would be enough to see her and Lady Lydia home from wherever they freed themselves.

If they could do so.

"I understand why Higbee might still want to wed Lady Lydia. If he did so, Polite Society might think there really was something between them. That they are a love match and have defied everything to be together, even raging gossip. But why me, my lord? Are you in need of my dowry?"

"Not really. It will be nice to have but I am not in desperate straits as Knight was."

"Then why me?" she pressed. "I made known I was not interested in your suit. That I wanted to have nothing to do with you."

His slow smile caused her to shudder.

"It is for that very reason that I have pursued you, Olivia. I have never been told no in my life. You denied my suit, publicly scolding me and warning me away. I cannot allow you to treat me in such a manner. You are far too independent. You need to be broken—and I am the man to do it."

His hand moved and fondled her breast. Disgust filled her.

"When I am done with you, you will have no spirit at all. You will be so meek and submissive, no one will recognize you, least of all yourself."

"How do you intend to break me?" she asked defiantly, her chin tilting upward.

"By taking you every night. Forcing you to bend to my will."

Horror filled her. "You would . . . rape me?"

"Ah, such a dirty little word for such an enjoyable activity. It will be a game we play, Olivia. I play it now with women in brothels. I tie them to the bed and do unspeakable things to them. Degrade them. Humiliate them." He paused. "I will do worse to you. I will shatter everything within you until you are docile. In the end, you will have no will of your own. You will be my puppet, dancing to whatever tune I play."

She jerked away from him, filled with terror, scrambling as far away from him as she could. He chuckled.

"I think perhaps I should start tonight. By the time we reach Gretna Green, you will be as malleable as clay."

Oliva turned away, staring out the window, not wanting him to see the tears that began to fall. Her mind raced and yet no coherent thoughts formed. She tried to slow it. She must come up with a plan. She must find a way for them to escape. They no longer had three days or more.

If they hadn't gained their freedom by tonight, they were doomed.

An hour later, the carriage began to slow. She saw they entered a village and looked for any sign as to where they might be. Higbee stirred and yawned loudly.

"I will see to the change of horses," Lord Cooperton said. "Watch them carefully." Leaning close to her, he whispered, "Behave, pet, else I will punish Lady Lydia for your indiscretions."

He brushed his lips against her cheek and she recoiled at his touch. Laughing, he exited the coach.

Higbee had removed the pistol from his pocket. Instead of pointing it at her as she expected, he rammed it into Lady Lydia's side. The girl squeaked, terror filling her eyes.

"They have decided the best way to control me is by threatening you," Oliva said to her friend. "I will do nothing to cause them to harm you," she promised.

Lady Lydia nodded, tears running down her cheeks. "I trust you."

They sat silently until Lord Cooperton rejoined them. Higbee pocketed his weapon and immediately fell back to sleep. Olivia kept watching out the window, hoping that Lord Braithwaite had gone to Hart. She knew Higbee hadn't seen the marquess and she doubted Lord Cooperton had since he was raising her into the carriage. That meant the two thought they left London scot-free. Again, she prayed that Lord Braithwaite had seen the fear on her face and had gone straight to Hart and shared what he saw. Hart was coming.

She had to keep believing that.

Another two hours passed and the carriage slowed. She knew it was time to switch horses again.

"We will need to stretch our legs when we stop," she told Lord Cooperton.

He shook his head. "I don't think so, Olivia."

"Then you will witness me piddle all over your fine seats. I don't think riding all the way to Scotland with that smell will be pleasant."

"Scotland?" Lady Lydia asked. "We are going to . . . Scotland?"

Olivia realized she had let slip their destination.

"Yes," Higbee said. "You and I will wed, just as my cousin and my dear friend, Cooperton, will do. They are to go first and then we shall speak our vows. You will speak them, my lady. You will have ridden hundreds of miles with me. Stayed in an inn a good three nights or so in my bedchamber. You will have no choice. You are already ruined. You were the minute you set foot inside this carriage."

Lady Lydia let out a sound that broke Olivia's heart, a keening that resembled an animal caught in a trap, knowing it was doomed.

She reached over and took the girl's hand. "It will be fine. Pull yourself together. We need to attend to our needs."

The carriage stopped and she looked to the earl. "Are you going to let us out of this carriage or not?"

"You are full of vinegar, Olivia," he said. "I am looking forward to wringing every drop from you."

Cooperton threw open the carriage door and climbed out. He held his arms out toward her. "Come on."

She allowed him to bring her to the ground, hating his hands upon her. They lingered and he laughed softly.

"I look forward to tonight," he told her before releasing her.

Higbee had disembarked and brought Lady Lydia out. The young woman looked a wreck, her face mottled red and her eyes swollen from crying for so long.

Olivia slipped her arm around the girl as the earl said, "The privy will be around back. I will escort you there. Knight, see to the change of horses."

She held on to Lady Lydia and whispered, "We will escape. I promise you."

The girl looked into Olivia's eyes. "I believe you. I am sorry I am falling apart."

"Being abducted does that," she said, bringing a smile to Lady Lydia's face.

It quickly fell, though, as she said, "I cannot believe they mean to take us to Scotland."

"Hush!" the earl said over his shoulder.

They fell silent until they reached the privy.

"Go first," he ordered Lady Lydia, pulling Olivia away and holding her elbow firmly.

She looked straight ahead, determined not to engage him in further conversation. Once her friend emerged, Olivia entered the privy. Not only did she attend to her business, but she also withdrew a sovereign from her reticule and clasped it in her fist. She emerged, her hand by her side, looking for an opportunity.

They returned to the carriage and she saw the last horse being harnessed. A groom finished as the young boy assisting him turned away. Higbee already sat in the vehicle. As Lord Cooperton moved to lift Lady Lydia inside, Olivia grabbed the wrist of the boy, who looked about eight.

Quickly, she pressed the coin into his hand and whispered, "They abducted us. Tell the duke who comes looking we were here."

She released his wrist and moved toward Lord Cooperton, hoping to distract him.

"Will we dine at the next stop, my lord? I have not eaten since this morning and we obviously have missed teatime."

He brought her into the carriage and followed behind her, slamming the coach door.

"Yes. The next stop will be our last." His eyes gleamed at her. "Are you looking forward to tonight, Olivia? I know I am."

She only hoped Hart wasn't far behind and would find the only breadcrumb she had been able to drop.

CHAPTER TWENTY-EIGHT

HART AND WYATT didn't speak until they reached where Hart believed the horses would need to be exchanged. The two men exited the carriage. Hart still worried about how the London traffic had slowed them down, putting them an hour and half behind, most likely.

Blevins had already climbed from the driver's seat and said, "The team has a little more in them, Your Grace. I think we can do another ten miles before we switch out."

"See they are watered but left harnessed," Wyatt said. "Not too much. We don't need them to be sluggish."

"Yes, Your Grace."

"We should split up," Hart suggested. "If they stopped here, I want to speak to everyone who might have seen them."

He separated from Wyatt and went inside the station. A few tables and chairs were in the small space. He doubted the kidnappers would have allowed the women out of the carriage after such a short time but it was worth asking.

A heavy woman stood behind a tall wooden counter, wiping a mug. "Yes, my lord?" she asked. "What can I do for you?"

"Have you seen two ladies come in today? One has—"

"None, my lord," she interrupted. "Only two carriages have come through today. We don't see many heading north this time of year with the Season still so young."

"Thank you."

He left and went to the stables, where Wyatt was talking with a man.

"The first carriage came through early this morning. Only one passenger. The second was a Lord Coopville. No, Cooperton," he corrected. "He promised to come back this way before a week passed. Said these were his personal horses and paid a pretty penny to see them stabled until his return."

"Did Lord Cooperton have any traveling companions?" Wyatt asked as Hart joined him.

"No one else left the coach while we changed out the horses but I did see a woman gazing out the window as they departed. Right pretty she was."

"Blond?" asked Hart.

"Yes, my lord."

"How long ago were they here?" he asked.

The man scratched his head. "Not long. They left three-quarters of an hour ago, I'd say."

"Thank you." Wyatt tossed the man a coin.

They moved toward the carriage and Hart said, "At least we know they were here and that they are taking the main road. They must feel safe in doing so and will stick to it."

"We have certainly made up the gap between us. I told you my team was fast."

Yet Hart knew they couldn't maintain the same blistering speed. Blevins had said another ten miles. They would have to switch out after that. He could only hope the horses they received would be able to catch up.

They helped Blevins with the horses and then boarded the carriage again.

Wyatt looked at him with encouragement. "We will catch up to them, Hart."

"I hope so."

Once again, they rode in silence, each man with his own thoughts. They stopped to get fresh horses and Wyatt arranged for his team to remain behind, saying they would return for them sometime tomorrow. Since it had only been twelve miles since they last stopped, they didn't bother to ask about a sighting of Cooperton's vehicle, knowing it wouldn't have stopped again so soon.

"We will change horses again at the next station," Wyatt said. "It will be one I am certain they did the same. It will also allow us new horses earlier than usual. That will give us an advantage."

Hart tried not to think of Olivia but couldn't help it. She and Lady Lydia had to be frightened, being taken in broad daylight against their wills. By now, if their abductors hadn't already told them, Olivia would have figured out where they headed. Although he hadn't been familiar with Gretna Green, she would know of it from her time in society. Once again, he fantasized of ways to punish Cooperton and Knight, all of them ending in death. The soldier in him was in hot pursuit of the enemy. There would be no retreat.

It would be a fight to the death.

He tried to think of happier things. His two nights in bed with Olivia and all they had discovered about one another. The thought that even now, she might carry his child. He longed for her to see Deerfield Park, as well as accompanying him on a tour of his other properties. It was something he had planned to do after the Season. Now, he would do so with his duchess.

If he could get her back. No—when he got her back.

Blevins steered the carriage off the road and he glanced out the window, seeing they had arrived at their next destination. He threw back the door and leaped from the carriage, ready to question everyone here.

A small boy came running over. He stopped in front of Hart, looking up, and asked, "Are you the duke? The lady said a duke would be coming."

Hope filled him as Wyatt joined them.

"Blevins is handling the horses," his friend said.

Hart turned back to the boy. "Yes, I am a duke, young man. Who is this lady and when was she here?"

He grinned. "Oh, she was very pretty. Blond hair and eyes a little blue and a little gray." The boy reached into his pocket and held up a coin. "She gave me this and said to tell you they was ab . . . ab . . ."

"Abducted?" he prompted.

The boy brightened. "That's it. She said to tell the duke they were here."

He reached into his pocket and handed the boy a new coin. "Here is another for you, lad. When was the lady here?"

"Not a quarter-hour ago, my lord."

"We must hurry," he said to Wyatt.

"It will take another ten minutes to switch out and harness new horses. We will catch up to them at their next stop."

"I think so, as well," he agreed. Looking at the boy, he asked, "What is the next place travelers might stop if they headed north?"

The boy shook his head. "Don't know, my lord. We can ask my father. Come on!"

He ran toward the stables and they hurried after him.

"What's the next stop for people on the road, Father?" the boy asked eagerly. "These lords want to know."

"That would be Dorville, my lords," the man said. "I would suggest you stop there for the night. They have a large inn and your horses can rest and be ready first thing in the morning."

"And if I went past there? Where would I stop?"

The man told him, saying the small village would be too far down the road. "You don't want to travel after sunset, my lord. No, Dorville's where you'll need to stop."

They thanked him and returned to their carriage, assisting Blevins and then climbing inside the vehicle.

"I doubt we'll catch them on the road. They are most likely half an hour ahead of us now," Wyatt commented.

"But we will certainly reach them in Dorville," Hart said, steel in his voice.

"What are you planning to do?" his friend asked, his brow

furrowed.

"You don't want to know."

"Actually, I do," Wyatt countered. "I know you want to wring the life out of them, Hart, but you can't."

"Why not? If Meadow had been taken, you would be calling for their blood."

"You're right. I would. But cooler heads must prevail."

"I thought dukes were invincible. I could kill the both of them and would not be charged with murder."

"No, that's true," Wyatt said. "But you don't want what you do to affect how Olivia looks at you."

"What do you mean?"

"She loves you," his friend said. "Just as you love her. If you kill her worthless cousin and Cooperton, that will always be between you. Taking a man's life is not something lightly done. You know that—because you and I have killed many times in the name of England's king."

Wyatt paused. "Even if they deserve death, do you want Olivia—and Lady Lydia—to see you kill them? They already have undergone a traumatic experience, being kidnapped and thinking they will be forced to wed their abductors once they reach Scotland. Do they really need to see you murder two men before their eyes?"

"I hadn't considered that," he said hesitantly.

"You must," Wyatt insisted. "Killing these two men will seep like a slow poison into your relationship with Olivia. She will wonder about the man she fell in love with. It will taint everything between you. I know you, Hart. You don't want to risk that. Not when you have a chance to build a life with a remarkable woman. To have a family. To finally have love."

Anguish filled him. "But they must pay, Wyatt. How can I let them walk away without any kind of punishment?"

Wyatt regarded him a moment. "You shouldn't take their lives. But you can take everything else away from them. Their money. Their reputations. You can bring them to their knees.

And I promise, the Terrors will help you do so."

He raked his hands through his hair in frustration. He knew Wyatt was right. Bringing death to a man in war was one thing. Killing in a civilized society would bring shame. Gossip. Ostracization. He couldn't allow it to color his relationship with Olivia.

"You are right," he finally said. "I cannot have their deaths on my conscience, no matter how vile their actions are. But I will snap them in two. Stomp on them. I will see that no one will wish to see them. Speak to them. Do business with them. They will be so broken they will never be able to be put back together."

"Good. The Terrors are with you. We will all see this comes to pass."

Strangely enough, relief filled Hart. Olivia wouldn't have to see him with blood on his hands. No guilt would weigh on his conscience. His heart told him she would approve of this plan.

A calm settled over him and continued until they arrived in Dorville. Blevins had been told to stop in the inn's yard. He did so and Hart and Wyatt emerged from the carriage.

Immediately, he glanced around and saw another carriage of quality. As Wyatt and Blevins arranged for the horses to be looked after overnight, Hart stopped a groom.

"Is this Lord Cooperton's carriage?"

"Yes, my lord. His party arrived a few minutes ago. Be you friends with him?"

He shook his head. "No. Far from it. He is the worst of men." Vehemence laced his words, causing the groom to take a step back.

"Is his lordship inside?" he inquired.

"Y-yes," the groom stammered.

"And did he have another man and two ladies who accompanied him?"

The groom nodded. "They went inside the inn," he said shakily.

"Thank you." He turned and found Wyatt had joined him. "Lord Cooperton and his party arrived recently. Are you ready to join them, Your Grace?"

Wyatt nodded solemnly. "Ready when you are, Your Grace."

OLIVIA LOOKED AT the food the innkeeper's wife placed in front of her. They had been escorted to a private room upstairs, which Lord Cooperton had requested before bringing his party into the inn. The main room below had been filled with others supping and drinking. No one took much notice of them as they entered and followed the innkeeper up the stairs. She tried to catch the eye of someone but the men present were more interested in the food and ale before them than a stranger walking by.

She had no appetite but knew she better force herself to eat something in order to keep up her strength. She lifted the fork to her mouth but set it down again, despair filling her.

The woman finished pouring them glasses of wine and said, "Your two rooms will be ready by the time you finish dining, my lord."

Olivia glanced to Lady Lydia, who absently twirled her fork on the plate. If she heard the woman, she did not react. She probably thought the two of them would be in one room and the men in another. Little did the young woman know that she was about to be deflowered by Higbee.

How to get out of this?

Forcing the fork to her mouth again, she swallowed a bite of meat and chewed it, swallowing painfully. Lord Cooperton had made sure they had no contact with anyone since their journey began. Even if Olivia had jumped up and begged the innkeeper or his wife to help her, she doubted that would have occurred. Cooperton was an earl. No one would dare cross him, much less believe what she said about him.

As she forced another bite into her mouth, she thought of what was to come. Should she fight him? Or would that encourage him to hurt her even worse than he intended?

Olivia decided she would lie passively and let him do whatever he wished. At some point, he would fall asleep. When he did, she would slip from the bed and room. Find Lady Lydia. And they would make their escape.

"You are too quiet, Olivia," chided Cooperton. "I am used to your sparkling conversation. I understand Lady Lydia's shyness but I expected more from you."

"I have nothing to say to you, my lord," she said stiffly. "I thought you preferred a docile woman."

She gazed down at her plate. The few bites of food she had eaten felt as if it would come back up.

Cooperton's fingers brushed her cheek. "What fun would it be if you submit without a fight, my dear?" He glanced to Lady Lydia. "I am sure even this young lady will fight Knight."

"What?" Lady Lydia looked at the earl. "I don't understand."

Higbee chuckled. "He means when I have you tonight."

Still, the girl looked blankly at them.

"Ah, you don't understand, do you?" the earl said quietly, malevolence oozing from him. "We may be headed for Gretna Green and marriage but Knight and I will consummate our unions with our chosen brides tonight."

Lady Lydia shot to her feet, her face drained of color. As she sputtered, Olivia knew this might be her only chance.

As both men stared at the young woman as she struggled to speak, Olivia came to her feet, lifting her heavy plate and slamming it into Lord Cooperton's face. As he shouted, she grabbed Higbee's plate and did the same, striking him so hard his chair tipped back and he fell backward, his head hitting the ground hard.

Higbee didn't move but Lord Cooperton grabbed her wrist, his fingers so tight that she thought he might break her bones. Quickly, she took her wine goblet and tossed the liquid into his face. As he blinked, she smashed it against the wooden table. Glass shards went everywhere.

Olivia took the jagged piece still in her hand and held it against the earl's throat.

"Let go of me," she ordered.

"No."

She applied a slight bit of pressure and saw blood spot his cravat.

"I will push this as deeply as I can into your throat," she promised. "Do not test me, my lord."

"Do it," Lady Lydia encouraged.

She heard the door crash open behind her. Cooperton tried to jerk away from her. He only succeeded in knocking her off-balance. As she stumbled, the jagged edge of the glass ripped his throat. The earl screamed, releasing her and bringing his hands to his wound. Bright red blood appeared, soaking his cravat.

"Fetch a doctor!" he cried hoarsely, panic in his eyes.

"Do it yourself," a familiar voice said.

Olivia turned and saw Hart there, larger than life. She ran to him, throwing her arms about him, babbling incoherently.

He smoothed her hair and murmured reassuring words to her, words that she didn't comprehend. She only knew Hart had come and he would take her away from this place.

She raised her tear-stained face and he kissed her. His kiss tasted of love and protection and comfort.

She broke it. "You came."

"Yes, thanks to Lord Braithwaite. He saw your abduction and found me straightaway. Wyatt's fast team of horses helped us to catch up to you."

"Lady Lydia!" she cried, pulling away.

Olivia saw Wyatt had an arm about her friend and had offered her his handkerchief. She mopped her eyes, saying *"thank you"* over and over.

"Lydia?"

The young woman glanced up. "Olivia!"

They ran to one another and embraced, both weeping profusely.

"We are safe," she assured her friend.

Hart and Wyatt came to stand beside them and Wyatt said, "Indeed, you are safe."

"Thank you," she said, wrapping her arms about Wyatt and kissing his cheek. "You are a good friend to Hart to come this far."

"Anything for a Terror and his bride-to-be," Wyatt said humbly.

Lord Cooperton staggered toward them. "Are you going to let me die?" he asked, pain filling his eyes.

"You kidnapped me and promised to rape me," she said evenly. "Why should I help you?"

He blinked, tears falling from his eyes. "Because you are a far better person than I could ever dream of being."

His words struck her. She wasn't a cruel, vindictive person.

"We should help him," she said. "Much as I don't want to, I cannot let him die by my hand." She glanced back at the earl. "Sit. Keep pressure on your wound. A doctor will be here soon."

Cooperton collapsed into a chair.

Higbee began stirring on the floor and sat up, looking confused, rubbing the back of his head.

"I will see to a doctor," Wyatt said and left the room.

Olivia wrapped her arms about a shaking Lydia. "He cannot hurt you now."

"It doesn't matter," the girl moaned. "He already has. I have been alone in his company. He will spread that throughout London. I am ruined." Determination lit her eyes. "But I will refuse to marry him. My father knows what Knight is like. He will be sad for me but he won't force me into a marriage with the cad."

"No one will know what happened, my lady," Hart said. "I guarantee it."

He explained the story her parents were to give to any callers and concluded with, "Your reputation will remain pristine."

Hart went to Higbee and brought him to his feet. He took

Higbee into a corner and spoke to him quietly, handing a small pouch to him which she suspected was filled with coins. Her cousin nodded several times and left the room without meeting her eyes.

"What did you say to Higbee?" Olivia asked. "Where is he going?"

"Your cousin will make for Bristol in the morning," Hart said. "He will take the first ship bound for America."

"America?" she asked, shocked at the thought of Higbee leaving England.

"He will write to me with his address once he is settled. I have made clear to him that there is nothing for him here. When Lord Rivers passes—which will likely be a good many years—I will notify Knight and he can return home and claim his title and lands. You have no need to fear him ever again, Lady Lydia."

"Thank you, Your Grace," she said through watery eyes.

Wyatt returned with the local doctor in tow.

"He was downstairs having his dinner," Wyatt said. "I explained the earl had a terrible accident."

They huddled together while the physician went to Lord Cooperton and pulled up a chair. After a few moments, he had the earl move his hands and the doctor untied the bloody cravat, looking carefully and then winding it back around Cooperton's neck.

He stood and motioned. Hart went over.

"Your friend will need to be stitched up. I must return to my surgery for my bag."

"He's not my friend," Lord Cooperton said through gritted teeth.

"Friend or not, he needs to help you to your room. I will come and attend to you shortly."

The doctor left and Wyatt went over, asking, "Which is your room?"

"The last on the left," the earl said, his voice strained.

"Wait here," Hart instructed them as he and Wyatt got

Cooperton to his feet and helped him from the room.

Olivia and Lydia sat, holding hands, waiting for their return.

"I cannot believe His Grace convinced Mr. Knight to leave England," Lydia said.

"He can be quite persuasive," she said with a smile. "After all, he persuaded me to say yes to his offer of marriage."

"His Grace is most handsome. You make a striking couple."

"Remember, you are to attend our wedding on Tuesday," she reminded, thinking they would also need to invite Lord Braithwaite, as well, to thank him for his role in today's rescue. Perhaps Lord Braithwaite and Lady Lydia might make for an interesting couple.

Hart and Wyatt returned and the two women rose to meet them.

"The doctor has Cooperton's wound cleaned and stitched," Hart revealed. "He will stay the night in the inn. The innkeeper's wife will watch over him. We had an interesting talk. Lord Cooperton will return to his country estate from here. His Season is over. If and when he returns to London, he knows never to speak to us again. His brief brush with death may have actually convinced him to walk a different path in life."

"We are leaving for London," Wyatt announced.

"But it is dark by now," she said.

"My coachman is very skilled," Wyatt assured her. "We will have lighted lanterns. He will walk the horses so there will be no accidents. We can be back at the stage where my blacks were left. They will be rested enough by then and we can make it home shortly after dawn tomorrow morning."

"We think it best to make certain Lady Lydia is returned home before prying eyes are awake," Hart continued. "Her parents have put out the story that she has a nasty summer cold. She will remain home a day or two and then once more participate in *ton* activities."

They left the inn and made for the carriage, which Blevins already had readied. Two lanterns glowed.

"I will ride with Blevins and hold one of the lanterns and help him watch the road," Wyatt volunteered. "That will give you the entire cushion, Lady Lydia. Perhaps you can get some rest before we reach London."

Hart helped the ladies into the carriage and sat with Olivia, wrapping his arm around her and holding her close. Lady Lydia sat opposite them, stretching out her legs and leaning her back against the window. Soon, she was asleep.

"What a day," he said as the carriage rolled along, the motion soothing.

"What a month," she replied. "Who knew I would have already found my husband—and love—so early into the Season."

He smiled at her. "And think of the days and months and years we have ahead of us. Ones we will spend together, in love."

Hart's mouth covered hers and Olivia relished the man. His kiss.

And most of all, his love.

EPILOGUE

Deerfield Park—Late September 1813

HART AWAKENED TO nibbles on his earlobe. He growled and captured Olivia, flipping her so she lay with her back against the mattress as he loomed over her, her wrists pinned next to her head. He gazed down at this lovely woman. His wife. His duchess. In the five months of their marriage, they had learned a great deal about one another. Favorite foods and colors. Music they liked. Books they enjoyed.

And discovered exactly what pleased them in the bedroom.

For Hart, oddly enough, it was his ears. Little did he know how sensitive they could be—or how wicked his duchess was, teasing and tormenting him. Olivia's weakness had turned out to be the backs of her knees. He had only to graze them with his fingertips for her to sigh. If he ran his tongue there, she grew absolutely giddy.

"Are you needing my particular attention this morning, Duchess?" he asked, his voice low.

She licked her lips, still innocent in some ways, not knowing how much that gesture filled him with desire.

"I suppose so, Duke," she replied, fighting a smile and quickly losing that battle.

He bent and flicked his tongue across one of her nipples, enjoying her squirm as the bud hardened. Hart grazed it with his teeth and sucked upon it, thinking her breast fuller than usual. She began writhing beneath him and he pleasured her with his tongue and teeth in all the places that called out to him. When he entered her, she let out a long sigh, which soon turned to the sweet little noises she uttered when they made love. Their waltz of love was timeless yet new each time they came together.

Spent, he collapsed atop her, burying his face against her neck, enjoying the floral scent that always clung to her. Then he rolled, bringing her with him until she was on top.

Olivia rested her chin on his chest and gazed at him. "I wish we could stay like this all day."

"We can, love."

"No, we can't." She pushed against him and rose from the bed, allowing him to admire her naked form and the sweet curve of her hips. "You are going to take me on a picnic today. By the lake."

His heart stopped for a moment before it began beating again. He had finally told Olivia the details of that day long ago. When Reginald had tossed a frightened Percy into the water. And how Hart had swum as hard as he could but hadn't reached his brother in time. He had also come to realize that Percy's neck had been broken when he was thrown into the lake. And he had finally realized that his father probably knew that and kept it quiet to protect Reginald.

Olivia had insisted on going to the lake, a place Hart had avoided once he returned from war to claim the dukedom. They had sat on the bank for a good while without speaking and then she had asked for stories about Percy. As he recalled his little brother, Percy came alive to him again. Hart had avoided thinking of Percy for so many years. With his wife by his side, though, he found he enjoyed thinking about his shared past with his younger brother.

He also told her what he could of Ada. He didn't remember as much about his little sister because she had still been in the nursery when he was sent to Turner Academy. He did recall her smile and how Ada's eyes would light up when she saw him. She had called him *Hot* instead of Hart, not quite able to pronounce the *r* in his name.

His wife had encouraged them to come to the lake a few times each week ever since they had arrived at Deerfield Park. She had told him there was no reason for the one horrible memory of Reginald's actions to ruin the place that Hart had enjoyed being.

"We will make this our place, Hart," she had told him. "We will bring our children here."

He was no longer unwilling to go to the lake. He still felt a bit unsettled each time they arrived but the feeling passed quickly. In time, Hart knew his discomfort would disappear.

"Breakfast before picnicking," he told her. "Then I have some letters to write."

"I have menus to plan with Cook. We can go early this afternoon," she suggested. "Shall we say one o'clock?"

"Agreed."

He pulled her from the bed and wrapped his arms around her, kissing her deeply before releasing her. Olivia slipped on her wrapper and went back to her bedchamber to get ready for the day. They breakfasted together and then planned to meet in the foyer at one.

When they did, she had a picnic hamper at her feet and a blanket in her arms. He stuffed the blanket under his arm and took the hamper's handle in one hand. With his other, he entwined his fingers with hers. They strolled across the lawn and through the trees.

Once they reached the lake, he spread out the blanket on the grass. Olivia pulled off her slippers and used them to anchor two corners of the blanket since there was a slight breeze. The hamper sat on the third corner and he stretched so his feet rested on the fourth. His wife pulled out what Cook had prepared for them. Cold chicken and slices of a hard cheese. Two pears. A carafe of wine and goblets for them.

They ate their fill, returning what was left to the basket. Hart placed his head in Olivia's lap and she threaded her fingers through his hair, stroking it absently.

"This is heaven," he said, gazing up into her eyes. "You. With me. Here."

"Actually, we are not alone," she said.

"What?" He lifted his head, looking to his left and right, before returning it to her lap. "I don't see anyone."

"You won't. Yet." A smile played about her lips.

Hart frowned.

And then he beamed.

He shot up, facing her. "Do you mean what I think you do?"

She nodded, her smile radiant. "I have missed my courses twice now. I vomited my breakfast after you left the room. My breasts are tender and larger. Everything that my friends have told me would occur."

Hart chuckled, reaching out and caressing one and then bringing his palm to her belly.

"When?" he asked.

"I think late April. I am supposed to see the midwife tomorrow. I should have a better idea after that." She hesitated. "We will have to miss the Season."

"Who cares about the Season?" he said. "I had the one Season I needed. I found you."

He slipped his arms about her. "Next spring, we will be three. We will bring our boy or girl to this same spot and sit on this blanket. We will bask in the sunshine and count our blessings."

"Always," she said. "I count them every day. I love you so much, Hart."

"And I love you, Olivia, Duchess of Mansfield and mother of our child."

Hart rubbed her belly, thinking how it would swell over the next months. Then he touched his mouth to hers in a tender, wonderful, marvelous kiss, knowing his love for Olivia would grow stronger each day for the rest of their lives.

About the Author

Award-winning and internationally bestselling author Alexa Aston's historical romances use history as a backdrop to place her characters in extraordinary circumstances, where their intense desire for one another grows into the treasured gift of love.

She is the author of Regency and Medieval romance, including: Dukes of Distinction; Soldiers & Soulmates; The St. Clairs; The King's Cousins; and The Knights of Honor.

A native Texan, Alexa lives with her husband in a Dallas suburb, where she eats her fair share of dark chocolate and plots out stories while she walks every morning. She enjoys a good Netflix binge; travel; seafood; and can't get enough of *Survivor* or *The Crown*.

www.ingramcontent.com/pod-product-compliance
Lightning Source LLC
Chambersburg PA
CBHW071756190726

48292CB00003B/997